DON'T FORGET ME

A RIDGEWATER HIGH NOVEL

JUDY CORRY

ISBN-13: 978-1976585067

ISBN-10: 1976585066

Cover Design by Victorine E. Lieske

Edited by Precy Larkins

ALSO BY JUDY CORRY

Ridgewater High Series:

When We Began (Cassie and Liam)

Meet Me There (Ashlyn and Luke)

Don't Forget Me (Eliana and Jess)

It Was Always You (Lexi and Noah)

My Second Chance (Juliette and Easton)

My Mistletoe Mix-Up (Raven and Logan)

Forever Yours (Alyssa and Jace)

Protect My Heart (Emma and Arie)

Kissing The Boy Next Door (Wes and Lauren)

A Second Chance for the Rich and Famous Series

The Billionaire Bachelor (Kate and Drew)

Hollywood and Ivy (Ivy and Justin)

Her Football Star Ex (Emerson and Vincent)

For anyone who has ever felt invisible or forgettable.

CHAPTER ONE

BETTING on my best friend's love life was getting expensive. Seriously, I'd get a bigger return on my investment if I threw the money out the window.

It was the smirk on Ashlyn's face that tipped me off. I'd lost yet another bet.

"Time for another trip to the mall, Eliana." Ashlyn opened her locker which was next to mine.

I counted how many days had passed since her brother, Jess, started dating his latest girlfriend. Well, ex-girlfriend now. "They only made it nine days?"

"Yeah. I think that's a new record for him."

I shook my head as I spun my locker combination. "I thought he'd make it at least two weeks this time around. Olivia seemed way cooler than his usual type."

"Maybe that's what scared my commitment-phobe brother. She was smart, unlike his usual looks-over-personality type." Ashlyn's gaze wandered behind me. "Speaking of my brother..."

Jess walked up behind Ashlyn as students filtered out of the halls in a rush to leave for their after-school activities. Even though Jess and Ashlyn were a year and a half apart, they could be twins with their identical dirty-blond hair, tall frames, and the glowing Brooks family complexion. In other words, they looked nothing like me with my dark brown hair and barely five-foot frame.

"Nine days? You only made it nine days?" I asked Jess.

"You heard, then?" He squeezed his green eyes shut and sighed. "Which one of you is paying for the shopping trip this time?"

"Eliana, of course," Ashlyn practically sang. "She has way more faith in you than I do."

"I don't know why." I shook my head and scowled at Jess, though I could never really be mad at this. Him not having a girlfriend was always a good thing for me. It meant I wouldn't have to share him with anyone else. But I went on pretending to be annoyed and said, "This is the third time this year I've had to pay for your sister's accessory addiction."

Jess shrugged. "Well, three times isn't *that* bad."

I shoved his shoulder and he bumped against his locker door. "I didn't mean third time this school year. I was counting since January. That's not even two months. I'll have to ask my dad to increase my allowance if I'm gonna keep up with your dating schedule." Which I didn't want to do. Dad had been super stressed lately with work. Trying to land big client portfolios always took a toll on him, and his latest acquisition was no different.

Jess pulled his backpack from his locker. "This betting game isn't *my* fault. You do it to yourself. Maybe my relationships would last longer if my sister and best friend weren't always counting down their demise. Plus, isn't it better I break up with them when I know it's not going to work out, instead of stringing them along?"

"So when are we going shopping?" Ashlyn asked, ignoring her brother.

"Tomorrow after school?" I suggested.

"Sounds perfect!" Ashlyn snapped her locker shut and pulled her Chloé bag over her shoulder right as her boyfriend, Luke Davenport, came around the corner. Unlike Jess, Luke and Ashlyn had been dating for months.

And then there was me. I'd never had a boyfriend. Period. I'd never even kissed a guy. So who was I to judge Jess? At least he asked girls out. That was more than I could say for the other guys in Math Club.

Ashlyn sashayed over to Luke and kissed him like they were saying goodbye instead of hello.

"Get a room," Jess said under his breath.

I just laughed. Ashlyn and Luke were gross. Cute, but gross.

When they finally broke apart, Ashlyn smiled back at us and said, "I'll see you guys later."

Jess and I shut our lockers at the same time, and headed toward the parking lot near the PE building where Jess always parked his lime green Camaro. His baby was less likely to get scratched there.

The air was frigid when we walked outside, the ground dusted with a skiff of white powder that hadn't been there at lunch time.

"Here," Jess said, offering me his arm. "It looks pretty slick right there." He pointed to the area on the sidewalk where the rain gutter emptied.

"Thanks." I linked my arm through his as we tread carefully down the icy slope to his car. He opened the passenger door for me and dropped the keys in my lap so I could get the heat blasting while he scraped snow off the windows. We'd done this routine so many times since he started driving us to school two years ago, we didn't have to think about it anymore.

Once the windows were clear, Jess banged the ice scraper on the bottom of his sneakers—yes, even his tires were too precious for that job. He climbed in and held his reddened hands against the heater vents.

"It's freezing out there."

"It *is* winter." I shook my head as he shivered in his short-sleeved t-shirt and jeans. "Maybe one of these days you'll decide to wear your coat. You do know we live in Ridgewater, New York, not the Bahamas, right?"

"Y-yeah, y-yeah," he said through chattering teeth.

We had this discussion at least twice a week. But no matter how many times I told him to wear his coat, he refused. Coats weren't cool, and they got in the way of the other stuff in his locker.

"At least you stopped wearing shorts all winter. That's an improvement."

His lips quirked into a proud smile, and part of me felt like he only did those things to prove some kind of a point. *Guys.* I didn't understand why they'd choose to be cold all for the sake of looking tough.

His shivering slowed as we headed out of the parking lot toward our neighborhood.

"So, what was it this time?" I asked as we drove past the football field.

"What do you mean?" he asked, pretending like he didn't know exactly what I was talking about. We'd had this conversation so many times.

"Did she snort when she giggled? Breathe too heavily? Crack her knuckles?" Seriously, you'd think Jess was a player with the number of girls he'd dated, but he wasn't. It was more like he was looking for a specific girl, and he was having a hard time finding her.

"None of those things." He glanced briefly at me and shrugged. "She was too... I don't know...insecure?"

"Of course she was insecure!" I didn't know whether to laugh or throw my hands in the air. "She's seen how many girls you've gone through."

Jess sunk back into his leather seat. "Maybe there's something wrong with me."

"You're just really picky. But picky can be a good thing."

"Kind of like how you're so picky you've only ever liked guys like Ryan: all the charm, all the muscles, and the dark hair and eyes to go with it."

Of course, he would bring up my infamous crush on our old neighbor. He and Ashlyn had teased me plenty over the years.

I played along like I always did, even if the unrequited crush still stung. "You forgot the dazzling smile."

"Oh yes, how could I forget?"

He stared out the windshield as we waited at a stoplight. The wipers swept the falling snowflakes away. "Maybe I should take a break from dating for a while. I'll be leaving for Cornell in a few months anyway."

I chewed on the inside of my cheek. I hated thinking about him moving away for college in half a year. I was a junior and would be left behind. Sure, I'd still have Ashlyn at school next year, but she wasn't Jess.

When I turned back to him, he was studying me instead of watching the stoplight. He frowned when he noticed me scowling. "Hey," he squeezed my knee and shook it, "Ithaca's just over an hour away. We'll see each other all the time."

But what if we don't? What if he finds a new best friend? What if he gets so caught up in college he forgets about everyone back home? What if he finds *the* girl who he'll finally choose over me?

My stomach soured at the thought. One day he would find someone, and she'd steal my best friend from me.

HOURS LATER, after Jess and I finished our homework, I crossed the lawn to the white two-story Colonial next door. Even after my parents renovated it, our house wasn't quite as big as the Brooks', but it was a good size for the three of us. I walked through the red front door and set my backpack on the hardwood floor. Mom was in the kitchen, her back turned to me as she transferred a batch of cookies to the cooling rack.

She was baking?

That was the last thing I expected to find when I came home. She usually spent her afternoons watching her favorite soap, *As the Sun Sets*. Or shopping.

But baking? No, not my mom. Unless she turned into some robotic Stepford-wife type while I was in school. Or she was secretly an alien doppelganger.

I eyed the cooling rack. Well, the chocolate chip cookies did look pretty charred. So maybe Mom hadn't been inhabited by an alien after all.

"Hey, Eliana." She looked over her shoulder, a smudge of flour across her cheek. "I don't know why I offered to bring homemade cookies to your piano recital tonight. I should have picked up a dozen from the bakery and put them on a plate like I usually do."

"These *might* be okay." I grabbed a cookie. It was crisp and heavy. Had she accidentally used cement instead of flour?

She watched with hopeful eyes as I took a bite.

Crunch!

I tried chewing it for a few seconds before spitting the burnt cookie in the sink.

"Maybe we should stop by the bakery on our way to dinner tonight."

Mom nodded. "Let's do that. Your dad should be home soon so we should have time before our reservation." She tossed the rest of the cookies in the trash. "How was school today?"

"Pretty good. I think I passed my test in Trig." I filled a glass with water from the fridge to wash down the burnt-cookie taste. "I have a Spanish test tomorrow, so Jess helped me study. Oh yeah, and I have to take Ashlyn shopping again."

"Jess broke up with *another* girl?" She shook her head. "You girls need to stop betting on him and his string of girlfriends. If your dad knew how much of your allowance went to Ashlyn's wardrobe, he wouldn't be so happy to give it to you."

After taking a sip from my glass, I said, "Who do you think taught me the art of gambling?"

My mom hmphed as she scraped the remaining cookie dough into the garbage. "Obviously, he didn't teach you well."

"Jess says he's done dating for now anyway, so that takes care of the problem."

"Oh?"

I pushed a strand of hair off my face and tucked it behind my ear. "He says it's pointless since he's graduating soon anyway."

She raised an eyebrow. "How much do you wanna bet he doesn't even make it one month?"

"Mom!"

She laughed as she set the mixing bowl in the sink. "I was joking, honey. You know I don't believe in gambling."

"What's this talk about gambling?" My dad's rich Italian accent interrupted us. He strolled into the kitchen, his tie already loose over his blue dress shirt and his dark hair tousled like he'd been running his fingers through it on his drive home.

"It's nothing, Dad. We're joking around."

"Good," he said before grabbing my mom about the waist,

pulling her into his arms and kissing her like he hadn't seen her in weeks.

"Gross. Can't you at least wait for me to leave the room before you start making out?"

"No. It's good for children to see how much their parents love each other. It helps them feel safe and secure." Dad winked before returning to make out with Mom.

I rolled my eyes. You'd think they were newlyweds, not a middle-aged couple who'd been married for almost twenty years. Seriously, they were almost as bad as Ashlyn and Luke these days.

"I'm gonna get dressed for my recital," I said since there wouldn't be much time after dinner. "Hopefully you'll come up for air before I'm back downstairs."

As PDA as they were, I couldn't keep a smile from sneaking up my face when I walked past them and down the hall to the staircase. Things had been rocky a few years back before my mom went to rehab for her alcoholism, but now they were better than ever. It was the kind of love story people dreamed of: high-powered Italian businessman falls in love with the cute girl in the coffee shop and asks her to marry him after only a few dates. It was a great love story. And my dad was right—the way they were together did make me feel safe. And I believed as long as you had a happy family, life was good.

On our way out the door, my dad's phone beeped. He pulled it from his pocket, his eyes tightening as he read the text.

"What is it?" my mom asked with concern.

My dad pressed his eyes closed for a moment. "It's John from work. There's something I need to take care of." He patted his hand on the side of his leg as if deciding what to do. "How about you guys go ahead to Alessandro's so we won't be late for the recital. I'll meet you there."

"Are you sure, honey?" Mom set her hand on his arm.

He nodded and bent over to give my mom a hug and a kiss, followed by a hug and a kiss on the cheek for me as well. "You girls have fun. I'll join you when I can." He handed Mom the keys to the Audi and waited for us to pull out of the driveway before going back inside the house.

"WHAT CAN I get you ladies to drink?" the red-headed waitress asked when she stopped by our table, her pad and pen ready.

I smiled at her. "Raspberry lemonade, please." I could drink a gallon of the stuff.

Mom bit her lip, still trying to decide. "Umm..."

"We have an excellent wine list," the waitress offered. "May I suggest the 2002 Cabernet Sauvignon?"

It was probably the most expensive wine they served.

I held my breath when my mom's eyes moved to the wine list, and bounced my knee as a bit of anxiety tightened my chest. I didn't know why I reacted that way after all these years.

A moment later, she smiled at the waitress. "I'll have the raspberry lemonade as well."

My muscles relaxed as the waitress jotted down my mom's order. "I'll be right back with those." With a smile, she turned and headed back to the kitchen.

"Will you text your dad to see how much longer he'll be? I left my phone at home," Mom said as she looked over the dinner menu. Why did parents always forget their phones? Was it their way of proving they weren't addicted to them like they accused their teens of?

Whatever. It didn't matter. I did as she said before turning back to my own menu.

The waitress came back with our drinks and took our orders.

"Any response from your dad yet?" She glanced anxiously at her watch.

I clicked my phone on and smiled at the picture I'd set as my wallpaper—Jess, Ashlyn, and me at their family's cabin last Fourth of July. But my dad hadn't responded.

"No text yet. Maybe he's still on the phone with John," I said. "He seemed stressed about whatever the text said."

My mom nodded. "He did. I know he's been worried about a few of his clients with the recent changes in the stock market. Hopefully, everything's okay. Your dad could use a break. Maybe we could head to Martha's Vineyard for a few days and give his blood pressure a much-needed rest."

"That would be nice." Though it would be freezing this time of year. At least the house we usually rented had a huge fireplace to stay warm by.

The waitress set our plates in front of us a while later. I took a bite of my *pasta all'Amatriciana.* The pancetta and tomato taste filled my mouth.

"Did he text you back yet?" My mom turned to look at the restaurant's entrance, checking.

He had never missed our weekly dinner at Alessandro's before.

I checked my phone. Still nothing. "Should I call him?"

"Sure."

I called, but it immediately went to voicemail.

"What's wrong?" Mom asked when she saw the confusion on my face.

"His phone went straight to voicemail. Maybe he's driving here now?"

But he never showed up at dinner. I sent him another text on our way to the car, so he'd know we'd left.

We stopped by the house for a plate to put the cookies on before going to the recital. My dad's truck wasn't in the garage, and when we walked into the kitchen, we found a note waiting for us on the granite counter.

Sorry, I messed everything up. It's better you not know anything.

-Paulo

CHAPTER TWO

"WHAT?" I dropped the box of cookies and grasped for the paper. He messed everything up? "Do you know what he means?" I asked my mom, the note shaking in my hand.

She looked as confused as I felt, her dark blue eyes full of fear.

"Let's call him," I suggested.

Mom grabbed her phone from the counter and dialed. I anxiously strummed my fingers on the counter as we waited for him to pick up.

"It went straight to voicemail," she said, more fear growing in her expression.

"Try again."

She dialed again, only to end up with the same result.

Mom slumped on a chair as I ran upstairs to their bedroom, scared about what I might find. I took one step inside and my stomach dropped. Their room was a mess. His dresser drawers hung half open, their contents ransacked. I ran to the closet to see if his suitcase was still there, but it was gone. The safe was open as well, but instead of looking like a mess, it was empty. He took mom's jewelry? What would he need diamond necklaces for?

I stormed out of my parent's bedroom and tore down the stairs. Mom was still sitting in the kitchen, staring at her phone in shock.

My heart twisted in my chest as I continued down the hall and into Dad's office. Maybe there was some hint in there about what was going on.

I rushed to his desk and yanked open a drawer, then another and another, searching for something, anything, that would give me a clue about what was happening. The problem was, I had no idea what I was looking at. It looked like a bunch of bills and receipts.

I rifled through the papers on his desk, searching for his laptop in the mess. But it wasn't there.

What was going on?

It didn't make sense. Hadn't he landed a huge account? Why would he suddenly run?

The note said he was sorry about messing everything up. But what had he messed up? Was that what John had texted him about?

I pulled out my phone to try calling my dad. Maybe he'd pick up for me, if not my mom.

This *had* to be some kind of joke. He wouldn't just up and leave us. He loved us.

His voicemail greeted me. I hung up and called him again, but he still didn't answer.

I called him again, and again, and again, until my hands were trembling. When his voicemail picked up the last time, instead of immediately hanging up and redialing, I listened to his cheerful message. "This is Paulo. Sorry I can't come to the phone right now. Leave me a message and I'll get back to you. *Ciao*." I fought back tears, an ache forming in the back of my throat as I waited for it to beep.

"Where are you, Dad?" I asked with a shaky voice. "What's this note supposed to mean? What did you mess up? What's going on?" My voice broke, a sob escaping at the thought that he really may have left us. "Why is it better we not know?" I hung up, not having anything else to say since all I wanted to do was cry and scream at the same time.

Where was he? How long did he plan to be gone? Why had he cleaned out the safe? He hadn't acted any different this afternoon when he got home from work. Had that been his plan all along, to pretend like he was going to take us out for a night of fun before abandoning us? To make promises for the future, like getting me a car and coming to my big concerto performance next month...only to run away? My gaze went back to his desk. Peeking out from under a piece of paper was his phone. It was sitting right there. It felt like my dad had kicked me in the chest. We had no way to track him. He didn't want us to find him.

But then I had an idea. Maybe I could find out what John had texted him about. That might tell me something.

I powered on his phone, feeling the first flutter of hope. But it didn't prompt me for a security code like it should have. Instead it gave me prompts for setting up my new phone. My dad had restored it to the original factory settings.

I threw the phone at the bookshelf across the room. As it shattered, so did I. My body shook as desperate sobs burst through me, tearing through my body and leaving me completely empty.

Ding dong.

I held my breath and listened for my mom to answer the door. A deep, unfamiliar voice spoke. In a matter of seconds, loud footsteps stormed through the house. Someone was running toward my dad's office. I jumped out of the chair, banging my knee on the desk. Was I in danger? Or were these guys here for my dad?

"Eliana! Eliana!" Mom called, growing louder as she got closer.

Two men burst through the door, followed by my mom. The men were dressed in dark jackets with the letters FBI printed on them.

FBI?

"Mom!" I ran to her and fell into her arms. "What's happening?"

She wrapped her arms around me, and we both leaned against the wall for support. "They're looking for your father."

WE WERE TOLD to stay in the living room as the FBI searched our house, looking through every corner and drawer—invading our personal space without a care for our privacy. When the FBI finished scouring the house, they asked to speak with my mother alone. But she was so shaky and nervous that she insisted I stay with her.

We sat in our living room with two of the agents—they were the type to wear perpetual frowns on their faces. The senior agent, a sixty-something man with a silver mustache, started asking questions. His partner, a middle-aged man with biceps bigger than my thighs, took notes.

"Are you aware that your husband embezzled money from his clients?" the older man asked, his eyes scrutinizing my mom.

Embezzled money? What?

"No. He wouldn't..." My mom cleared her throat. "Paulo wouldn't do that."

"We have a mountain of evidence that says he did."

"He was framed. I'd know if my husband was breaking the law. We don't keep secrets from each other."

The agents looked at each other, telling me they didn't believe my mom at all.

"Did you have any indication that your husband would be going out of town? Did he mention anything to you?"

"No." My mom's voice broke. "We were supposed to go to dinner tonight. I had no idea."

The older agent turned to me. "What about you? Did your father say anything to you before he left?"

"He didn't say anything." I shook my head, worried I'd say something wrong and get in trouble. "He just left a note."

"Note?" The agent stilled and squinted his eyes. "What note?"

"The one on the counter." I stood up.

"No. You stay here. I'll get it." The middle-aged agent turned on his heel and left the room.

I held my breath the whole time he was gone. Had I just offered evidence to help them arrest my father? I wanted to run after the agent and tell him to stop. But my mom reached over and squeezed my hand.

The agent was back a couple of minutes later. "Where did you say that note was?"

I cleared my throat and glanced at my mom, wondering why he hadn't found it. She nodded for me to tell him.

"I thought it was on the kitchen counter. That's where we read it when we got home."

Had Mom done something with it? When I looked at my mom, her eyes gave nothing away.

The agent went back to the kitchen. I heard him moving things around, imagined him looking in every cupboard and corner, even in the garbage. But he returned a few minutes later with empty hands.

"Maybe one of the other agents grabbed it," my mom suggested.

"Let's hope they did. If we find out you're hiding things from us, it will only make things worse for you. As for now, we're taking your husband's fleeing as an admission of guilt. And until he comes back and turns himself in, we'll have to freeze your accounts."

My mom gasped. "You can't freeze our accounts. How will we survive?"

"It was never your money to begin with. I suppose you'll have to *earn* your money the old-fashioned way."

MY PHONE BUZZED as soon as the FBI left.

Jess: **Is everything ok?**

He'd probably seen all the cars and commotion.

Me: **No.**

Tears pricked at my eyes again. Everything was not okay. Everything was a mess.

And it probably wouldn't be okay any time soon.

Had my dad left town for a couple days, or had he left the country for good? His passport hadn't been in the safe. If he was guilty and had any idea of the consequences, it was likely he'd never come back. He wouldn't choose to go to jail.

Jess was on my doorstep a minute later, panting as if he'd sprinted all the way over. "What's going on? Is everyone okay? Did something happen?"

He searched my face for any clues.

"My dad's gone."

Jess straightened. "What do you mean he's gone?"

I looked to the side and wiped the tears out of my eyes, hating the fact that I was crying in front of him. "He left a note saying he was sorry for the mess he made, and it was better for us not to know anything." My voice wobbled, and a sob sneaked up in the back of my throat. "I don't think he's coming back."

Jess pulled me into his arms, hugging me tight against his chest. "That doesn't make sense. Is there anything I can do?"

I sniffled and shook my head.

"He'll come back. This has to be some sort of misunderstanding." Jess sounded so sure.

"Even if he does come back, he'll go right to jail. The FBI says it might be for twenty-five years." My voice grew more and more hysterical as the reality of everything fully hit me. We couldn't go twenty-five years without him.

"Hey." Jess pulled me into his arms again and rubbed my back. "It's gonna be okay. My parents can help your mom find a job. And you guys have money in the bank, don't you?"

I shook my head against his chest. "The FBI said they're freezing our accounts until my dad returns. We have nothing."

THE NEXT FEW days were a long, horrible blur of FBI agents coming in and out of the house, taking statements from me and my mom and searching every corner for more clues about my dad. I held my breath every time the doorbell rang, dreading every moment when our privacy was invaded by complete strangers. The media also tried relentlessly to get more information on this hot story. To avoid having my picture plastered all over the newspapers and social media, I stayed inside.

Jess and his family helped my mom and me in a search of our own, contacting all the people who might know something more about my dad. But no one knew anything. And even though they said they would do all they could to help, I knew if my dad didn't want to be found, he wouldn't be. He was too smart for that.

My mom had barely eaten anything since that last dinner at Alessandro's. She wouldn't leave the house. She didn't shower. She spent the days in bed crying. Her already small frame was becoming thinner and the dark circles under her eyes were looking worse. It reminded me way too much of how she'd looked a couple years ago when things had been bad with her alcoholism, and it twisted my stomach into knots.

In addition to watching my mom for any signs of a relapse, I tried to gather any financial-type documents I could find. But when it came down to it, there was nothing left that the FBI hadn't taken as possible evidence. We didn't even know the passwords for any of the online accounts my dad had, since he'd always been the one to handle paying the bills. We would have to wait for the bills to come in the mail before we'd know where we stood.

On Saturday afternoon I decided to cash in my silver coin collection. My dad had taught me to *freeze some of my fruit* in case of an emergency. Now definitely seemed like an emergency, so Jess and Ashlyn helped me take the coins to a pawn shop. When all was said and done, I only had eight hundred and thirty-six dollars—not nearly enough for me and my mom to get by on for very long.

"MOM, you have to eat something. You're wasting away before my eyes." I held a spoonful of broth up close to my mom's lips, but she stared stoically ahead at her bedroom wall.

She wore her blue bathrobe today, and her chestnut hair was falling out of the braid I'd put it in yesterday.

When she didn't respond, I said, "If you don't eat this on your own, I'll have to take you to the hospital and they'll stick you with an IV."

She slowly opened her mouth.

I spooned the broth in and she eventually finished the bowl. She barely pecked at the small piece of bread I offered her, so I took the dishes to the kitchen to wash them.

A few minutes later, Jess knocked on the French doors in the dining room, his six-foot frame hunched over as he peeked through a square of glass. I waved him in.

"How are things this evening?" He shoved his hands in the pockets of his dark blue jeans as he leaned against the counter beside me. "Is your mom any better after you showed her the cash?"

I set the sponge down and looked at him. "She actually finished her dinner tonight."

"That's progress." He gave me an encouraging smile.

"I guess." I turned back to the sink and scrubbed the dishes again. "It's like I'm taking care of a baby. I have to do everything around here."

"She's hurting right now." His brow furrowed over his green eyes. "Her life was turned upside down. That's not something you just get over."

"It's happening to me too, you know!" I scrubbed the plate in my hand even harder. "But you don't see me starving myself and laying around in bed all day. Instead, I've been doing all the cooking and digging to trying and figure out how to make things work. I even called my piano teacher and told her I had to quit. I gave up my concerto with the orchestra!" The plate broke and sliced my finger. "Ugh!" I dropped the broken plate and sponge, and gripped the sink.

"Are you all right?" Jess leaned over and inspected my hands.

I squeezed my eyes shut for a moment as I tried to gain control of my temper. A few deep breaths later, I felt marginally better. "I'm okay."

He scooted behind me, grasped my forearms and lifted them

so I had to release my death grip on the sink. "Let me clean up the plate while you take care of that cut."

"Fine."

A few minutes later, when I came back after bandaging my finger, I found Jess with his hands in the soapy water.

"I don't think I've ever seen you willingly do the dishes," I commented as I watched him place a cup in the top rack of the dishwasher.

"Come on." He shook his head and smiled the kind of smile that made it easy understand why so many girls at school were dying to date him...even knowing his horrible dating record. "You know I do the dishes at my house all the time."

"Sure, but you usually complain for twenty minutes before you trudge over to the sink."

He moved to put the sponge away. "I can stop if you want."

"No, no, please continue." I leaned back against the counter. "I'm not complaining. Just amazed."

"Well, I'm glad I could amaze you for once then." He winked as he put a handful of silverware in the dishwasher's utensil basket.

I hesitated before asking my next question, not sure I wanted to know the answer. "So...um, has your dad found out anything more?" His dad owned several successful businesses in town, so he had a lot of connections. I hoped he would be able to discover something.

Jess frowned. "Not really. Just a bunch of investors who got screwed over. I guess my mom's sister was one of them."

I pinched my eyes shut. If I closed my eyes, maybe everything wouldn't seem so real.

But hearing there were actual clients of my dad who had lost real money because of him...well, it just made it a lot harder to pretend like it was a big misunderstanding.

Jess shook his head as he rinsed another plate. "I'm sorry."

I sat down on the stool behind the counter. Nothing made sense. Sure, my dad gambled in Atlantic City every once in a while, but I never thought he did anything illegal.

"Anything else?" I asked when I found my voice again.

"No." Jess finished loading the dishes, and started the dishwasher. "It's like your dad disappeared into thin air."

It did seem like that. His family in Italy hadn't heard from him, and his passport hadn't been flagged at any airports. It *was* like he disappeared into thin air.

CHAPTER THREE

I WENT BACK to school on Monday. Big mistake. Thanks to the news and social media, everyone had heard about my dad and the rumors had run wild. It seemed like everyone had their own theories on why he needed to steal so much money.

Down the hall on my way to meet up with Jess, Ashlyn, and Luke for lunch, I overheard Kelsie Perkins, the captain of the drill team, talking to her friends Hannah and Madison.

"I heard he was supporting his other family in New Jersey." Kelsie's voice drifted over the sound of other students talking by their lockers. "He's been switching off between them for a few years, that's why he went on so many *business* trips."

My stomach shrunk in on itself as I continued past her, pretending I hadn't heard her.

How did she know he'd gone on a lot of business trips? She didn't even know my dad.

But apparently neither did I, or I would have foreseen some of this. Could Kelsie be telling the truth somehow?

Tears threatened to drop as I shuffled through the sea of people making their way toward the cafeteria. The bathroom was around the next corner. If I could keep the tears at bay until I made it into the stall, I would be okay. I would not cry in front of people. It was bad enough I'd cried in front of Jess last week. *Costas don't cry,* my dad had always said. *We don't let anyone know when we're down. We keep ourselves to ourselves.* The last time I'd cried in school had been in second grade when I fell off the monkey bars at recess. I would not do it again.

I tilted my head down so no one could see my face and turned the corner, crashing right into someone's chest.

"Sorry," I mumbled, not looking up as I stumbled back.

A hand grabbed my arm. "Hey wait, Eliana. What's going on?" I lifted my gaze and found myself in front of Jess. He examined my face before asking, "What happened?"

I shook my head. I couldn't talk right now, or my voice would crack and I'd lose it.

"Do you wanna get out of here?" he whispered.

I nodded.

"Let's go." He led me down the hall and out the doors. Once we'd made it to the safety of his car, he asked me what was wrong.

The black leather interior was comforting with its familiarity in a world spinning out of control. I bit the inside of my cheek and willed the tears to evaporate back into my head. Once I was sure I could talk without any emotion breaking through, I said, "Everyone's been talking about me all day."

"I'm so sorry." Jess reached across the console and pulled me into a hug.

I sighed, feeling the comfort from his embrace. Jess and I didn't usually touch so much, but ever since my dad left, Jess seemed to know when I needed a hug to keep me from breaking apart.

A moment later I took a breath and leaned back against the seat. "They're saying he got involved in some sort of cult and had to give his leader a ton of money to keep us safe. Or that he gambled away all our money and had to embezzle everyone else's to keep us afloat." I sighed again. "And right before I ran into you, I overheard some girls talking about how my dad had another family hidden somewhere else that he had to support." I shook my head. "All morning I tried to tell everyone that the rumors weren't true...but what if they are? What if my dad has another daughter or son somewhere out there? What if he's with them now?" My voice was borderline hysterical. "He *has* gone on a lot of business trips over the past few years. And now that I know better, I doubt they were related to work. Maybe he was attending some other little girl's piano recitals all along."

Jess's eyebrows scrunched together, telling me he was as confused as I was. "I doubt he has some other family hidden somewhere. For now, let's stick with the idea that he got in way over his head, panicked, and that he'll come to his senses and come back home soon."

ALL THROUGH THE next month I held on to the hope that my dad would come back and magically fix everything. But when March arrived and we still hadn't heard anything from him, the last of that hope shriveled up and died. He was really gone. For good. I tried to be strong for my mom and make the best of everything, but I was screaming and crying and freaking out in my head. I was barely getting any sleep anymore and my grades were reflecting that. And when I tried to figure out how to make everything work without my dad in the picture, I came up with nothing. I had no idea what we were going to do.

My mom was hunched over a piece of paper when I walked in the door after school one day.

"What are you looking at?" I sank onto the stool beside her at the kitchen island. She was eating and showering more regularly now, so at least that had improved in the past month. Her hair was even combed into a ponytail, and she had taken the time to put on actual clothes instead of her blue robe.

"It's our mortgage statement." She sighed.

I inspected the bill, hoping the number at the bottom may have somehow been a lot less than the amount of money we had left. But no, it was way more than we could afford.

"What are we going to do?" I asked. "We're going to lose the house."

"I don't know. Your dad took care of all our finances. I never had to worry about any of it." She tossed the paper onto a stack of bills in the middle of the table.

"Will we have to move?" My chest tightened. Did we even have anywhere to go?

"I can't do that!" My mom shook her head, her eyes fearful. "I love this house!"

I looked around the kitchen at the beautiful cabinets I'd helped my mom paint creamy-white last summer. I looked at the granite countertops my dad had installed for my mom's fortieth birthday. This was our home. We'd put a little piece of our souls in with each improvement we made. All my memories were tied to this place. But as much as I loved it, I knew we couldn't stay here. And it would be better to leave on our own than be forced out by the bank.

"I love this house as much as you do, Mom. It's where I grew up. It's where my friends are. But we have to do something." I stopped, hating that I needed to be the one to think of solutions. After a minute, I asked in a calmer tone, "Could we try to rent out the house? That way if things get better, we could always move in again."

My mom closed her eyes, as if to shut out the situation we were in.

I touched her shoulder. "We have to do *something*."

She turned her blue eyes back to me, and in them I saw the anxiety of a woman who had lost everything and didn't know where to begin picking up the pieces of her shattered life.

"We could ask the Brooks if we can stay with them for a while," I suggested.

My mom shook her head. "I will not ask them for any more help. They've already done too much."

"But we can't afford to rent anything. We've already gone through most of the money we had and you still haven't even started looking for a job."

She clenched her teeth and gave me a look that made me stop talking. "I'll figure things out. I just need more time."

But we were almost out of that, too.

I HAD to get out of that depressing place. I texted Jess to see if he could hang out. He was stuck working on a project with Kelsie for their Adult Roles class, so I texted Ashlyn. She suggested we go out for some retail therapy, though she'd be the only one buying anything. I still hadn't taken her out to make good on the bet we'd made before the crap hit the fan. But she told me not to worry about it. Still, I was embarrassed I couldn't afford a pair of cheap sunglasses anymore. I couldn't even afford a pack of gum.

Our first stop was Ada's Smoothie Shack, where Luke was working today. After Ashlyn and Luke said "I love you" about ten times, Ashlyn and I sat at a table.

"Are you and Luke done drooling over each other, then?" I asked once Ashlyn peeled her eyes away from her boyfriend and seemed to remember she was with me.

"Yes." She sighed. "Doesn't he look so cute in that apron?"

"Sure." More like ridiculous. Luke was an all-state linebacker this year. The orange apron he sported looked out of place with his huge shoulders and buff arms.

"So what's going on with your mom today? I'm guessing she's the reason you texted."

"We have to move." I pouted as I played with my straw.

"What?" Her eyebrows lifted. "Why? I mean, I guess I can assume why... But you can't leave us! Did your mom get a job yet?"

My shoulders slumped. "She hasn't even started looking. She tells me she's been busy all day, but most of the time she just looks out the window for hours...almost like she's still waiting for my dad to walk through the front door after a long day at work."

"Oh, Eliana." Ashlyn reached across the table. "That is so sad."

A quiver of emotion tried to break through as I thought of how bad things were. I stuffed the feelings back down. I would not get emotional in the food court with all these people watching. I took a sip from the Very-Berry smoothie Ashlyn bought me and waited for the moment of weakness to pass.

"Anyway, that's why I had to leave. I couldn't stand sitting in that house today, knowing it would be one of the last days I'd live there." Phew. That was good. I didn't detect the slightest tremor in my voice. I hurried and changed the subject. "Did Jess say how long he and Kelsie would be working on their project?"

"No. Though I'm pretty sure Kelsie will try to make it last all night, maybe trick him into taking her out on a date while they're at it."

I grimaced. "I don't know how he can't see how fake she is with him."

"I'm pretty sure the main reason she wants to date him is because he's the only guy from our school going to Cornell next year. I overheard her talking to some girls at drill practice about how she wants a boyfriend on her arm at freshman orientation."

"That's not a good reason to date someone," I said.

"She also thinks she'll be the one to cure Jess of his short attention span when it comes to girls."

"I'm all for Jess learning how to date someone for longer than a week. I just don't want Kelsie to be the one to break the curse.

"Me neither. I can't stand her," Ashlyn said.

I took a sip from my smoothie and realized that with all the craziness going on in my life, I'd lost touch with what was going on in Ashlyn's life. "So what's new with you? I feel like I've been such a bad friend lately."

"Oh, things are great." She beamed and set her cup down. "Luke asked me to prom."

"That's not until like May, right?"

"Yes, well." She waved her fingers to someone behind me—probably Luke again. "He wanted to make sure I knew he *wanted* to take me and that he wasn't doing it because he's my boyfriend."

"How thoughtful of him." How would it be to have a guy do something like that for me? Sometimes it would be nice to have someone there to hold me when I felt like I was breaking apart.

"Remember that bet you and Jess made last spring?"

"Which one?" I'd made way too many bets with my best friends to remember them all.

"You know, the one about prom."

Ah yes. That one. I'd felt so left out last year when everyone went to prom without me, that in my mopey state I'd whined about how I probably wouldn't get asked this year either. With the recent dip in my social status, I was sure to win that bet at least.

"So you also remember that Jess promised that if you were both single this year's prom, he'd take you himself." Ashlyn smiled. "Well, he said he was swearing off girls for the rest of the year...so it looks like you'll have a date after all."

Just what I needed. A pity date.

"Don't get your hopes up too high. You know as well as I do that Jess isn't good at living the single life. Prom is still two months away. He'll probably have gone through at least two girls by the time May rolls around, especially if Kelsie gets her way."

IT ONLY TOOK a week to find tenants for our house with the help of my mom's friend across the street, Mrs. Hillyard. Her son was relocating to Ridgewater from Connecticut with his wife and three kids, and the proximity to grandma seemed to be a huge selling point to the couple. Apparently, built-in-babysitters are all the rage for young parents. They put down a deposit and gave us the first month's rent, along with signing a year's lease. My mom and I had three weeks to get into a new place.

Since Mom still didn't have a job, I had no idea how we could afford to live anywhere. But she surprised me a couple days later by telling me she'd called her brother, Peter, and that we would be moving across town to live with him.

"Are you sure that's a good idea?" I asked. The last time we dropped by his house he was so drunk he forgot to put pants on before answering the door, giving me insight into his "boxer or briefs" preference that I didn't need to know. And the time before that, he didn't even recognize me—and I'm his only niece.

"We don't have many options at the moment, honey. It'll be fine." That was all my mom had to say about our future living situation. Which made me even more apprehensive about moving.

Despite my misgivings, we began packing up the house the next day, finding things to sell since we would need money more than furniture at Uncle Peter's place.

One thing I couldn't bear to part with was the baby grand piano my dad bought me for my twelfth birthday. Instead of putting the piano for sale online, I found it a temporary home in the Brooks' music room. Macey, Jess and Ashlyn's thirteen-year-old sister, was taking lessons anyway and she was excited to practice on such a nice instrument.

One day, I came home from school to find my mom cranking the wood-burning stove. She was stuffing my father's belongings into it instead of packing them away to put in storage.

"What are you doing?" I ran over and yanked my dad's favorite baseball cap from her hands. Had she been drinking on the sly?

"A little de-junking." Mom picked up the photo album from their wedding.

"Don't burn that, Mom! What if he comes back?" I grabbed it from her before she could throw it in. "What if this is all some big misunderstanding? You can't replace these."

"What if he comes back? Just a big misunderstanding?" My mom scoffed. "You think I'd take that fraud back? He left us, Eliana!" Her voice shook with rage, and she slammed the door of the wood stove shut. "He fed us a million lies, told me he loved me and that forever wouldn't be long enough, and then he left us to deal with his mess." She sat down on the hearth and put her head in her hands. "He's not coming back," she sobbed. "He's not ever coming back. And the sooner we accept that, the better off we'll be."

CHAPTER FOUR

A COUPLE OF WEEKS LATER, Jess, Luke, and I drove up to my uncle's house with a load of my bedroom furniture. One look and I wanted to turn around and go back home. Uncle Peter's house was as much of a disaster as it had been at Christmas time when we last stopped by. The yellow paint was faded and peeling. The yard was a mess, with trash strewn everywhere. I was afraid to see what it looked like on the inside.

"Is this it?" Jess parked his dad's black Silverado.

I double-checked the address my mom had given me. I hadn't driven here without her before. "This is it." My throat tightened as humiliation drowned me. "Um, can you guys wait here while I find out which room is mine?"

"Sure," Jess answered. "We'll wait in the driveway."

Luke swallowed. "Yeah, we'll just get ready."

I hurried out of the truck before they could see the tears welling up.

I rang the doorbell. "Hi, Uncle Peter," I said when a short, stocky man with a dark, bushy beard answered the door. He was wearing pants and didn't *look* drunk... Maybe this wouldn't be as bad as I'd feared.

"Hi, Eliana," he answered. "Come on in and I'll show you the place."

Once inside, the heavy odor of cigarettes assaulted me. It was so thick, I could barely breathe.

"This here's the living room," Uncle Peter said as I inspected my new surroundings. We'd never come inside this far before. He made a ton of money on the role-playing game app he'd created in college. I'd been wrong to assume any of it had gone toward fixing up the inside of his house. Mom said he wanted to keep his small fortune a secret, but I didn't think he'd keep it *this* much of a secret. The living room carpet had stains all over and could have been there since the eighties. It was likely it hadn't been vacuumed since then either. A leather recliner in the corner and a huge TV on the wall were the only nice things about the room. The rest of the furniture looked as worn as the carpet.

Just off the living room was the kitchen, which was so cluttered I doubted anyone could cook in it. The kitchen sink was piled high with dirty dishes, and the garbage overflowed with beer cans and takeout boxes. My stomach churned. How could Mom think living here would be okay? We didn't need any more problems to deal with right now.

I forced myself to follow my uncle through the rest of the house as he mumbled explanations, pointing at the different rooms. The main floor had a single bathroom. Upstairs, there were three bedrooms and a bathroom that we would all have to share. My queen-sized bed would barely fit in my new room, and I'd probably have to sell my desk.

My uncle left me and I took a minute to compose myself before going out to Jess and Luke. *It's better than being homeless,* I told myself as I tried to ignore the fact that my nose was still burning from the stench in the air. *But was it really?*

My mom pulled up to the curb a few minutes later in her silver Audi. I rushed outside, not looking at Jess or Luke, to catch her before she climbed out of the car, jumping in the passenger seat and shutting the door.

"We can't live here, Mom," I said with as much force as I could. "It's a disaster in there. There are beer cans everywhere. It looks like Uncle Peter had a booze fest last night or something."

Her gaze traveled from me to the house and back to me. She pursed her lips. "I know it isn't ideal. But we don't have anywhere else to go."

"But, what about your *problem*? You can't—"

She shook her head and stopped me with her eyes. "I'll be fine. I haven't had a drink in five years. If I didn't need a drink in the last month since your dad left us, I won't need one now."

"But..."

"We'll deal with it, Eliana." She opened her door and stepped out of the car. There was no point in arguing any further. We were desperate. We had nowhere else to go.

Maybe Mom was right. Maybe she would be fine.

But could *I* survive this?

I stepped outside the car into the fresh March air and took a much-needed deep breath. Luke and Jess were unloading my bedroom furniture from the truck, so I told them where to take it. They were nice and didn't say anything about the house, and I was starting to get over my embarrassment about the whole situation...that was, until Ashlyn arrived with her little sister Macey and her mom with another load of boxes.

"I'm so sorry, Eliana," Ashlyn said as soon as she stepped out of her mom's Escalade, a look of deep pity in her blue eyes. "I kept hoping my mom was driving the wrong direction as we rode here."

"Nope, this is my uncle's house." I forced a smile. "I'm sure it will look fine once we have a chance to get moved in." *And spend an entire month scrubbing it down.*

"If you say so." Ashlyn gawked at the house with a look of pure disgust. I couldn't help but notice how her mother wore the same expression as she stepped out of her SUV in her designer outfit.

I was carrying a box of my things up the stairs when I overheard hushed voices coming from my new bedroom. I stopped on the stairs to listen.

"It's a dump," Ashlyn whispered. "We can't let her live here."

"I know," Jess replied. "But there's nothing we can do about it. They had to move and this was their only option."

"I wish Mom and Dad would let her move in with us."

"You know they'd never let her live with us as long as I'm there. Plus, her mom said no."

"I don't know why. It's not like you're *ever* gonna try anything. But whatever," Ashlyn said. "I just feel so bad for Eliana."

IT ONLY TOOK me two days to get my bedroom set up the way I wanted—there are only so many ways you can arrange your furniture when it barely fits in the room at all. I scrubbed down the walls, swept and mopped my bedroom floor, and opened all the windows to try and get the cigarette smell out of my room. I hoped once I got it smelling better I could simply keep my bedroom door shut all the time and hopefully keep the stink from coming back, because I really, *really* didn't want to be the stinky girl at school.

Mom found a job as a waitress a couple of weeks later. She worked the evening shift most nights. I didn't see much of her, but at least we had some money coming in. It wasn't much, but we could buy groceries as long as my uncle let us stay there rent free.

Since my mom was gone most evenings, I tried to spend as much time at Jess and Ashlyn's house as possible. It was weird being at Uncle Peter's place with him and his friends when they were all drinking and watching TV. Uncle Peter was pretty laid-back, and not that he was a bad guy or dangerous to be around... but he had a lot of friends coming in and out of the house most evenings, and I didn't feel comfortable being there without my mom.

"How many people do you bet are already passed out?" I asked Jess when he dropped me off one night. It was ten o'clock, and I knew if I distracted him long enough, I could buy an extra half hour before I had to sneak through the back door to avoid whatever party Uncle Peter was throwing.

Jess eyed the clock on his dash with a whisper of a smile on his lips. He knew what I was doing. I did it every night. "I'm gonna say one person so far. The night is still young."

"And I'm gonna bet no one is passed out yet. Like you said, the night is young."

"Maybe they're sitting in there chatting about politics and ideas tonight," he said. "I mean, Brandt seems like the kind of guy who listens to talk radio every day. And I'm pretty sure I saw Plato's *The Republic* poking out the top of Davey's pocket yesterday."

I laughed. "I'm pretty sure that was a pack of cigarettes."

"You're probably right. The lighting was pretty bad."

"Yeah, his favorite vomiting spot in the bushes isn't lit very well. I'll have to tell him to try the bushes beneath the porch light next time."

I didn't mention the fact that Uncle Peter was actually a genius or that he'd said Davey was only like this because he was under a lot of stress. It probably wasn't nice of us to joke around this way. But sometimes the only way to get through this situation was to joke about it.

"I wish there didn't have to be a next time." Jess rested his hand on my shoulder. I looked up at his face. A serious expression replaced the jovial one he'd sported a second before. "I'm sorry you have to live like this."

"It's okay," I said. I was kind of used to being around drunks, even if Jess didn't know it.

"No. It's not. This is not okay." He waved a hand in the direction of the house. "You shouldn't have to live here. What kind of father abandons his family? It's been almost two months and you still haven't heard anything from him." He raised his voice, his eyes hard. "How could he do this to you and your mom?"

I'd never seen Jess so frustrated before. Yes, I knew he didn't like what had happened to me, but he'd never shown this much anger at my father before.

As if on cue, Davey and his wife burst through their door across the street, yelling a string of profanities that made my ears bleed. If that wasn't disturbing enough, their two young kids were standing in the doorway crying for them to stop.

Jess and I were quiet as we watched the family. A couple of minutes went by before Davey stomped his way across the street and into Uncle Peter's house, leaving his wife to usher her distressed kids back inside.

When things calmed down again, I turned back to Jess. There was sorrow in his eyes. When he spoke, he sounded defeated, his temper having dissolved into sadness and hopelessness. "I wish you still lived next door."

"I know." I offered him a faint smile, my eyes searching his as I leaned back in my seat. There wasn't anything more to say about it, and we didn't need words anyway. We could read in each other's eyes how we both felt about the situation.

"So what do you think about this Friday?" Jess asked eventually.

"You mean the party Ashlyn was talking about?"

"Yeah."

I lifted one shoulder. "I don't know. I was gonna try hacking into my dad's email again that night."

"Can't you do that any other night? Why Friday?"

I sighed, knowing he'd called my bluff. "I mean, the bonfire sounds like it could be fun. But I'm not so sure about hanging out with the drill team again."

"Some of them are nice."

"*Some* being the operative word."

"I know Madison and Hannah aren't your favorite people."

Or Kelsie. But I couldn't say anything bad about her in front of Jess. Ever since they worked on that project together, Kelsie had been as sweet as high fructose corn syrup to him. And from what Ashlyn had overheard it sounded like she was positive he was on the verge of asking her out, but I hoped he wouldn't. He had his no-dating plan after all. And she wasn't good enough for him, anyway. He always talked about how he wanted a nice girl he could chill with. Kelsie was definitely not nice...at least, those rumors she and her friends spread about me weren't.

I'd never told Jess that Kelsie was the one responsible for spreading the whole *second family* rumor. And I was pretty sure she was also responsible for the latest favorite about my dad being in the mafia. I'd thought about telling him but knew Kelsie would find a way to make things worse if I did. She'd probably start spreading rumors about me being in love with Jess or something. So instead, I pretended the rumors didn't affect me.

"How about this?" Jess asked. "Let's go and see how the party is. And if at any point you feel like leaving, we can. Ashlyn's been talking about it all week. I need to be a good brother and at least show up for a few minutes."

“Okay,” I said. “As long as we can leave whenever I want.”

"That's what I like about you. You're always so enthusiastic about my sister's social events,” Jess said sarcastically

“You know me.” I smiled, grabbing my backpack and making ready to sneak inside the house. “I’m sure it will be the best night of my life.”

CHAPTER FIVE

FRIDAY, Jess and I drove to the woods behind the Brooks' lake house near Lake Oneida. We walked down a short trail and found a large group of kids from school hanging out around the huge fire.

As soon as we joined the crowd, Kelsie walked over to us with a big smile on her face.

"Hey Jess," she said, giving him a quick hug before stepping back. "I'm glad you could make it."

She gave me a polite smile, though I'm pretty sure she was gritting her teeth behind her pink glossy lips. "It's nice you could tag along too, Eliana." As if I hadn't been invited at all.

I forced a smile. "Ashlyn couldn't stop talking about this, so we decided to check it out."

"I bet." She turned her attention back to Jess. "I've signed up for a tour of Cornell's campus tomorrow." She looped her arm through his and led him closer to the fire. I followed a step behind them. "And I thought I could check out some of the dorms. Are you planning to live on campus?" She looked up at him with her big brown eyes. "I thought it would be fun to live in neighboring dorms."

"Uh...sure." Jess swallowed. "I mean, I'm not sure where I'll be living yet."

"Great! I'll make sure to take lots of pictures, and we can make plans."

Make plans? Did she think they were a thing or something?

"Yeah." Jess scratched the back of his neck. "Sounds great, Kelsie."

"Great!" She beamed before leaving us.

"What did the Ice Queen want?" Ashlyn asked when we reached her and Luke.

"Your brother, of course," I answered, a hint of my dislike coloring my voice.

Jess scowled at me. "She was asking about my plans for next year."

"So she's already planning the wedding?" Ashlyn made the gagging gesture.

Jess shook his head. "You guys are crazy. Kelsie was being thoughtful."

Ashlyn and I looked at each other. Guys could be so clueless sometimes.

An hour later, a group of us formed a circle on the logs around the fire. Everyone decided to swap first-kiss stories. It was quite entertaining. Some were hilarious while others were so awkward I got anxious listening to them. How was I supposed to ever even get to that point if I knew it was most likely going to turn out horrible anyway? Only a few people sounded like they actually had a perfectly romantic first kiss.

"What about you, Eliana? Tell us about your first kiss," Madison said.

"Yeah, I would love to hear all the juicy details," Kelsie

added, her eyes flitting between Jess and me. Was she worried Jess had been my first kiss or something?

After looking at the expectant faces around the circle, I finally answered. "No. That's okay. You can skip me."

Yeah, another attempt at hacking my dad's email would have been much better than this. I knew I should've said no to coming.

Madison gave me a sly grin, and looked sideways at a couple of her friends.

This was going to be painful.

I shifted my weight on the log and braced myself for the blow.

"Was it really that bad?" Madison asked with a smirk on her face.

My heart constricted in my chest. She already knew the answer. Was this her way of rubbing it in my face?

I peeked at Jess, who was frowning next to me. Ashlyn mouthed something to Madison, her eyebrows knitted together as she shook her head.

Madison grinned back at Ashlyn, and focused on me again. "Come on, Eliana. We're waiting." She looked at her friends again and snickered.

My face burned flaming hot.

"There's nothing to tell," I said.

"What do you mean by nothing?" Kelsie asked. "Nothing to tell as in it was so forgettable it's like it never happened? Or have you actually never kissed a guy?"

I looked down, wishing the dirt below would swallow me up.

Madison took that opportunity to gasp at the obvious. She turned to the group. "Eliana's never kissed a guy." She looked back at me. "You do like guys, right?"

"Real nice, Madison!" Jess stood and glared at her. He turned to me and held his hand out. "Come on. Let's get out of here."

I took his hand and let him help me up.

Ashlyn and Luke stood as well. "Yeah, this is dumb, anyway," Ashlyn said.

Jess guided us through the crowd scattered around the picnic area before releasing my hand. I could feel Madison's gaze burning a hole into the back of my head as we left.

"Sorry about those guys," Ashlyn said as we walked down the trail toward the parking lot. "I can't believe Madison did that."

I shrugged. "It is pretty ridiculous. I mean, how many junior girls haven't kissed a single guy yet?"

Ashlyn put a hand on my shoulder. "It's really not all it's cracked up to be."

"Hey," Luke said. "What's that supposed to mean?"

Ashlyn patted Luke on the arm. "I didn't mean it like that, honey. Kissing you is perfect." She turned back to me. "What I meant to say was that it isn't always amazing. For example, my first kiss was with Trenton Wilber." She shuddered. "If I could take that back I would."

I smiled, remembering when she'd told me about her first kiss in middle school. Trenton apparently had an overactive salivary gland and had forgotten to swallow before kissing Ashlyn. We'd laughed for days about how her dog, Hank, would have been a better kisser.

We were silent for a moment, focusing our attention on navigating the uneven ground in the darkness. I was relieved when we made it out of the trees and into the parking lot.

"Well, I guess I'll see you at home, Jess." Ashlyn raised her eyebrows and nodded at her brother like she was trying to communicate something to him. Then she leaned over and gave me a hug. When she stepped back, she said, "I'm sorry again about Madison. Having virgin lips is nothing to be ashamed of. I think it's cool you're waiting for the right person to give your first kiss to." She gave Jess one more look. "I'm sure it will happen sooner than you think."

I glanced at Jess to see why Ashlyn kept looking at him like that. He still looked irritated from Madison and Kelsie's comments.

Once we were alone, I asked Jess, "Are you in a hurry to get home?" It was only ten, after all. Uncle Peter's party was just getting started.

"Not really."

"Good, because I'd rather not go home yet. Wanna walk by the lake?"

"Sure." Jess stuffed his hands in his pockets and headed to the trail that led to the lake.

We walked in silence under the light of the full moon, stray branches scratching at my jeans. I pulled my jacket on to ward off the chill in the air now that we were away from the fire.

We found a log to sit on at the edge of the woods overlooking the lake. I leaned my elbows on my knees and rested my chin in my hands. "Sometimes I forget how pathetic I am."

"What do you mean by that?"

I sighed. "I'm a junior in high school and still haven't kissed anyone."

"That doesn't make you pathetic," Jess said. "It simply shows you aren't easy."

I scoffed. *More like I'm a pariah.* I didn't say it though, because I knew Jess would make a point to disagree with me, even if it was true. "What is it about touching lips to someone else's that's so appealing, anyway? I mean, when you think about it that way, it's kind of a weird thing to do."

Jess laughed. "Only you would think about kissing like that."

"Well, it's true." Jess was looking at me like I was the strangest person ever. "Wipe that smirk off your face," I said, shoving him, and he almost fell off the log. "I've had seventeen years to think about it, and I still don't understand what the hype's all about."

Jess grinned. "That's only because you've never done it."

I sighed. He was right. I had no idea what it was like.

"And you can't tell me you never thought about kissing Ryan Miller. I saw your notebooks with his name written all over them." He raised his eyebrows.

"Yeah, okay. So I thought about it." I shrugged. *But a lot of good daydreaming ever did about it.* "I wish I could just get it over with. I mean, I'd probably kiss the first guy that offered. Heck, I should just kiss you."

Jess started coughing and pounded his chest.

Crap! I clasped my hands to my mouth. *Way to make things awkward, Eliana!*

"Sorry, that came out wrong." Stupid, stupid, stupid. "That would be weird." I picked at the bark again for a moment before daring a glance at him.

"No." Jess looked thoughtful, pushing his lips into a pensive frown as he shrugged. "It wouldn't be *that* weird. I mean, what are friends for?" He smiled and nodded. "I've heard of guy and girl friends practicing kissing with each other before. Why shouldn't we?"

"Wait, are you serious?" I asked.

"Why not. I mean, it's not like we're going to be all weird about it, right?"

I nodded, feeling slightly less awkward. "I'm sure people do it all the time."

"Okay. So...your first kiss." Jess sat up straighter and angled toward me. "You're sure you're really ready to give it away? You know you can never get it back again."

"I just wanna get it over with."

"Ouch." Jess winced.

"Sorry, that sounded bad." I hurried to touch his arm. "What I meant was, I've built it up so much in my mind that I've made it into this huge thing it probably won't be. I just want to jump off this cliff, so it won't be as scary next time."

Jess looked at me carefully. "Are you sure?"

I nodded and scooted closer to him, angling myself so we faced each other. If this was anyone other than Jess I'd be dying of humiliation right now. But he'd played house with Ashlyn and me when we were little. He knew everything about me, and he got me in a way nobody else did.

But even though all that was true, nervous tingles spread across my face and fingers.

Jess leaned toward me, lifting a hand to my neck to tilt my head just so. I tried to take a mental note of everything he did. I'd need to remember every step in the future—well, for when I get the chance to kiss someone for real in the future, hopefully.

I closed my eyes and puckered up as his face came closer. Just when I thought we were about to do it, he stopped. I opened an eye to peek, only to find a whisper of a smile playing on his lips.

"Last chance to back out." His warm breath caressed my skin. So close.

"Not happening." I squeezed my eyes shut again.

"If you say so."

In a moment, I felt his lips press against mine. An instant later, he pulled away.

I slowly opened my eyes to find him leaning back with a triumphant smile.

I held still, a little bewildered. "That's it? Seventeen years of stressing over how it would be to kiss a guy, and that's all it is?" I hunched over and faced forward again.

Jess pressed a hand to his chest. "You really know how to deflate a guy's ego. I didn't think it was all that bad."

"I didn't mean it like that and you know it. Kissing that way is fine, but I probably could've figured it out without any practice. I thought you were going to teach me how to kiss someone for, you know...longer." I sighed. "Like if I was going to kiss someone for more than half a second, what should I do?"

"So you're saying you want me to teach you more than the basic peck?"

I bumped my shoulder against him. "That would be correct, Einstein. I mean, you're the one who said friends could practice with each other."

"We'll need to stand up." Confused, I squished my eyebrows together. "It's more comfortable than sitting on this log," he explained.

He got up, pulling me with him. He was almost a foot taller than me.

"Hmm..." He pursed his lips, noting our height difference. "Maybe you should stand on the log, Shorty."

"Okay." I sighed and stepped up, holding onto Jess's shoulders for balance. "Is that better?" We were now almost at eye level.

He nodded. "So, do you really think you can handle all this?" He gestured to himself with a grin. "I've been known to sweep unassuming ladies off their feet."

"Yes, Jess, master of all things romantic, I think I can handle all that."

"Then try not to get swept off your feet." He took a step closer, reaching an arm behind my waist to steady me. "I'm about to teach you my best moves."

"Uh-huh." My stomach knotted as he moved even closer. He looked straight into my eyes with an intensity I'm sure made girls faint in the past.

He really did know how to turn on the charm when he tried. Maybe this wasn't such a good idea. Maybe I wasn't really ready for this kind of a kiss.

He slowly ran his thumb across my lips, causing my heart to hammer in my chest. I tried to quiet my heart, but it didn't seem to realize this was a practice kiss. "I hope this lives up to your high expectations," he whispered, his voice slightly shaky. Could he be nervous too?

I drew in a ragged breath, trying to think of something funny to lighten the mood, but couldn't find any words. What was happening to me?

Jess slid his hand behind my neck and pressed a soft, lingering kiss to my lips. Warmth immediately spread throughout my body. I didn't know exactly how to respond, so I stood there with my hands still on his shoulders as he coaxed my lips to part slightly. He kissed me once again before pulling back and looking me in the eyes.

"So far you're doing good," he whispered near my ear, sending chills down the back of my neck. "But can I give you one tip?"

I couldn't speak, so I nodded.

"You don't just kiss with your lips." He guided my hands off his shoulders, entwining my arms around his neck. He held me tightly around my waist, pulling me against him. "You kiss with your whole body."

This time, his lips were tender and slow against mine. My hand moved, without consulting me, to brush along his jaw, while the other slipped from his neck to grip his shoulder tight. My body was responding on its own accord because my brain had turned to mush, unable to control my limbs.

This was way better than the initial peck he'd given me. I finally understood the appeal of making out. Was this how it would feel to kiss any other guy? Or was Jess just really good like he'd bragged about earlier?

I didn't understand what was happening, but I knew something was changing. Electricity buzzed through my veins as we kissed, like something inside that I didn't even know existed was coming to life.

Our kiss slowed eventually until it ended with a short peck. Jess unwrapped his arms around me, and I pushed away to give him some space.

"That was interesting." Jess ran a hand through his hair, taking his time in looking at me.

I stepped down from the log and dug the toe of my shoe into the dirt. "Yeah. Very educational."

Jess shoved his hands into his pockets. "Very." He chuckled awkwardly. "I, uh...I hope you now know what to expect in the future."

I swung my hands at my sides, one hand in a fist as it bumped into the palm of the other. "I-I think I do. You're a very good ki... ah...teacher. Thanks."

CHAPTER SIX

"HOW WAS the rest of your weekend?" Jess asked as we drove to school together Monday morning.

"It was long. I tried hacking my dad's email, but it was pointless." Actually, I'd spent most of Saturday and Sunday thinking about the kiss. I'd wanted to call Jess to talk about it, but couldn't get up the nerve, hoping he'd call me first.

"Did the Easter bunny pay you a visit?" Jess asked.

"Nope." I put my hands on my lap and picked at my cuticles. "I don't think he got the memo that I moved."

"Well, we're too old for that stuff anyway."

"Yeah." I hadn't expected my mom to do anything since we couldn't afford any extras right now. She did at least have the night off, so we had dinner with Uncle Peter and his best friend Brandt, which turned out to be okay, I guess. Brandt was a nice guy. He was intimidating at first glance. Seriously, he was built like an ox. But he and Uncle Peter told a ton of jokes, so that was good. My mom hadn't said much the whole night, but that was fine since my mind had been occupied with thoughts of Jess anyway.

An uncomfortable silence stretched on as Jess and I each tried to think of something else to say, though I could only think of the way his lips had felt as they moved with mine, and the feel of his arms snug around my waist. I shook my head. I shouldn't be thinking about that right now. He would totally notice the flush on my cheeks.

Jess fidgeted with the radio, only listening to each station for a couple of seconds before switching on to the next. I guess love songs weren't what he was in the mood for at the moment.

"The weather is nice today," I commented, looking out the window at the clear blue sky above us.

"Yeah it is," he said, looking everywhere but at me.

This was soooo awkward. Obviously, he regretted that kiss. I needed to talk to him about it, and make sure he knew I wasn't expecting things to change between us. I may have enjoyed the kiss—enjoyed reliving it all weekend—but that didn't mean it was a good idea for us to try kissing again. He had his infamous dating record to scare me away from even attempting that. I would not become another two-week fling, only to lose my best friend in the process. No thank you. I needed stability in my life...even if kissing him was like heaven.

There wasn't enough time to talk in the car now, since we were almost to school. But I would definitely talk to him after school. We needed to get this whole mess sorted out so we could get back to normal.

We were standing by our lockers, waiting for the first bell to ring, when Kelsie walked up to us with her Gucci bag on her arm, looking like the supermodel she was destined to be.

"When are we going on that date you promised me?" She smiled coyly at Jess, biting her plump bottom lip. Weren't they just going to get together and talk about her visit to Cornell? Had Kelsie translated that as an official date? Or had they talked about going out when I wasn't around?

"Oh, um." He looked at her, to me, and back to her again. "I don't know..."

He clearly didn't want to make me feel bad. I needed to show him it didn't bother me in the least that he still wanted to hang out with Kelsie.

I pasted on a huge smile. "Yeah, you guys should totally hang out this weekend. You'd have a blast together."

Jess hesitated a moment before speaking, quickly glancing at me once more. I nodded enthusiastically, so he'd know I was completely fine with him asking her out. Jess frowned, looking confused as he said, "Umm, do you want to hang out on Friday night?"

Kelsie smiled, showing off her ultra-white teeth. "Friday is perfect!"

Jess swallowed. "I'll pick you up around seven?" His eyes darted to mine again.

"Great! I have so much to tell you about Cornell!" She turned and left us as the warning bell rang.

SINCE LUKE WAS WORKING and Jess was with Kelsie, Ashlyn and I went to a movie at her family's theater Friday night. We loaded up at the concession stand, making good use of the family's 100% discount, and found our seats in the back of the theater.

"Did Jess tell you what he and Kelsie are doing tonight?" Ashlyn asked as we waited for the movie to start.

I shook my head. "No, I didn't ask. Jess didn't seem to want to talk about it." Things had been off between us all week. I almost wished I hadn't asked Jess to kiss me, just so we could get back to normal. He'd always been so open about his love life before, but now it seemed like he wasn't talking about his plans with Kelsie because he thought it would make me feel bad.

"I'm still surprised he asked Kelsie out." Ashlyn put a handful of popcorn in her mouth.

"Why do you say that?"

She looked at me like I was missing something obvious. "Because he can't keep his eyes off you." She paused and furrowed her brow. "You can't tell me you never noticed."

"He looks at me like he looks at anybody. That's kind of this weird thing people do when they hang out with someone."

Ashlyn chuckled. "Yeah, and he was only furious at what Madison did because he's your friend. I mean, come on, Eliana." She turned in her seat to face me. "He was mad because she was rubbing it in his face that he hadn't had the guts to kiss you yet."

I looked down at the popcorn in my lap like it was the most fascinating thing I'd ever seen before. "Why would anyone think he'd want to kiss me? We've been best friends since I was four. You don't go around kissing your best friend."

"What were you guys doing out so late Saturday night anyway? I got home a full hour before Jess."

I shrugged. "We hung out by the lake and talked."

"Talked? What about?"

"I was frustrated and embarrassed about everything, so I told him I wanted to get my first kiss out of the way." I covered my mouth, knowing I'd said too much.

"You what?!" Ashlyn gasped. "Did you guys kiss?"

I nodded slowly and peeked up at Ashlyn. Her eyes looked like they were about to pop right out of her head.

"He actually did it! I thought when he didn't say anything that it meant he hadn't done it," she said as if more to herself than me.

"What are you talking about?"

"Was it good?" She leaned closer.

I blushed, remembering how amazing the kiss had been. Visions of his warm lips moving with mine and the feel of his freshly shaven face against my fingertips popped into my head. "Yeah, it was good."

"Then why the heck is he with Kelsie tonight?"

I shrugged. "You, of all people, know the short lifespan Jess's relationships have. How many of his ex-girlfriends have stayed on good terms with him?"

"None."

"*Exactly*. As great as that kiss was, it couldn't mean anything. It would mess everything up between us. So, when Kelsie asked Jess when he was gonna take her out, I told them what a great idea that was."

Ashlyn's jaw dropped. "Why would you tell him to go out with Kelsie? We hate Kelsie!"

"It all happened so fast." I squeezed my eyes shut briefly then looked back at Ashlyn. "What else could I do?"

Ashlyn shook her head. "No wonder he's been depressed all week."

He was depressed?

I waved the thought away. "If he ever felt romantic feelings for me, he wouldn't have dated half the girls at school."

"Well I can't pretend to understand the reasoning behind everything, but I doubt he would kiss you if he didn't want to."

I CALLED Jess the next day, hoping we could hang out so I could get a better read on whether that kiss had meant anything to him or not. But he said he was busy and couldn't hang out.

Sunday, he had church and family stuff.

By Monday, I had everything that I was going to say to him planned out. I'd had plenty of time to think it through, rehearsing the words over and over in the mirror so I wouldn't mess up.

With no appetite for breakfast, I packed a peanut butter sandwich in my backpack, in case I could stomach it later. It wouldn't do me any good if I fainted from low blood sugar before I could even talk to Jess.

Jess honked for me outside, so I grabbed my backpack and checked myself in the mirror before leaving my room. I'd taken extra time on my hair and make-up this morning, not wanting to have a single hair out of place when I got in his car.

I walked down the stairs, careful not to wake Davey, who was sleeping on the couch—he and his wife must have had another fight. I opened the front door with hardly a sound.

Jess, I sighed to myself, *the quietly handsome boy with the most beautiful green eyes a girl could get lost in.*

I practically danced down the sidewalk to the car. Lost in my thoughts, and excited about the possibilities today might bring, I didn't notice someone was in the passenger seat until I reached for the door handle.

I almost jumped out of my skin when I saw Kelsie sitting shotgun. In *my* seat. From the sour expression on her face, she looked like she'd bitten into a lemon.

She climbed out and let me get into the backseat.

"Hey, Jess." I slid in behind him.

"Hey." Jess looked at me through the rearview mirror as Kelsie climbed back in. He put the car in gear and pulled away from the curb without another word.

Kelsie twisted in her seat to face me. "I didn't know this part of town was included in our school district." She glanced at my uncle's house.

"It's not." My face burned with humiliation. I doubted she'd spent much time in this part of town, if ever. "When I moved here, Jess offered to drive me to school so I wouldn't have to switch."

Kelsie smiled at Jess. "How sweet of you, Jess," her voice oozing with false admiration, "helping little Eliana out like that." I hated how she always called me *little* Eliana, as if just because I was short it made me like a kid still.

"I pretty much forced my services on her." He winked at me through the rearview mirror. "She tried to refuse at first, but when I told her I'd switch schools right along with her, she finally agreed."

I smiled back at him, feeling my humiliation subside. Why was Kelsie in the car anyway? Did her fancy Jag break down or something?

I didn't say much else the rest of the ride to school. I had hoped to get everything out in the open between Jess and me this morning, but Kelsie had foiled that plan. Once again, I'd have to wait until later. Maybe I could pull Jess aside during lunch and get everything figured out.

But as soon as we got out of the car, Kelsie sashayed right up next to Jess. He smiled and reached over to hold her hand.

I stumbled and barely kept myself from face-planting.

This couldn't be happening!

Jess shouldn't be smiling at Kelsie.

He shouldn't be holding her hand and looking at her like she was the sun his earth orbited around.

But it was happening. And I had a front row seat to it all.

"I'll see you guys later. I need to get something from the library before class," I lied. I quickened my step and rushed past them into the school building. I could hardly keep the tears from falling down my face, giving my feelings away for everyone to see.

I ran into the girls' restroom and locked myself in a stall as the tears trickled down.

Why was I crying?

This was what I'd wanted, right? This would keep our friendship the way it'd always been. This would ensure things wouldn't get weird between Jess and me.

"Eliana? Are you in here?" Ashlyn's voice echoed in the bathroom. "I saw everything. Are you okay?"

I grabbed some toilet paper and dabbed at my eyes, embarrassed I was even crying in the first place.

"Yeah, I'm fine," I choked out. Why couldn't my voice cooperate and be steady when I needed it to be?

I took a deep breath and came out of the stall.

Ashlyn pulled me into a hug as soon as I stepped out. "I'm so sorry, Eliana."

"Don't be. This is a good thing." I sniffled. "Don't tell Jess about this, okay?"

After making sure my makeup still looked fine, Ashlyn linked her arm through mine and we went to our lockers. Jess and Kelsie were there. They didn't even seem to notice us as we pulled out our books. Which was fine.

"C'mon, let's get to class." Ashlyn eyed her brother and his new girlfriend with a look of annoyance. "We need to make wagers on how long *that* relationship will last."

I shook my head as my heart panged. "I don't feel like betting this time."

Ashlyn regarded me with sadness in her eyes. "Okay, Eliana. I don't really feel like betting on this one either."

CHAPTER SEVEN

AS FAR AS I KNEW, Jess never gave that kiss a second thought. Our friendship went back to normal, at least on his side of it. Even though I told myself not to feel anything, that this was for the best, my chest hurt every time I saw him and Kelsie together. But he was so busy with Kelsie these days I didn't think he even noticed I'd changed. And somehow, Kelsie managed something none of Jess's other girlfriends had. She asked him to make her a priority, in a way girls always hope their boyfriend will make them a priority, and for some reason...he did.

So for the first time in our friendship, someone else was more important to him than me. We still had our ride to and from school each day, but besides that, any other time we did get together was chaperoned by his girlfriend. Most times I opted to stay home or go to the library instead.

Junior Prom came and went. Jess never had to fulfill his promise to take me. Not because I had a date, but because *he* did. I kept waiting for the day when he'd tell Ashlyn and me about his and Kelsie's breakup, but that day never came. Somehow, she was the girl who had been able to break the curse. And I hated her all the more for that.

SCHOOL ENDED, Jess graduated, and I started working at the Brooks' movie theater. I had worked there last summer too, so it was an easy adjustment. Ashlyn had most of the same shifts I did, so it was fun to hang out with her as we sold moviegoers their popcorn, drinks, and candy.

But as my social life leveled out, it seemed like the universe was determined to keep my mom and me from spending much time together. About a week after I started working evenings at the theater, Mom got switched to the day shift at work. We were like passing ships in the night. She would get off work as I was leaving. I worried that with nothing else to do at night, she may get sucked into spending time with my uncle and his friends, and her temptation to drink might finally win.

It had been a long night at the theater, opening night for the big superhero movie fans had been waiting months to see, when it hit me what special day it also was. My parent's wedding anniversary. July eighth. It would be their twentieth year together.

Why hadn't I realized it before?

"Do you think it's okay if I take off early tonight?" I asked my supervisor, Derek, once the nighttime rush had passed.

An annoyed look crossed his face. "It's a busy night, Eliana."

"Please," I begged. "I just realized it's my mom's first anniversary without my dad there. I need to make sure she's okay."

He seemed to think about it. "Fine. You can go after you check the girls' bathrooms."

I finally made it home around ten-thirty. I crept through the back door, hoping I wouldn't find my mom moping in her bed all alone. She needed someone. She needed me.

"Come on, Annie," I heard Brandt's voice carry from the living room.

"No," Mom's voice sounded. "I changed my mind."

I peeked. My mom was sitting on the couch next to Brandt who wore an easy smile. He held a glass of wine in front of her. "We found the last bottle of your favorite wine. If that's not a sign that you should still celebrate tonight, I don't know what is."

"My husband left me. I shouldn't be celebrating our twentieth anniversary." Mom crossed her arms.

"Then don't think about that. Give yourself a break. I'm tired of seeing you sulk in the corner all night." He lifted the glass closer to her face.

She stared at the liquid, seeming to have an internal battle.

Please tell him no, Mom. You know what alcohol does to you. I silently prayed.

After a minute, she perked up. She was going to tell him no.

Good job, Mom.

She smiled at Brandt and shrugged. "It *is* my favorite. I might as well celebrate it with someone."

"That's my girl," he said.

"Mom!" I called out once I realized what was about to happen. "I need to talk to you."

Her eyes found mine; there was a deadness in them I hadn't noticed before. "Not right now, Eliana." She grabbed the glass from Brandt. "Mom needs a vacation." Without another word, she lifted the glass to her lips and gulped down the red liquid.

I watched, frozen, as she drank. Something in her demeanor changed the moment the wine touched her lips. Like she felt a freedom of sorts. All the memories from my childhood came rushing back to me. Images of her sitting on the couch, glassy-eyed as I practiced my piano, or one of her searching the cupboards for all the bottles my dad had hidden when he realized how bad her drinking had gotten. The memory of her pushing me so hard I collapsed into the coffee table and got a bloody gash on the side of my head. Visions of how she used to scream and scream at me about how it was my fault she was like that. How I was so spoiled that my dad had to work all the time to pay for my toys. Then there was the image of her sitting in the car, shoulders slumped as Dad and I drove her to a rehab clinic in New Hampshire. Alcohol was the demon that turned my mom into a person I hated. A person who had no self-control, who didn't care about anyone but herself and when she would be getting her next drink. Mom's alcoholism was also my family's darkest secret. It was something we did not talk about. With *anyone*.

Her glass was empty. Satisfied, she leaned back into the couch cushions and smiled like she hadn't smiled since my dad left.

CHAPTER EIGHT

AUGUST BURNED hot and humid as it did every year. The day I'd been dreading since last winter finally came. It was Jess's last day home. He'd be moving to Ithaca in the morning, and then it would just be Ashlyn and me.

The sun was blistering hot, the humidity suffocating, as I sat on the porch waiting for Jess to pick me up. If he didn't show up soon, I might be tempted to go sit in the kiddie pool with Davey's kids across the street. That would be much better than going back inside to hang out with my mom and her favorite drinking buddy, Brandt.

I'd hoped her anniversary drink would be a one-time thing, but one drink turned to two. Bottles turned into cases until she was helping Uncle Peter pick the alcohol selection for each evening—there was a lot more red wine than there used to be. When I tried talking to her about her drinking, she told me to mind my own business and let her make her own choices. It seemed like since I was almost eighteen, my mom had decided she could be done with raising me. She'd put in her time. Maybe I should be happy I was so free to come and go as I pleased, and that I didn't have anyone watching my every move. Wasn't that what teenagers were supposed to want?

Instead, it just made me realize how insignificant and forgettable I was to the people I cared about most.

And if my own parents could forget me so easily, would Jess even bother keeping in touch with me?

Normally I'd tell myself that it was impossible, that our friendship was too important to him...but what if I was wrong?

I shook those thoughts away. I needed to stop throwing a pity party and focus on today, because at least for today, life would be good. Jess had promised me one last day together, like old times, before he went off to Cornell with Kelsie. And that was all I wanted. One last, normal day where I didn't have to think about my messed-up home-life, or how everything was changing. I needed normal. I *craved* normal.

My makeup was just beginning to melt when Jess's Camaro rolled up to the curb. I wiped the sweat off my forehead and trotted down the steps, hoping he had the air conditioning on full blast.

"Sorry I'm late," he said when I opened the door. "Lunch with Kelsie's family went late."

Kelsie...

Think positive thoughts. Be happy. Be normal. Don't be jealous. Think. Positive. Thoughts!

"Did you even hear what I said?" Jess asked.

"Um, sorry?" I gave him a guilty smile.

"I was wondering if you wanted to grab some ice cream before heading to Little York Lake." Jess switched the AC on high, probably noticing my sweaty hairline. "You look like you could use some cooling off right about now."

"Ice cream and Little York sound great."

We drove to the nearby ice cream shop, and since we were both chocoholics, we each ordered Extreme Chocolate Meltdown shakes with extra brownie bites mixed in. Then we headed out of town. Little York Lake was such a great hideaway about thirty minutes away. There was an old playground with the tallest metal slide I'd ever seen, along with a bunch of picnic tables and tent sites that sat beneath tall pine trees.

Kids were running all over the playground when we arrived, enjoying the last bit of summer left before school started. Jess and I sat on the grass overlooking the playground, on the old quilt he kept in the back of his car.

"How was meeting Kelsie's sister?" I asked, following through with my plan to keep everything normal. Friends asked friends about what they did with their girlfriend's family, right? And apparently, things were getting more serious between Kelsie and Jess, because her family sure made a big deal out of him meeting her sister and her family for the first time.

"It was fine. Her sister was nice." His eyes wouldn't meet mine as he pumped his spoon in his shake.

"That's good."

He cleared his throat. "So, we'll be leaving around nine in the morning. Do you wanna come over for one last breakfast together before I leave?"

My heart sank. "I have to work in the morning. I traded Josh shifts so I could hang out with you tonight."

His eyes looked sad. "So this really is it before I leave, huh?"

I nodded, trying to keep the panic out of my chest. How had this day snuck up on me so fast?

We sat in silence for a while as we finished our shakes, watching the people at the park. About twenty feet away, a couple was sitting on a bench together, looking to be in their mid-thirties. They were holding hands, smiling proudly as they watched their two little kids go down the slide. They reminded me of how my parents had once been.

I looked around, people-watching now. There was a dad on

the swing with his baby girl sitting on his lap. His wife stood in front of them, her phone held up to capture the father-daughter moment. They all looked so happy, smiling and laughing at each other.

I couldn't help but think that my life used to be like that. I was the little girl whose daddy constantly doted on her. I'd been the little girl in the fluffy dress and bouncing ringlets, who ran to my daddy every day when he got home from work, wrapping my arms around him in a tight hug. But life wasn't like that anymore. Part of me wanted to warn the little girl, before she got her hopes up, that her fairytale life might not be happening.

Before long, she'd probably have the FBI stopping by her house off and on to see if her dad had been in contact with them since he disappeared.

Two squirrels scurried past. I followed them with my eyes until they ran past the bench with the middle-aged couple on it.

"Is she doing what I think she's doing?" Jess turned to me with a crooked smile.

I screwed up my face. "It looks like she's popping his zit." Indeed, the man was bent close to his wife who had both hands on his face, looking like her fingers were pinching a pimple.

Jess laughed. "Now that's true love right there."

"Some couples are so strange. They could at least wait to do that in private."

I hadn't noticed the clouds darkening in the sky above us until I saw families gathering their things and rushing to their cars with the first drops of rain. It would start pouring soon, so we packed up our stuff and headed for Jess's car.

I glanced at the time on the dash. It wasn't even seven yet, and I was nowhere near ready to say goodbye. This would be our last time together before he left for Cornell. I needed to prolong the night as long as possible. *Who knows when we'd get to hang out alone again?* Kelsie was going to have him all to herself in

Ithaca, and I could only imagine how much shorter his leash would be after that.

"What should we do now?" Jess drummed his fingers on the steering wheel.

I shrugged. "I know we planned to do *all the things* tonight, but I think I'd be happy sitting here in your car, watching the rainstorm." I meant it as a joke, but he seemed to take my suggestion seriously because he reclined his seat and settled in.

I followed suit.

"Are you ready to be a big-shot college guy tomorrow?" I turned sideways and propped myself up on my arm to be more comfortable. The rain had cooled things off, so thankfully, it wasn't too hot to sit in the car without turning on the air conditioning.

"I don't know about the big shot part, but yeah, I'm excited to live on my own. It'll be nice to not have my parents nagging me about my future 24/7." He and I had opposite problems. His parents were very involved in his life and had extremely high expectations, while my mom couldn't care less what I did anymore.

As he talked about his class schedule and all the things he was looking forward to, I studied him. The way his eyes lit up when he talked about a class he was excited for, and how his mouth formed around the words he spoke. I watched how his eyebrows knit together when he was trying to remember something, and noticed how he moved his hands as he spoke.

I would never admit it to anyone if they asked, but Jess was beautiful. Everything about him was perfect.

I would miss him so much this year. The summer had been hard enough with him splitting his time between Kelsie, work, and me. How was I supposed to survive nine more months?

Then it hit me. We may never get to hang out like this again. Earlier, he'd mentioned something about going to his grandparents' resort next summer. After that, I would be heading off to college too. I planned to apply to Cornell and Ithaca College, but I would also be applying to other schools.

I hoped to get a scholarship, and if I did, I would be going to whatever school gave me the best one. I might be in a completely different state than Jess after this year.

Anxiety hit me with an intense force at the thought of things never going back to normal again. All this time I'd been waiting for things to change, to get better, but even my relationship with Jess would never go back to the way it was before my dad left. Why did things have to keep changing all the time? It wasn't fair!

I wanted to be in this moment with Jess, talking in his car as the rain poured all around us. But the pressure in my chest grew the more I thought about how things would be without him. I would die if we drifted apart, too.

Jess furrowed his brow, deep creases stretching across his forehead. "What's wrong?"

"I'm realizing what saying goodbye to you tonight really means." I drew in a deep breath, trying to gain control of my emotions again. I didn't want my tear-filled face to be his last memory of me.

He took my hand and squeezed my fingers. "I'll be back. It's not like I'm leaving the country or anything."

"I know." I sniffled and wiped at my eyes. "I'm going to miss you, that's all."

He moved his face closer to mine and spoke in a low voice. "I'll miss you too." He tucked some hair behind my ear. "So much."

I nodded and looked down, feeling my heart throb as I looked at our hands together. Did he realize what he was doing to me? I wasn't supposed to like him. He was my best friend. He had a girlfriend.

He placed a hand on my shoulder and leaned his forehead against mine.

I lifted my eyes to look at his face, to try to read what emotions might be there.

His eyes were squeezed shut as he breathed in a shaky breath.

"Is everything okay?" I whispered. *Please tell me what's going through your mind. Do you ever think about that kiss?*

He opened his eyes, a torn look flitting across his face. "Yes. Sorry, I..." He shook his head, released my shoulder, and turned to look out the windshield. "Sorry, I'm being weird. It's been a long day."

"Yeah?" *Had he almost kissed me?*

We were quiet for a while, watching the rain.

"How are things at home?" he finally asked.

"They're fine," I lied.

Keep yourself to yourself, my dad's voice sounded in my mind like it had so many times when my mom hurt me before. I didn't know why I still listened to him, it's not like he deserved to matter to me anymore. But for some reason he still did. And for an even stupider reason, I still wanted to be daddy's obedient little girl.

Jess narrowed his eyes. "Are you sure things are fine?"

"I'll be fine." I looked away, and then turned to him again, a fake smile on my face.

Jess nodded slowly, still not looking like he believed me. But instead of asking further, he turned the key in the ignition and said, "How 'bout we get some dinner."

MIDNIGHT ROLLED AROUND and Jess took me home. It was still raining, so he grabbed the umbrella out of his trunk before walking me to the back door.

"Try not to forget about us non-Ivy League people," I said when we stood on the doorstep under the yellow glow of the porch light. I wanted to say more, something funny that might lighten the mood, but I couldn't think of anything.

"I'll be back for fall break before you know it." He pulled me into a tight hug.

I leaned into him and breathed in his cologne, committing his scent to memory. Jess was a great hugger, and it was comforting being so close to him. He just felt...good.

When Jess pulled back, I thought I saw tears in his eyes.

"I'll see you soon." He hesitated a moment before pulling me in for one more hug.

"I'll be here," I said, my voice breaking along with my heart. *Don't forget me.*

He turned and headed down the path back to his car. I shivered, feeling cold all over as I watched him walk away. Jess was the sun in my life, and I wondered if I would ever make it out of the darkness now that he was gone.

CHAPTER NINE

GOING BACK to school without my best friend stunk. Jess and I still texted, but it wasn't the same when I didn't get to see him every couple of days. He was loving college life, though, and all the freedom that came from being away from home, so I tried to be happy for him at least. But I couldn't seem to manage being happy for myself. I was a senior, so I should have been excited about my final year of high school. But I wasn't. Even though most of the rumors about my dad had died down, I still couldn't shake the feeling that everyone saw me as the girl who was left behind. And not just by my dad. Now by my best friend, too. So many days I worried my mom would leave me completely behind too.

When I was younger, her problem with alcoholism had happened more slowly. She'd been able to hide it from us for years, seeming normal in public. But now she didn't seem to care. Most days I worried she'd smash up her car on her way home from work after a stop at the liquor store, or that I'd come home from school to find she'd died from alcohol poisoning.

Just to cope with my fear on the days I didn't have work, I

would head to the library to finish my homework. Then, I'd lose myself in a novel so I could pretend to be the main character, and that the life I was living now was actually the one that was pretend.

A FEW WEEKS into the school year, I was delivering a stack of papers to the school office for my math teacher, Mrs. Carver, when I heard a familiar voice sound behind me.

"Is that Eliana Costa?"

I slowly turned my head and almost dropped what I was carrying. "Ryan?" I furrowed my brow. "What are you doing here?"

Ryan Miller, the boy who had lived across the street from sixth through tenth grade—also known as the guy I'd been ridiculously infatuated with during those years—was sitting on one of the green chairs in the waiting area.

"I just moved back," he said, his legs crossed and stretched out like it was the most natural thing for him to be back at our school.

"Moved back? Didn't your dad get a pretty good job in Manhattan?"

"New job, and new boss...who turned out to be his new girlfriend." He sighed as he pulled his legs in and shrugged one of his broad, linebacker shoulders. "My mom and I moved in with my grandparents for a while. Divorce sucks!"

"Wow, that stinks." A pit formed in my stomach. "I'm sad to say that I sorta know what you're going through."

He raised his dark eyebrows. "Your parents got divorced?"

I shook my head. "Not a divorce, exactly. My dad screwed over a bunch of clients and ran off before he was caught."

"Seriously?" His eyebrows shot up further. "When did that happen?"

"Last February." I shifted the stack of papers nervously in my hands. "We haven't heard from him since."

"Wow." His mouth fell open.

"It happens." I shrugged, and looked at his chest...a very well-defined chest. He was huge. They'd probably beg him to be on the football team, even though they were well into the season.

"Can I help you?" The secretary, Ms. Haslam, came from behind the desk. I whirled around. "Yeah, um, Mrs. Carver wanted me to bring these to you. She said you'd know what they were for."

The woman reached her hand across the counter. "Yes, I'll take those. Thank you." She smiled my dismissal and looked behind me to Ryan. "Mr. Miller, your schedule is ready if you want to take a look."

I tucked some hair behind my ear and turned back to Ryan who was approaching the counter.

"Well, it was good to see you again." I had to crane my neck way back to see his face. "I hope you enjoy your first day back."

"Thanks." Ryan smiled, displaying the dimple in his right cheek that I had always wanted to poke. "Despite everything, it's actually good to be back."

I walked out the door, proud that for the first time in my life, I'd been able to talk to Ryan Miller without blushing and losing my train of thought.

WHEN I GOT TO LUNCH, I told Ashlyn all about running into Ryan. I was telling her what he'd said about why they had moved back when I felt someone walk up behind us.

I turned around and almost choked on my chocolate milk.

Ryan was standing a foot away. I swiped at my mouth with a napkin, hoping I didn't have spaghetti sauce smeared all over my face, and turned in my chair to face him. All six-foot-three inches of him.

"Hey, Rapunzel." Ryan whispered his old nickname for Ashlyn.

"Ryan!" Ashlyn jumped up and gave him a hug. "I can't believe you're back!" She stepped back and punched his arm. "Eliana told me she saw you! If you hadn't come over I would have kicked your butt!"

"You couldn't hurt me if you tried." Ryan grabbed a chair from the table behind us and sat so we were the three points of a triangle.

"Whatever." Ashlyn folded her arms. While I could hardly utter a complete sentence to Ryan in the past, Ashlyn was the exact opposite. She and Ryan had carried on like you'd expect a brother and sister to do. "How have you been?"

"I've been all right," he said, showing us his confident smile.

"Been busy stealing all the hearts of the girls in Manhattan?" Ashlyn asked.

He shrugged and tilted his head to the side. "It's not something I can turn off."

And I had to agree with him, since I was one of the girls who had her heart stolen away years ago. Some guys attracted girls without even trying, and Ryan's personality was magnetic.

"How's your family doing? What's my buddy Jess up to these days?"

"They're great," Ashlyn said. "And Jess moved up to Ithaca last month to attend Cornell."

Ryan raised his eyebrows, impressed. "Cornell? That's Ivy League, right?"

"Yeah, nothing but the best for Jess," I said, more than happy to brag about my best friend. "He even got a full-ride scholarship." Though, unlike me, he could have attended it without the scholarship.

"Impressive," Ryan said. "Will he be back in town anytime soon? I'd love to catch up with that guy again."

"He'll be here for fall break," I answered.

"When's that?"

"The same weekend as homecoming," Ashlyn said, since that's how her brain worked. She measured time by events that were happening in her life, while I measured in days, weeks, and months.

"And when exactly is that?" He held up his hands. "Sorry. New guy."

"Under two weeks from now. It's on October twelfth," I said. Even though I was pretty sure I'd be sitting this dance out, like I had all the others, I'd been counting down to it. There was a certain time frame that guys usually asked girls to dances at our school. Ranging from three weeks in advance to a week before. If a girl hadn't been asked by the Saturday before the dance, it was pretty certain she wouldn't be going. That gave the guys at school a week to realize I existed.

Ryan pointed a finger in my direction. "I forgot how quick you were."

"Is that a bad thing?" I hadn't meant to sound like a know-it-all.

"No. It's great. Being smart is cool." Ryan glanced at the clock on the wall. "Well, I'll let you get back to your lunch. I just wanted to catch up real quick." He stood and tucked his chair under the table beside us. But then he suddenly turned around again. "Hey, Eliana, are you still as good at math as you used to be?"

"I guess so. Why?"

"I was wondering if you could help me go over some of the stuff from Stats. Mrs. Carver said you used to tutor? We weren't quite this far along at my old school."

Ryan Miller was asking me to help him? If only my twelve-year-old self could see me now.

I nodded. "I could probably do that."

His smile broadened. "Awesome! Is Wednesday before school too soon?"

I pretended to think about it before answering. I didn't want to appear like I had nothing else going on in my life. "Yeah, I can do that."

"Cool." He took a step back. "I'll see you then."

Once he was gone, I turned back to my food. Did Ryan Miller just ask me to spend time with him...without Ashlyn or Jess? That had *never* happened before.

I tried not to read too much into it. Crushing on Ryan Miller was a bad habit I'd never been able to break in the past. But maybe this could be a good thing. I needed a distraction, and maybe a good old crush on Ryan would get me to move past the impossible feelings I had for Jess. Plus, it would be fun to have something, *or someone*, to look forward to seeing again. Who knows, maybe I'd found a guy to trick into being my homecoming date.

TWO DAYS LATER, Ryan and I sat in the west corner of the school library, hunched over our notes as I helped him figure out one of the math problems he was having trouble with. I was wearing my favorite shirt today, which also happened to be red—Ryan's favorite color—so I hoped he'd notice it and maybe also notice what a great date I could be for homecoming. It might not be true love or anything like that—I wasn't ready for that anyway—but it could be fun.

"Have you and your mom found a house yet?" I asked when

we'd finished the assignment that was due today. If I was going to get him to ask me to the dance, I needed to show him that I cared about his life, right?

Ryan leaned back in his chair and rolled a pencil around his fingers. "We looked at a bunch of places last night, but so far, *no bueno*. If our old house was available, it would be perfect. My mom wants to move into the old neighborhood."

I nodded. "It was a nice place to live."

His eyebrows squished together. "Was? You don't live there anymore?"

"No. We rented the house out after my dad left."

"Dang. Where do you live now?"

I stared at a spot on the table. Did he mind going out with girls whose families couldn't afford a mortgage payment anymore? "My uncle let us move in with him for now. He lives in Westside."

"I didn't know that was in our school district."

"It's not. But they let me stay since I've already gone here two years." Okay, enough about me. We needed to talk about him. Guys loved talking about things they were good at. "I heard they got you to join the football team."

Ryan folded his arms across his chest. "Yeah. Coach Hobbs called me into his office my first day back. I was happy they wanted me. It would have sucked to miss playing my senior year."

Next step: compliment him. "You must be pretty good." Well, try to compliment him. Wow, I'm horrible at this flirting thing.

"I do okay. What about you? Do you still play soccer?"

I shook my head. "I didn't have time for it this year. I'm taking a lot of honors classes."

He nodded like that was cool. Did he prefer sporty girls over bookish girls? "Still getting straight A's, I assume?"

"I'm trying to get a scholarship somewhere, so I'm keeping my grades up."

"Good for you. I hope you get one."

Hmm, was that a neutral reaction?

I sighed. Ryan was hard to read.

I looked out the library window before us. There were a lot more kids in the halls now. He'd probably want to leave soon to hang out with his buddies before the bell rang. My time was almost up.

"So, who are you going to homecoming with?" he asked.

I almost choked. Did he read my mind? I cleared my throat. "Actually, I'm not going yet."

He leaned his head forward, baffled. "That's crazy. I figured someone asked you already."

"Nope. Not yet anyway." *I won't turn you down if you ask.* The sad fact was that I probably wouldn't turn anyone down. Maybe I should have Luke make one of his famous "Boyfriend Wanted" posters. It sure had created some excitement for Ashlyn last fall. "What about you? Who are you taking?"

"No one yet. Being gone for a year kind of took me out of the dating scene at our school."

Oh no, he'd realized I wanted him to ask me and now he was backing off.

His friend Mark appeared and interrupted us, saving me from making an even bigger fool of myself.

"Hey, Ry," Mark said. "I gotta tell you something real quick."

Ryan looked at me apologetically before getting up and walking over to one of the bookcases behind us.

Mark spoke in a low voice, but I could still hear him. "I heard Bridgett and Ashton broke up last night. She's totally free for you to ask to homecoming."

My heart, which had inflated with hope throughout the morning, shriveled inside me like a popped balloon. Bridgett had been Ryan's girlfriend before his family moved away. I should have known he'd want to date her when he got back. He'd probably been hoping something like this would happen all along.

"Are you serious?" Ryan whispered back. He slapped Mark on the shoulder. "You rock, dude!"

Ryan rushed back to the table and stuffed his books into his backpack. "Thanks for all your help this morning, Eliana. You're a lifesaver." He threw his backpack over his shoulder and pushed his chair under the table. "See you later."

"Yep. See you."

I sank in my chair and watched through the window as he strode down the hall, coming to a stop in front of Bridgett Maynard. I didn't need to see the rest of what happened after. I already knew. People like Bridgett and Ryan were genetically destined to be together. I didn't know why I even thought I had a chance.

Like I expected, Ryan and Bridgett were holding hands by lunchtime.

CHAPTER TEN

AFTER FAILING at getting Ryan to ask me out, I pretty much gave up on going to the dance. I didn't know why it meant so much for me to go to homecoming, but for some reason it did. It seemed like something every senior girl should experience. And for once, I wanted my life to be normal.

I didn't necessarily have a crush on any of the guys at school, none of them were Jess, so I had no idea who to smile at more. Well, I *thought* smiling at guys might help my chances. I was friends with all the guys in Math Club, but half of them had already asked girls, and the other half would probably be skipping the dance to play computer games online instead. I already overheard Hayes and Brady talking about the science fiction movie marathon they were planning for that evening.

Ashlyn asked me to go dress shopping with her after school that Friday, which I agreed to do, even though it was sure to keep my pathetic-ness fresh on my mind. We drove to the Destiny mall in Syracuse, where she scoured the stores for the perfect formal. I tried to seem like I was happy for her and her luck with having a wonderful boyfriend who didn't mind coming to a high school dance even though he'd graduated.

"What do you think about this one?" Ashlyn asked, holding a pink, knee-length dress in front of her.

"It's beautiful." I moved to examine the dress more closely. It was gorgeous, with a layer of lace over satin. I moved my hand to check the price tag and quietly gasped. I could buy three months' worth of groceries for the cost of the dress.

Ashlyn noticed me eyeing the price tag and forced an embarrassed smile. "I know it's pricey, but my dad said I could charge it to the credit card."

This reminded me of how different our situations were now. I dropped my hand from the dress. "I'm sure Luke will love it. Now go try it on." I pushed her toward the dressing room. "I bet it fits you perfectly."

"It better." She closed the door behind her. A couple of minutes later, she emerged with the dress on. "What do you think?" she asked, twirling around.

I sat up in the chair. She looked amazing—the pink color brought out the glow of her tanned skin. No wonder Luke could never keep his eyes off her. "I think this could be the one. What do you think?"

She sighed and ran her hands down her dress. "I'm in love."

I laughed. "Good."

I pulled off my heels and rubbed my aching feet, regretting my dumb idea to wear them today. I'd figured maybe guys never noticed me because I was so short. But like all my other attempts—curling my hair yesterday and wearing lipstick the week before—the added inches hadn't given me any more luck. Just blisters. I was running out of ideas and time.

"You should try on a dress, Eliana," Ashlyn said as she studied her reflection in the mirror beside us. "You could still get asked, and you don't wanna be rushed at the last minute."

I shook my head. "No, that's okay. I'm pretty sure I'll be sitting this dance out too."

"Come on." She turned to look at me, hands on her hips. "Grab a few and try them on. It'll be fun."

It *would* be fun to try one on. I glanced back at the rack with the teal-blue chiffon dress I'd eyed earlier, my fingers itching to touch the soft fabric. I hadn't worn a fancy dress in a long time. "Okay. But just one." I turned on my heel and strode toward the rack, taking the dress with me to the dressing rooms.

A couple of minutes later, I examined myself in the mirror. The dress fit like it was custom-made for me. And miraculously, it gave me some curves. *Maybe I should wear this dress to school on Monday as a last-ditch effort.* I shook my head at the ridiculousness of that thought. That would put me in the *do-not-ask-the-crazy-girl* zone for sure.

"Are you decent?" Ashlyn called from the other side of the door.

"Yeah."

"Then get your butt out here. I want a full-on fashion show."

I opened the door, and as I stepped out, Ashlyn's jaw dropped.

"You look stunning! Like, seriously. You should get the dress even if you don't go to homecoming. It would be a crime to not get a dress that was made for you."

I shrugged. "It would be dumb to buy a dress I have no reason to wear."

"You still have a week to get asked. We should at least ask the store to hold it for you, just in case."

I did have some money saved for college. I could use some of it for this.

I looked longingly at my reflection one more time, trying to imagine what it would be like to wear this dress to a dance. But me getting asked to a dance was such an unbelievable dream that

I couldn't even summon the image of it in my head. I sighed. "It's okay. If I do get asked, I'll know where to find it."

"Let me at least get a picture of you wearing it." She pulled out her phone. "Smile."

I did as she said, posing with my hand on my hip.

Ashlyn inspected the photo. "You look hot!" She returned her phone to her pocket. "Are there any other dresses you want to try on before we leave?"

"No." I didn't think there could ever be a dress more amazing than this. "I'll just change and I'll be ready to go in a minute."

Ashlyn had me hand her the dress over the door so she could put it away while I finished putting on my normal clothes. It was probably a good thing she did, or I may have been tempted to hang on to it forever.

AFTER ASHLYN DROPPED me off at the library, also known as my new hang-out spot that kept me away from "home," I got a text from Jess.

Jess: **How was shopping with Ashlyn? Did she try on a billion dresses?**

Me:**Just about.**

Jess: **Exciting. *rolls eyes* Did you try any on just in case?**

Me: **One, but it was probably pointless. At least I'll get to hang out with you even more while you're here for the weekend.**

Jess: **All those guys at school must be blind, or stupid. But their loss is my gain.**

Me: **Yeah, right. Thanks for trying to make me feel butter.**

Me: ***better. Not butter. Stupid autocorrect.**

Jess: **Any guy would be lucky to take you to Homecoming.**

Me: **Apparently no one got that memo.**

Jess: ***Checks sent mail folder* Dang it! My secretary forgot to send the memo out two weeks ago. I can have her resend it if you want.**

Me: **Meh…it's ok. I won't mess with fate. Apparently, she thinks it's better for me to hang out with my best friend when he's home for fall break instead of dancing with some guy I've never talked to anyway.**

CHAPTER ELEVEN

FINALLY, it was October twelfth. Homecoming had come, but an invitation had not. So while all my classmates would be enjoying a magical night, I decided to throw a party of my own and definitely not think about how much fun everyone else was having. I wouldn't even think about the fact that Jess had cancelled his plans to come home for fall break, saying he had a study group he couldn't miss. Nope, I definitely wouldn't think about that.

I holed myself up in my room with my laptop and all sorts of goodies tossed on my unmade bed. After taking a bunch of online quizzes to pass some time, I discovered that my *real* age should be twenty-three, Belle was the princess I most resembled, and I was destined to marry a Mr. Darcy-type guy and have four kids. My fake life sounded way better than reality was turning out to be.

Deciding I'd spent enough time "learning" new things about myself, I moved on to the next activity of the night. I was turning on my favorite K-Drama when I heard a knock at the back door.

It was probably Davey trying to hide from his wife again, so I didn't bother getting up.

A minute later there was another knock. *Why isn't Uncle Peter getting that?*

Then I remembered Uncle Peter had actually trimmed his beard this week and was in NYC showing a new app idea to a couple of guys. I paused my movie and slid out of bed and down the stairs.

The knock sounded again. "Coming!" I called out as I fiddled with the lock. "Sorry, my uncle must be..."

I opened the door and my jaw dropped to the floor. Standing there, on my back porch, was Jess. He wore a black tuxedo, his hair styled to perfection, and he looked good—like take-my-breath-away good.

He held out a bouquet of peonies.

I put a hand to my chest, trying to catch my breath. "What are you doing here?" I managed to ask, though it came out more like a sigh.

A huge grin stretched across his face. "I came to see if you wanted to go to homecoming with me."

"You... But... What?" My brain stopped working. I couldn't manage to form a simple response. "I thought you said you had a study group this weekend."

He shook his head. "I made that up. I had to surprise you somehow."

"But you're a cool college guy now, why would you want to go to a dumb high school dance?"

Jess smiled. "Because *you* deserve to go to a high school dance, Eliana."

"What about Kelsie?" There was no way she knew about this.

"She'll be fine."

"I don't want this to cause a fight," I hedged. "I really am fine with my movie and junk food."

"You might be. But I'm not." He took a step closer and held

the flowers out. "I have to make up for not taking you to prom last year. So, Eliana, will you go to homecoming with me?"

I almost melted.

Then I remembered something.

"But I don't have a dress." I looked down at my ratty gray sweats.

"Don't worry, Cinderella, your fairy godmother took care of everything." Jess jumped off the porch and pulled a teal blue formal dress out from behind the bush by the door.

I covered my mouth with my hand. He was holding the exact dress I'd been coveting at the mall a week ago.

"You didn't," I whispered.

"I did." He held it out for me. "And it would be a crime for this dress to go unworn. So Eliana, will you *please* go to the dance with me?"

"Yes!" I leaped onto the porch and threw my arms around him. "Of course I'll go with you."

He laughed and hugged me back. "Good." His voice was muffled against my shoulder, and I got a whiff of his cologne. I stepped back before any old feelings could bubble up.

He called behind him, "She said yes, Ashlyn. You can come out now."

"What? Ashlyn?"

A giggling sound came from behind the bushes. A second later, Ashlyn sauntered into the house, already wearing her pink dress with her hair in an elegant up-do.

She hugged me. "I told you to get the dress."

My eyebrows knit together. "Did you know about this all along?"

I inspected their faces, and they both looked guilty of conspiring together.

"Of course she knew," Jess answered for Ashlyn. "You don't

think I'd be able to pick out a dress like that all on my own, did you?"

I shook my head, resisting the urge to cry. "I can't believe you guys did this for me."

"Well, that's what friends do." Ashlyn smiled and tugged on my arm. "Now let's fix that hair."

AFTER EATING the most delicious dinner I'd had in a long time, we drove to the school. Jess and me in his Camaro, Ashlyn and Luke in Luke's Jeep. On our way to the dance I decided to come up with a game plan for the night. Step one: Don't trip on my dress. Step two: Have fun at the dance. It had been all I'd thought about for weeks, I needed to make sure to enjoy the moment to the fullest. And step three, which was the most important step of all: Don't let my mind run off with any romantic notions of Jess and me being more than friends. Taking me to the dance was just something nice he was doing, and I needed to try not to make things awkward between us by letting it slip that I had feelings for him.

Jess gave me his arm as we walked into the school. The usually drab gym had transformed into a magical wonderland fitting the dance's theme, "Midnight Fairytale." Fake trees wrapped with twinkling lights marked the rope-lit path to the dance floor. Quite a few students from the drama department had taken the theme to heart, dressed in full-on fairytale costumes. I almost didn't recognize some of them at first glance. Nena from AP English had forgone her typical goth makeup and black clothes, and instead looked brilliant in a blue knee-length Cinderella dress and light makeup. I hoped this wasn't a one-night look for her. She looked so much better when we could actually see her face. Madison, the girl who'd taunted me last year for having never kissed a boy, was standing in the corner with her minions Natalie and Hannah. Was it be possible that nobody had asked them either? I tried to keep a smug look from my face at the thought that karma had finally kicked in. My eyes next spotted Ryan and Bridgett, dancing near the refreshments table, holding each other close.

Jess led me further onto the dance floor. My stomach tightened when he rested his hands on my waist, pulling me into his arms for the slow dance. I couldn't help but remember the last two times we were this close, when we said goodbye and that practice kiss that seemed so long ago.

I shook my head; I shouldn't be thinking about those things right now. I scrambled for something to say before he could read my thoughts.

"Are you sure Kelsie won't be mad about this?" I blurted out before realizing how stupid it was to bring up his girlfriend at that moment.

"No, she's the one who had the study group this weekend. She won't miss me."

"Well, that's good." I'd hate to be moved up even higher on her enemy list. "Thanks again for bringing me."

"It's my pleasure," he said, meeting my gaze. His eyes looked more blueish green than usual, probably matching the teal-blue of his vest. He leaned closer, whispering into my ear, "You look stunning in that dress, by the way."

Heat rose up my neck at his compliment. *Stunning?* Jess thought I looked stunning? I swallowed, hoping he hadn't notice my blush. "Y-you look good too." Jess in a tux...sigh.

I tried to push the nervous jitters from my stomach as we swayed to the music, but they would not go away. All my mind could think about was how nice it felt to be in Jess's arms, how they were the perfect fit for me. And how in the world could someone smell so good? His clean masculine scent was so addicting I might hyperventilate if I didn't watch myself.

I needed to stop noticing so many things about him. That would definitely not help me accomplish goal number three.

"How have you liked college so far? Is it like you thought it would be, or a lot different?" I asked.

"It's good." He shrugged. "The first week was super stressful and tiring, but I've got the hang of things since then."

"That's good."

"Any news about your dad?"

My chest deflated. "Nope. Still nothing. We have FBI agents contact us every once in a while, but they haven't found anything either."

"Does that mean the search for your dad is dead?"

"I guess. It's been eight months with no trace."

"Are they going to at least unfreeze your accounts so you can get back in your home?"

I shook my head. "I don't think so."

Jess let out a frustrated sigh. "That isn't fair. You guys are innocent."

"Yeah, but who knows if any of that money is even ours. It's probably all stolen anyway."

Jess frowned but looked like he was going to drop the subject.

"Is your mom still dating that guy? Brandt?"

"He practically lives with us now."

Jess scrunched up his nose. "That guy is huge. Is he nicer than he looks?"

I bit my lip. "He's okay."

"You need to get out of that place. I hate that you're living there."

And you don't even know what my mom is like now.

I forced a smile. "At least I'll be off to college in less than eleven months."

Jess looked like he was about to ask me something, but didn't; instead, he continued to lead me in the dance.

Ryan found us as soon as the song ended.

"How have you been, buddy?" He slapped Jess on the back and gave him a hug in a way that only guys can do. "I hear you're off to some fancy-pants university."

Jess smiled hugely. "I don't know about the *fancy pants* part, but things are great. College life is awesome."

"Good to hear."

I excused myself to go to the bathroom so they could catch up without me.

Madison, Hannah, and Natalie were primping in the mirror when I walked in the bathroom.

"So are you and Jess an official thing now?" Madison asked when I went to wash my hands at the sink next to her.

"No. Of course not," I said.

Madison glanced at her friends through the mirror. The way they looked at each other told me they didn't believe me.

"We're just really good friends." I shrugged before grabbing a paper towel.

"Sure." Madison nodded slowly. "Since it's completely normal for best friends to check each other out."

I crumpled the paper towel. "I wasn't checking Jess out."

Madison raised her eyebrow. "I never said it was you."

Was she saying that Jess had been checking me out? Had I been so focused on making sure he didn't notice my feelings for him that I'd been blind to any signals he'd been putting out? My fingers went all tingly at the thought. Could Jess actually *want* to be here with me?

I worked hard to keep from running back into the gym to find out. Jess and Ryan were finishing up their conversation when I got to them.

"So how's it been having Ryan back at school?" Jess asked

with a teasing glint in his eye. A slow song started in the background.

Ok...he was teasing me. Definitely not checking me out. Why did I believe Madison?

"Pretty much the same as when he was gone," I said.

He pulled me into his arms for another slow dance. "Really?

"Believe it or not, I'm no longer crushing on our old neighbor." *I found a new, old neighbor to crush on.*

He pursed his lips and studied my face as if deciding whether I was telling the truth. Seeming satisfied with whatever he saw, he asked, "So what are the qualifications a guy needs to get you to go out with him?"

My cheeks flushed, my mind scrambling for something to say. I tried shrugging nonchalantly. "I don't know. Breathe. Have a heartbeat." I tried to keep my tone light. "Why are you asking me this? It's not like I've been turning down guys left and right."

Jess tilted his head to the side in contemplation. "I think you make guys nervous and they don't want to risk being shot down because they aren't good enough for you."

I pulled my head back, completely confused. "Why would anyone be nervous around me? It's not like I'm this mean girl, am I?"

"No." He shook his head. "It's not that at all. You're so beautiful, and smart—it's kind of intimidating."

"You're talking to the girl no one's ever looked at twice, except for when I had rumors swirling around me and my family. I doubt I intimidate anyone."

He moved his cheek next to mine, the warmth of his breath on my ear. "You intimidate me."

My face grew hot. Intimidate Jess? How could that even be possible? He knew me better than anyone. He'd seen me at my worst, when my eyes were so red and swollen because I couldn't keep from crying after my dad left and my world was falling apart.

He'd seen the desperation in my eyes every night last year when he dropped me off and I kept talking to him about random things because I didn't want to go inside.

"I wish you could see yourself the way I do," he said after I'd been quiet for too long.

I nodded, feeling way too awkward. What was I supposed to say anyway? Did I intimidate Jess? What did that even mean?

Ashlyn and Luke bumped into us. "So, did you notice Shao and Rackelle came to the dance together?" Ashlyn asked, her lips red with the juicy gossip.

Jess's face fell slightly with the interruption, but he responded with, "I wonder how long they'll last this time around," while my mind still reeled and tried to catch up.

But as Ashlyn kept talking, I knew the moment was lost. And no matter how hard I tried, I couldn't get that moment back.

"I HAD A GREAT TIME TONIGHT," I said to Jess as we stood on my back porch after the dance. The moon was full and high in the sky, backlighting the soft clouds in a way that made me feel as if it was just Jess, me, and the moon still awake.

"Me too," Jess said, looking like he had something on his mind. "It was fun hanging out again."

"Yeah." I fiddled with my bracelet.

"I guess I better let you go." He rubbed the back of his neck. "I've kept you from your chick-flick long enough."

"I don't think I'll be getting to that tonight after all." I looked down at my hands, unable to ignore the nervous feeling growing in my stomach.

Jess chuckled awkwardly. "That's probably wise, I guess. I forget how much you enjoy sleeping." Was he stalling?

"Well, I'll let you go." I stepped toward him and gave him a hug. "Thanks again," I whispered, backing up.

"Anytime," he said. A hesitant look flashed across his face. Before I knew it, he leaned close, pressed a quick kiss to my cheek and spoke next to my ear, "It's nights like tonight that make me wish we could go back to last April."

He pulled back. His eyes were haunted.

I had a thousand things to say, but they all stuck in my throat. And before I could respond, he disappeared down the sidewalk and into the dark night.

I stood frozen for a minute. *What just happened?* Did he just bring up what happened Easter weekend? I thought I was the only one who ever thought about that. Could he, like me, have regretted what happened after that kiss? Did he wish he'd never gone on that date with Kelsie? Would everything be different now if I hadn't pushed him that way?

I walked inside and leaned against the door, ghosts of what might have been taunting me. *Did he really wish we could go back —go back to the day when everything changed?*

But I shook those *what ifs* away. Not everything had changed that day. Just me.

CHAPTER TWELVE

JESS WAS in hot water with Kelsie. Apparently, he'd never told her his plans about taking me to the dance, and she found out the next day when one of her friends sent her a picture of us dancing. They didn't break up though, which I didn't understand. Had I completely misunderstood what he'd said the night of homecoming? Hadn't he hinted that he wanted to go back to the weekend of that kiss and have a redo?

But maybe it was just my own wishful thinking.

Regardless, I still had no idea why he'd want to stay with her. She was a beast, way worse than any of his previous girlfriends that he'd let go of after only a couple weeks. But who knows, maybe she had some hidden qualities I didn't know about. She was in Ithaca with him at least, so that was convenient.

The next month passed slowly as I turned in my college applications and continued to spend most of my free time at the library. I saw my mom for a few minutes every day in passing, and lately those few minutes were more than enough. She was turning into that bitter, angry woman she'd been before, maybe even more so since now she was a poor drunk instead of a rich one. Dating Brandt wasn't helping anything either. Sure, he seemed like a positive enough guy, but all he had to do was worry about himself, he had no one else depending on him—just working during the daytime and partying at night. And from some of the things my mom said, it seemed like she was jealous of his freedom and wished she didn't have a stupid, needy daughter to tie her down.

Thanksgiving was lame. Mom had to work, so I ended up eating pizza with Uncle Peter and Brandt while they watched football all day. Jess and Ashlyn had gone to their grandparent's new resort in Dominica for Thanksgiving, so I couldn't even escape to the Brooks' house for a few hours.

Finally, the day I'd been looking forward to in forever came. November twenty-seventh. My eighteenth birthday.

I was an adult now!

In years past, my parents had always made a huge deal out of birthdays, spoiling me with more gifts than I could count. When my mom was sober, she had found a hobby in throwing themed birthday parties. When I turned thirteen I had a rock star party, and the next year we had a spa day for me and my friends.

For my sixteenth birthday, they'd rented a limo to take me, Ashlyn, and Jess to New York City for a couple of days of over-the-top activities.

I knew my mom couldn't afford to do anything big and crazy this year, but I secretly hoped she'd at least make me the traditional strawberry French toast she made each year.

I walked into the kitchen and found Mom and Brandt sitting next to each other at the table. This was a good sign. It was rare to see her up before I left for school. My mom's light brown hair was frizzy and falling every which way over her light blue bathrobe. She rested a cheek on her hand, much like she did on the days she had a hangover.

"Good morning." Brandt smiled at me, his brown eyes lingering a moment too long. "You look happy today."

I dipped my head and tried to return his smile. "I am happy." I glanced around the room, searching for evidence of breakfast. The kitchen didn't smell or look much different than it had last night, though. The sink still overflowed with dirty dishes, the peeling laminate counters cluttered with stacks of junk mail and empty wine bottles. My smile faltered until I remembered how she always set breakfast in the warm oven so it didn't get cold. I opened the oven door and peered inside. It was empty.

"What are you looking for?" my mom asked in a tired voice, turning her gaze in my direction.

I tried to keep any disappointment from showing on my face. "Nothing. I wanted to make sure I hadn't left anything in there last night."

I'd just have cold cereal again this morning.

I checked the clock on the wall. Ashlyn would be here in about ten minutes to pick me up. She didn't have drill team practice this morning and had offered to drive me to school so I wouldn't have to ride the city bus on my birthday. I washed a bowl in the sink, and found the box of cereal I kept hidden in the back of the pantry.

When I sat down to eat, my phone vibrated with a text message from Ashlyn.

Hey, Eliana. Luke gave me strep throat. I can't get you today. :(

Dang it! I checked the time, the city bus left the stop down the street in fifteen minutes. I'd have to hurry if I wanted to make it in time.

I quickly texted her back, and slipped my phone into my back pocket.

"Teens text their friends this early in the morning?" Brandt asked.

"Ashlyn was telling me she's sick today. I'm gonna have to ride the bus after all and I'm running late."

"I can give you a ride on my way to work," Brandt offered.

"Oh," I shifted in my chair and looked at my cereal bowl. "That's okay. I can take the bus like usual." I'd rather not be alone with him if I could help it...just to be safe. I still didn't feel super comfortable with the way he always sat a little too close to me when my mom wasn't around.

"Don't be silly, Eliana." Mom sounded annoyed. "Brandt offered to do something nice for you. The proper thing to do is to accept."

"It's okay, Annette." Brandt patted her hand and looked back at me. "Eliana was probably worried it was out of my way." Yeah, *that's* the reason. "But the construction site is not too far from your school. It's no problem at all." His smile seemed earnest enough. And maybe he was just being a nice guy willing to help his girlfriend's daughter.

"O-okay. Thanks," I said.

My mom straightened up and frowned into the mug she was holding.

"What are your plans for today?" I asked her, trying to have some sort of positive interaction between us.

She startled and shifted her gaze to me—apparently still out of it. After a beat, she answered. "Working, same as usual, in the never-ending world of waitressing."

I nodded, looking at my cereal as I swirled my spoon around.

"Do you have any tests today?" she asked.

"No, thankfully. That would kind of ruin my day." I hoped the hint would jog her memory.

She lifted the mug to her lips and blew in it. "And what's so special about today?"

Was she playing dumb in order to surprise me with something later today? I couldn't be sure. Maybe she was pretending to forget my birthday since she knew I was expecting something and she didn't want me to catch on?

"Oh, um, it's just Tuesday. I hate having tests on Tuesdays."

She pursed her lips and nodded her head thoughtfully as she slowly looked at Brandt. "You learn something new every day." She gave him a half smile, like she found something amusing. "I had no idea Tuesdays were a bad day for tests."

"Any day is a bad day for a test." Brandt laughed and winked at me.

I forced a smile at him, though his winking made my stomach turn. "I wish my teachers felt the same way."

Once I finished my breakfast, I decided to pass the time before Brandt took me to school by tidying up the kitchen. Since I didn't have to catch the bus, I had more time than usual to get to school. I washed the dishes, stacked the junk mail in a corner for Uncle Peter or my mom to go through later, and tossed the empty bottles in the recycling box outside. At least the kitchen would be nicer looking if my mom wanted to bake a cake later on. When it was seven-thirty, I grabbed my backpack and followed Brandt to his rusty old truck.

WHEN I GOT home from school, I brought in the mail, hoping to find a birthday card from my grandparents in Italy. They had always made sure to send something, even if it was just a card. But there was nothing with their name on it. Maybe they didn't know our new address. I sighed and added the junk mail to the pile on the counter. Someday Uncle Peter or Mom might decide to look through it.

Next to the mail I found a note from my mom. *I have to work a double-shift. There's leftover pizza in the fridge for dinner.* My shoulders slumped, and I let my backpack slide off my arm to the ground. I had held out hope that Mom was planning a big surprise after school, but it didn't look like that was happening.

I decided not to go to the library like I usually did on the days I didn't work at the theater. Uncle Peter was out of town again, so there wouldn't be any partying tonight. And my mom didn't sound like she'd be around, which meant Brandt shouldn't be home either. So I was safe to stay home, which I guess could count as a birthday present of its own. I took my backpack upstairs and studied in my room, taking a break for cold pizza around six.

I'd just finished writing a paper for Humanities when my phone rang. It was Jess.

My spirits lifted as I slid my finger across the screen to answer. "Hello."

"How's my favorite birthday girl doing?" Jess said, sounding cheery.

"Great, now that I'm talking to you," I said, feeling a brightness in my chest I'd been missing all day. Jess was the first person to wish me *Happy Birthday*.

"Did you do anything fun today?"

"Not really. I went to school, came home and did my homework."

"What? How did anyone let you be so lame on your eighteenth birthday? It's only the most important one you've had so far."

"Nah. It's okay." I leaned back on the pillows on my bed, pushing my laptop to the side. "It's like any other day of the year." I hoped that sounded convincing.

"You at least have plans to party tonight, right?" He sounded so sure.

I shook my head before realizing he couldn't see it. I found my voice. "Nope. No partying here. Actually, I'm the only one home."

"You mean your mom didn't even get the night off work?"

"You know she can't do that. We need the money." I wanted to leave it at that, but I needed someone to vent to. "Plus, I don't think she even realized today was my birthday."

"Are you serious?" I heard him draw in a breath and release it before speaking again. "How do you forget your only daughter's birthday?"

I rubbed a wrinkled spot on my comforter until it lay smooth. "I doubt she knows what month it is, let alone the exact date. Her life is the same every day: go to work, hang out with Brandt, go to sleep, wake up, and repeat." I sighed. "It's okay, though. I made myself a birthday cake and blew out the candles about an hour ago."

Jess laughed, but it was the kind of laugh that told me he didn't know if I was serious or not.

"Did you really bake yourself a cake? Because that would be sad."

"No, but I'm seriously thinking about it. Maybe I'll get all fancy and make a cheesecake or something."

"I have a great recipe if you need one," Jess offered.

"What? You know how to make cheesecake?" Did he even know how to heat up a can of soup?

"Heck yes!" He sounded so proud of himself, I could picture the big smile on his face. "Since living on my own I've been cooking a lot of different things. That's what happens when you get sick of eating Top Ramen for every meal."

"I'll have to see this so-called cooking in action before I believe it," I said.

"I'll make something for you sometime, and when your taste buds come back from what's sure to be the closest thing to heaven, you can apologize for doubting me."

I smiled. "You're on."

There was a pause on the line, and then Jess spoke in a quiet, concerned voice. "I'm sorry your birthday ended up being a total flop. I wish I could have celebrated it with you."

I relaxed my head on my pillow and curled up on my side, missing Jess so much it hurt. At least with him around my life had been bearable. "It's okay."

The line was quiet again for a while as I thought about how our relationship might have been if I hadn't messed things up last year. Too bad I couldn't go back in time and fix things.

"Jess?" I asked, not sure he was still there.

"Yeah?"

There was a thickness in my throat now. "I miss you." I wiped at a tear trying to escape out of the corner of my eye.

"Me too, Eliana." I heard an almost imperceptible sigh through the earpiece. "I think I miss you more every day."

AFTER HANGING UP WITH JESS, I ended up pulling out the scrapbook I had put together a couple years ago, hoping to get my mind off the present. Inside the thick binder was photo after photo of once-happy memories. There was the photo of my dad reading my favorite book to me on the leather couch in his office when I was four. A couple pages later sat a picture of my fifth birthday. Mom had done my hair in French braids the night before so it could be wavy for the party. In the picture, I was smiling from ear to ear, with Ashlyn on one side, Jess on the other, as we anxiously waited for my mom to cut the pink castle cake she'd had a friend bake. I choked back a wave of emotion, remembering how good things were when my mom wasn't drinking and my dad was around.

I kept turning pages until I came across a page from when I was ten. Beneath a picture of my dad and me fishing from a boat at Martha's Vineyard was a crumpled piece of paper with the first note Dad had written me. When my mom's drinking started the first time, he had made sure to always show me how much he loved me, going the extra mile to do nice things. When I was ten, he came up with the idea for us to write notes as a way to tell each other things we couldn't always say out loud. This particular message read: *I love you forever, Baby Girl.*

I ran my fingers over the paper, trying to ignore the pain the memory evoked in my chest. I couldn't help but remember what my return message had been: *I love you forever, Dad.* I hadn't been creative enough to come up with a different message of my own.

When my mom went to rehab a few months later, we told everyone she was visiting a sick aunt. It was then that I used these notes to tell my dad how alone I felt. And how sad I was that Mom was sick. He'd always written back with words of comfort, which helped me get through that difficult time.

We stopped exchanging notes a couple of years ago. Maybe I should have recognized that as the first sign that he was pulling away.

Feeling nostalgic, I pulled out a notebook and wrote the few sentences I would send if I knew how to reach him today.

I miss you.

Why did you leave us?

I still love you.

CHAPTER THIRTEEN

I WAS SNEAKING into the house after work Thursday night, when I overheard my mom talking to my uncle.

"You were smart to never tie yourself down like I did," came her tired voice from the living room. "If I hadn't gotten knocked up with a kid when I was twenty-three, I wouldn't be in this mess. I could have finished college and started my own company like I'd always dreamed of."

She paused, probably taking another long sip from her wine glass.

"Instead I got stuck with a colicky baby and had to drop out so I could take care of her while Paulo got all the accolades and awards because his wings never got clipped."

"You can't mean that," Uncle Peter said. "Eliana's a good kid."

My mom huffed. "Yeah well, a lot of good that did. Paulo still left us. He always spoiled her too much, and when he knew he couldn't afford the college his baby girl wanted to go to, he embezzled a bunch of money and split."

My dad embezzled all that money because of me? If I hadn't talked so much about going to an expensive school like Cornell, would he still be here?

Was everything my *fault?*

I snuck out of my hiding place on the other side of the wall and slipped up the stairs to my bedroom. I tried going to bed, but my mind wouldn't shut down. Was my mom telling the truth, keeping it to herself all this time and only venting when she thought I wasn't around? As much as I didn't want to believe what she said was true, I couldn't ignore all the whisperings inside that believed her. It was stupid for me to expect my parents to pay for college. Obviously they couldn't afford Cornell.

But I hadn't known we couldn't afford it. Dad had always been happy to buy me the things I asked for; in fact, he'd encouraged me to look into what my dream school would be. He'd been the one to drive me around campus as we talked over the pros and cons of Cornell versus a more local university like 'Cuse. He wouldn't have done that if he didn't want me to go there.

Would he?

But the facts were hard to change. We never had enough money in the bank to even pay for a semester at Cornell. So instead of telling his baby girl "no" for the first time in his life, he'd committed a huge crime and disappeared.

It was all my fault.

JESS TEXTED me the next day to tell me he'd made a last-minute decision to come home for the weekend and wanted to hang out. I wanted nothing more than to get out of the house, away from my mom and all the guilt her words had formed in my heart. So I slipped my phone into my pocket, tugged on my coat, and waited for Jess on the front porch. Thinking about the truth bomb Mom had dropped wouldn't do me any good, and I needed a break from everything tonight. So as soon as Jess showed up, I shoved my thoughts into a separate file in my brain, only focusing on the fact that at least Jess still wanted to spend time with me. Hanging out with him had always been like magic for my soul.

"What made you decide to come home so suddenly?" I slid into his car, the smell of his Camaro immediately taking me back to a time and place when things were much simpler.

Jess pulled away from my house. "Kelsie and I had another fight, and I needed to get away for a while."

"What was it this time?"

Jess exhaled. "More stupid stuff. Like she's been bossing me around a lot lately." He glanced over at me as he drove. "You know, telling me what to wear and how to cut my hair."

"She doesn't like your clothes? I love the way you dress."

"No. Apparently, my jeans aren't *skinny* enough." He rolled his eyes.

I scrunched up my nose. "Eww. I hate it when guys wear those skin-tight jeans." I reached over and grabbed his shoulder in mock desperation. "Please tell me you didn't cave to her demands. I don't think I can be seen with a guy who wears tighter pants than I do."

Jess chuckled. "Don't worry. I didn't." We drove for a moment before he spoke again. "Does it bother you when a guy hasn't shaved for a few days? I mean, do you think it looks sloppy?"

I hadn't noticed before, since it was dark in the car, but Jess had a few weeks' growth on his face. "It depends on the guy. Some guys can pull it off, others can't."

"So, what are the determining factors on whether a guy can pull it off or not?"

I cleared my throat. "Well, it depends on the shape of a

guy's face, the length of his hair, and his ability to grow a decent beard. Like, if it's patchy, I'd say he needs to stay clean shaven."

Jess nodded, but I could tell he wanted more. "What about me? I've been doing No-shave November with my roommates. Do I look as bad as Kelsie says?"

"Hmm, it's a little hard to tell in this light," I said, trying to avoid telling him what I really thought about how he looked, because he looked good. Way too good.

His shoulders slumped. "It looks that bad?"

He looked crushed; I couldn't let him think he looked terrible when he looked the opposite. "No, Jess. You look good with facial hair."

His lip lifted into a crooked smile. "How good is good?"

I blushed, realizing he wasn't going to let up the interrogation until I flat-out told him. "Let's just say that Kelsie's wrong on this one, because I don't normally like facial hair on guys my age and I think you may have changed my mind."

Was the heater on full blast? Because I was suddenly overheated.

"You think I can pull it off?"

"Um...yeah." I nodded, feeling my blush deepen.

Jess smiled and leaned back in his seat, content with my answer.

I, on the other hand, had a hard time relaxing the rest of the drive—having just admitted to my best friend that I thought he was attractive. I was curious, though. I'd never touched facial hair before, and I wondered how it felt. Ashlyn always talked about how she hated kissing Luke when he hadn't shaved, complaining about getting beard burn. But Jess's scruff didn't look too prickly. I couldn't help but wonder what it would feel like to run my fingers along his jawline. What would it feel like against my cheek? Or my lips?

"So is your beard scratchy or something?" I blurted out when we were walking into his house.

He stopped and turned to face me. "Why do you ask?"

"Well," I floundered for an excuse. "I-I guess I'm wondering why Kelsie hates it so much." I couldn't meet his eyes.

"Why would it being scratchy have anything to do with it?" He took a step closer.

I shrugged and tried to sneak past him down the hall, but he stuck his arm out, creating a barrier I couldn't get through. I backed into the wall trying to put a few more inches between us and said, "Well, you know." When he didn't appear enlightened by my eyebrow raising, I continued, "I figured she must not like the way it feels."

"Oh." He did a slow nod, finally catching my drift. "No, after a week or so it's pretty soft." He paused, scrubbing his fingers along his chin with a thoughtful look on his face. "Here." He leaned a shoulder against the wall I was trapped against, grabbed my hand, and lifted it to his face.

He moved my fingers along his cheek, back and forth, so I could feel his short beard.

My fingers trembled as they caressed his jawline. "You're right," I squeaked. "It is soft."

Our eyes met, and his narrowed as they searched mine. I knew he had totally noticed my trembling fingers, but must have decided to ignore it because in the next moment he let my hand drop.

I urged my heart to stop racing when he stepped away.

"My family is out tonight. So I hope you don't mind just hanging out with me," he said.

"That's cool."

Jess could turn into a band of feral monkeys and I'd still probably have a way better time here than I would at home.

"Are you hungry?" Jess walked to the fridge and ducked

inside. He pulled out a few containers of leftovers and set them on the counter.

"I could go for some of your mom's cooking."

"I know what you mean. Living at home did have its perks." Jess grabbed two plates from the cupboard behind him and dished a big square of lasagna on each. He covered one with a paper towel and popped it in the microwave.

"I thought you said you were eating pretty well since you're this gourmet cook and all."

Jess smiled. "That only happens once a week, my friend. The other six days I'm lucky if my roommates don't steal my leftovers, leaving me stuck with canned foods or frozen burritos."

"I still don't know if I believe that you're some cooking prodigy. I've never heard of cooking skills being genetic."

"They aren't. But there are these things called recipes, and if you have a good one that your mom emailed you, and you know how to measure ingredients correctly and follow instructions, you'd be amazed at what can happen." The microwave beeped so he switched out plates and put the hot one in front of me.

I cut into my lasagna and blew on it before taking a bite. I closed my eyes as I chewed to fully experience the awesomeness filling my mouth.

When I opened my eyes, I found Jess staring at me with a huge grin.

"What?" I covered my mouth with my hand, suddenly feeling self-conscious.

"You're cute when you eat." He filled two glasses with ice water before taking his food out of the microwave and sitting on the stool next to me.

"I'm glad I could amuse you." I took another bite, this time keeping my eyes wide open as I swallowed.

We ate in silence for a few minutes before Jess spoke

suddenly. "Would you think I was crazy if I decided to take next semester off school?"

I almost dropped my fork. "What? Why would you do that?"

"I don't know if pre-med is for me, after all."

"Are the classes too hard?"

"They're hard, but that's not it. I'm just not interested in it like I thought I'd be. I realized the main reason I got into it was because my parents always wanted a doctor in the family. I think I only did it to impress them." He sighed. "It sounds dumb. I'm like the biggest people pleaser ever, it's ridiculous."

If Jess had a fault, that was it. Though it had been nice when I'd needed so much help from him last year.

"Is there something else you want to study?"

"I'm not sure. I've been thinking about a lot of different things. Culinary school even made the list."

"Really?"

His face fell. "You think it's a dumb idea too?"

"No, not at all. I'm just surprised." I narrowed my eyes. "Who told you it was a dumb idea?"

He looked down and swallowed. "Kelsie. She thinks I'm throwing my future away, going after some random dream. She thinks I should choose a career with more stability."

"Kelsie doesn't know what she's talking about." All she cared about was status and money. All summer she'd bragged and bragged about how her boyfriend was going to be a rich doctor, possibly surgeon someday, as if she'd already envisioned herself as his trophy wife.

I almost said my thoughts aloud but bit my tongue at the last second. I knew once I got started I wouldn't be able to stop. I had watched Jess get bossed around by that girl way too much since they started dating, and I had come close, on several occasions, to telling Jess what I really thought about Kelsie. But I didn't want to say anything, only to have Jess get mad at me and not want to hang out anymore.

"Are you going to tell your parents about your plans?" I asked.

He shifted in his seat, his gaze trained downward. "I want to. I mean, I need to. I just haven't found the right moment. You know what I mean?" He looked up, meeting my eyes. "That brings me to my second choice."

"You have another choice to make?"

"Yeah. I was talking to my grandma over Thanksgiving break about all this stuff, and she said I should take the semester off and come help them out at their resort."

My eyebrows shot up. "Are you serious?" Only Jess would hesitate to go on an extended vacation to an island resort.

Jess nodded. "I'm just...I don't know." His eyes were wide, his mouth downturned. "Can you tell me what to do with my future? That way, if I choose wrong I don't have to blame myself."

"And you could blame me instead, right?" I set my fork on my plate and pushed it away from me. "Sorry Jess. This is your life. I can't make that decision for you."

"I guess I have a lot of thinking to do." Jess took our plates and rinsed them in the sink. "Hey, so how did the rest of your week go? I felt so bad after our conversation on your birthday. I still can't believe your mom forgot."

If only that was the worst thing that had happened this week.

"It's fine. My week is much better now that you're here." I smiled, hoping he'd drop it. I had done such a great job of forgetting my problems this past hour, I'd almost felt normal again.

Jess narrowed his eyes and searched my face. His tone was serious when he spoke. "You're not saying something. I've known you for way too long to believe you when your face tells me you're keeping a secret."

What should I tell him? Should I tell him everything about

my mom? Should I finally free the family secret and let him know that my mom was an alcoholic and had been for a long time? It would be nice to have someone to talk to about it, someone to understand what my life was really like.

But my dad's words played through my mind. *Don't let anyone know when you're down. Keep yourself to yourself.*

A war rivaled on in my mind. Why was I still letting my dad influence me? He was gone. He left us and hadn't even tried to contact us. He didn't even send me a birthday card.

Maybe I'd just tell Jess the most recent thing. My dad only told me to keep the drinking a secret.

"My mom blames me for everything. She says my dad embezzled all that money to help pay for college next year."

Jess's eyebrows squished together. "What?"

"My parents were never good with their money, and I think he freaked out when I started talking about going to Cornell like you." At least, that's what I guessed from what I heard.

"You can't blame yourself. Your mom shouldn't blame you either. Your dad is the one who made that choice. He's the only one at fault."

I nodded, my chest lightening. If telling him just that one thing made me feel better, maybe I should tell him everything.

But before I could say more, Jess said, "You know what we need to do?"

"What?"

"We need to get you out of town for the day. We could get the old gang together, head to the lake house, and celebrate your birthday the way it should have been celebrated the first time." He leaned closer. "What do you think?"

A day at the Brooks' family lake house. That sounded like heaven right about now.

"Who exactly would be coming to this birthday bash of mine?" *Please don't say Kelsie. Anyone but Kelsie.*

"We could keep it pretty small. Ashlyn and Luke, of course, and maybe also Ryan. It'll be like old times."

"Let's do it!"

Maybe I hadn't told Jess everything about my mom being an alcoholic, or what it was like when I was younger. But I had told him enough for him to make things better. And it wasn't like my mom had gotten abusive again.

CHAPTER FOURTEEN

WE MET AT THE BROOKS' house the next morning at ten. Ryan had brought along Bridgett, so that made for an interesting dynamic. Two couples and Jess and me.

So close to being like a triple date, but oh so far away.

"Okay, guys. This is the plan." Jess came to where we all stood by his dad's black Silverado. "I was thinking that since Ryan hasn't been there for a while, he and Bridgett might want to ride in the truck with me and the gear. Ashlyn and Luke can drive his Jeep over, and Eliana, you can ride in whichever car you prefer...though I suggest you come with me since Ashlyn and Luke can be pretty gross sometimes."

"Hey!" Ashlyn pouted. "We're not that bad, are we?"

"Um, sorry, Ash, but your brother's right." I looked at Jess. "I'll go with you if there's still room up front."

Jess smiled. "Of course. I saved a spot about your size, just in case."

"Great."

I went to climb in the passenger side door of the truck, but found Jess had put the cooler right in that seat. *I thought he said there was room up front.* Had he meant for me to sit in the back with Ryan and Bridgett? That would be awkward. I mean, I knew Ryan okay, but I didn't know Bridgett that well. She was one of those quiet but gorgeous girls, and so we never really talked—two awkward introverts together never worked out so well.

Ryan and Bridgett climbed in the back passenger side, so I went around to get in on the other side. But when I got there, Jess stopped me.

A sheepish look spread across his face. "I put a bunch of gear back there too, I didn't want it to get rained on. When I said I saved a spot just your size, I meant it." He opened the driver's door and gestured for me to look inside. He was right, there was just enough space up on the bench seat for us to squish in close.

"Should I go in the Jeep? I didn't know how tight a fit you were talking about earlier." But Luke was already pulling out of the long driveway, turning onto the street. "Looks like we're squishing," I said, and grabbed onto the steering wheel to heft myself into the high-clearance truck.

Jess jumped in next, and when he shut the door there was no space left between us. Like, zero space. I never would have thought much about our proximity a year ago, but now it was all I could think of. We were *so* close. Our thighs, sides, and shoulders were practically welded together.

"Are you good?" Jess asked, turning his green eyes on me.

Had he done all this on purpose? *Should* I be reading into this?

I wanted to.

"Um, yeah. I'm good." I cleared my throat and tried to find something to busy myself with. Seatbelt. Buckling my seatbelt would be a great distraction. I felt around behind the cooler for the seatbelt, until I realized it was on the other side. I reached behind my left side and accidentally touched Jess's butt. "Sorry!" My face flamed.

Jess laughed. "Don't be."

I turned a darker shade of red and fumbled around until I found the dang seatbelt hiding in a crack. I had to feel around the cooler to find the latch. I was starting to sweat in my jacket, and was sure Ryan and Bridgett could see how flustered I was. Why couldn't I act cool? It's not like we hadn't sat this close before.

"Do you need help?" Jess asked when he noticed my struggle to secure the belt.

I blew a wisp of hair out of my face and sighed. "Probably. Are you sure you didn't put this cooler here to torture me?"

I looked over my shoulder just in time to see his smirk.

That boy! Ugh. He was enjoying this.

I resisted the urge to punch him and instead handed him my seatbelt. "You do it!"

He placed my seatbelt right back in my hand, then jumped out of the truck, ran around to the other side and pulled the cooler back so I could click the buckle in.

"Got it?" he asked, lifting his eyebrows.

"Got it." I turned forward and crossed my arms.

"Now that was entertaining," Ryan said from behind me as Jess walked in front of the truck again. "It's almost like Jess had planned to give you such a hard time."

I shook my head. Of course he did. I should have remembered how much he loved to tease me when we went on trips to the lake house. I could only imagine the other shenanigans he had planned to "cheer" me up this weekend.

After buckling himself in—with ease, I might add—Jess pulled the big truck onto the road. I glanced out the passenger window to gaze at my old house as we drove by, my chest tightening with longing. I missed that house so much. I missed having my own bathroom. I missed having a peaceful, clean place to feel secure in. I even missed being able to open my bedroom window without worrying about hearing Davy and his wife screaming at each other.

"So, I was thinking," Jess said, bringing me back to the here and now. "Before we head to the lake house it might be fun to do some things that only eighteen-year-olds can do."

"We're getting lottery tickets?" Ryan asked, his voice full of way too much excitement.

Jess laughed. "No, I hadn't even thought of that, actually."

"Getting a tattoo?" Bridgett offered. "I'm totally getting one when I turn eighteen."

I made a face. "Um...definitely not happening." Spur-of-the-moment tattoos had never made much sense to me.

"Ok, then what else is there?" Ryan asked.

"Get my first credit card?" I guessed. What else was left?

Jess shook his head and grinned. "We're gonna watch Eliana register to vote."

"Woohoo." Ryan's voice was flat, exuding anything but excitement. "I bet that's exactly what she wants to do."

"I registered to vote on my eighteenth birthday," Jess said matter-of-factly. "What's wrong with that?"

"Dude." Ryan reached a hand to Jess's shoulder and gave it a shake. "Don't admit to things like that. You're totally killing any game you're trying to ha— Ow!" There was a shuffling in the backseat like Bridgett had elbowed Ryan in the side. Then they had a whispered conversation, one that made it sound like Ryan thought Jess and I were in a relationship and had no idea that Jess already had a girlfriend. "*But they were at homecoming together,*" Ryan whispered in a not-so-whispery voice. Seriously, he would never be allowed back in a library if that's as low as his voice could go.

I peeked at Jess, to see if he noticed what was going on. He was rubbing his neck and his cheeks looked more flushed than usual.

Now if this wasn't awkward I didn't know what was.

A few seconds passed before I found my tongue. "I wouldn't mind registering to vote. That sounds fun."

"I was joking. You know that, right?" Jess laughed uncomfortably.

"Well, call me weird, but I still think I'm gonna do that when we get to the lake house. I can do it online, right?"

"Yeah," Jess said. "It's pretty easy."

Ryan spoke up, "So Jess, uh buddy, it just came to my attention that you're dating someone? Kelsie Perkins? Is she meeting us at the house?"

Jess's grip tightened around the steering wheel. "No. We broke up last night."

I frowned and looked at him confused, though my stomach fluttered at the thought of him being free. He didn't say they were taking a break last night, just that they had a fight.

He seemed to notice my confusion because he said in a lowered voice, "I called her after I dropped you off and said I was done. I felt bad doing it over the phone, but I couldn't wait any longer."

My eyebrows dipped together. "Really?" What would have made him change his mind last night? Had I missed something?

"Hanging out with you helped me realize how wrong she is for me. I wasn't happy. I don't know if I ever was. It's hard for me to remember why I dated her in the first place, and it boggles my mind that it lasted so long."

What was I supposed to say to that? I couldn't say I was sorry about the breakup, because that would be about the biggest lie ever told. So I said, "If you need to talk about it, I'm here."

There was a soft smile in his eyes. "I think I'm going to be okay. But thanks." He reached down and squeezed my knee. "You're too good to me."

The rest of the drive was a lot less serious. Ryan and Jess entertained Bridgett and me with hilarious stories from when we were younger. I may have grown up with those two, but I had no idea about half of the mischief they got into. It was weird that I had been so infatuated with Ryan back then that I hadn't really seen Jess. Yes, Ryan's personality was magnetic and he was easy on the eyes and fun to be around. But Jess was those things, too. Just in a quieter way.

It only took about half an hour to make it to the lake house. It was a beautiful two-story, rustic-looking cabin with huge windows overlooking the lake. Seeing it brought back memories of summers spent here with my parents and the whole Brooks family. I hadn't been here since before my dad left. A hollow feeling entered my chest at the thought of him never being at this house again with me. It shouldn't be that way.

"Are you coming, Eliana?" Jess was standing beside the truck, watching me.

"Yeah, yeah." I nodded. "Sorry, I was just remembering last time we were here."

I scooted to the edge of the seat to slide out. Jess held out his hand to assist me to the ground, and I took it. His touch was steady and warm, and I wished I could have his hand keeping me steady forever. But once my feet were on the ground, Jess hurried around to the other side of the truck to grab the cooler.

Ryan and Bridgett grabbed the other gear from the backseat, so I followed uselessly behind everyone into the house. The main floor had a kitchen with a small dining room, a living room, a master bedroom, and a bathroom. Upstairs had a big loft area with another bedroom and bathroom. Once everything was inside, the guys worked together to get the fire burning in the wood stove. Ashlyn pulled me aside to talk in the master bedroom.

Ashlyn's eyes practically glowed when she shut the bedroom door. "Did you hear that Jess broke up with Kelsie?"

"I'm not taking you shopping, if that's why you dragged me in here," I joked, since we'd never actually placed a bet on how long this relationship was going to last.

"You should have bet me this time, because you always had more faith in him lasting longer than I did." Ashlyn laughed and plopped herself onto the bed, patting a spot next to her for me to sit. "But in all seriousness, do you still have feelings for him? I know you asked me not to talk about it last year...but if you still feel the same, now's your chance."

I shrugged and picked at a spot on one of the fluffy white throw pillows. "Isn't it dumb to go after someone when they're on the rebound?" Especially your best friend? There was a reason I didn't dare try last April. So much could go wrong. I couldn't afford to mess up my friendship with the one person who truly understood me. The one person who had always been there.

But what if he broke up with Kelsie because he had feelings for me? Why did everything have to be so complicated? I cared so much about Jess, but would I risk losing him in order to see if there was a chance of something more? Especially right now when everything else sucked?

"Ugh." I threw myself into the pillows. "Why is it so complicated?"

"Well, if you're worried about putting yourself out there, I don't know, try flirting with him or something?"

My chest tightened at her suggestion. "Has he ever said anything to you about this?" She had to know if he liked me back or not. They *were* brother and sister.

"He's never said those exact words. But he likes you, Eliana. I know my brother, and the way he treats you and looks at you... there has to be more than friendship there."

My chest loosened with her words. But would I dare do anything? I didn't even know how to flirt.

When Ashlyn and I joined the rest of the group in the living area, my eyes were drawn to Jess. He was hunched down, still working on the fire, his sleeves rolled up to his elbows. His forearms flexed as he shoved a log into the stove, the muscles and veins more defined than they were the last time we'd been here. In his plaid shirt and jeans, he looked like a lumberjack, especially with the scruffy beard he still hadn't shaved.

It was funny that he was so insecure about his beard. But I guess it made sense. Jess had always commented negatively on how he looked. I guess being friends with Ryan hadn't helped in that area either. A few years ago, Jess and Ryan had gotten into lifting weights at the school. But while Ryan easily bulked up, Jess had to eat almost constantly, chugging protein shakes and still only gained a few pounds. And even after all that hard work, all the extra muscle he'd built slipped off him when Ryan moved away and they stopped working out together.

But not all girls wanted the beefy guys. Some liked the tall, toned blondes who wore blue plaid shirts that made them look like a lumberjack.

A really cute lumberjack.

I watched him for a minute before realizing how obvious I was being. But thankfully, after a quick glance around the room, no one seemed to have noticed my stare.

Once the fire was roaring, he shut the stove's door and got up, wiping his hands on his jeans.

"So what do you have planned for Eliana's big birthday bash?" Ashlyn asked Jess. Ryan and Bridgett were cuddled up on the love seat while Luke had his arm around Ashlyn's waist. I stood dumbly with my hands tapping my sides.

"Well," Jess said. "I'll admit that this whole thing was thrown together rather last minute. Sorry about that, by the way." His eyes met mine. "But I brought stuff to make lunch, and then I was thinking we could take it easy, play some games, maybe watch a movie." He slipped his hands into his pockets and shrugged. "I don't know. What do you guys wanna do?"

"Do you mind if Luke and I take a walk around the lake while you make lunch? I want to see if our old tree house is still there."

"Sure," Jess said.

"Yeah, a walk sounds nice," Ryan interjected. "Bridgett and I want to check out the lake, I haven't been back here since before I moved to NYC."

"Yeah, sure. I'll make you all lunch by myself." Jess placed his hands on his hips, looking disappointed that everyone wanted to bail on him.

I raised my hand to my side. "I can help make lunch." I may not be that great of a cook, but I could definitely help him make sandwiches or something.

"Cool. That's awesome. We'll be back in about forty-five minutes." Ashlyn tugged on Luke's elbow, seemingly in a big hurry to get outside. Was she trying to help me get some alone time with Jess to work on her plan?

Ryan and Bridgett stood too and pulled their coats on. "Yeah, thanks for making lunch, guys."

And in a matter of seconds it was just Jess and me.

All alone.

And he was single.

I hope I don't mess this up.

CHAPTER FIFTEEN

"WHAT'S FOR LUNCH?" I asked when Jess pulled cutting boards and a frying pan from the cupboards. I'd never made sandwiches with those things, so I had the feeling I may have gotten myself in way over my head. Me and cooking did not get along well.

"I remembered that your favorite food is fajitas, so I was thinking we could make those."

"Aren't those hard to cook?"

"They're not that hard. Plus, I've made them before."

"Well, as long as *you* know what you're doing, I'm okay watching you show off those cooking skills you bragged about." I smiled and settled into a bar stool.

"I don't need to show anything off." He stopped his preparations, raised an eyebrow, and gave me a knowing smile. "Oh, I see. You think you're going to watch me slave away in the kitchen while you sit there looking pretty."

I squished my eyebrows in confusion and tried to ignore the fact that he'd said I looked pretty. "You want me to help you cook?"

"Is that so hard to believe?"

"Kind of, considering I've been living on sandwiches and cold cereal for the last year. And I'm pretty sure you haven't forgotten the whole glass-shard pie incident from last Thanksgiving."

"It's not like you're the first person to set a glass casserole dish on a hot burner."

"Yeah. But most people don't scrape the glass shards off the pumpkin pie and serve it like nothing happened."

"No one complained about eating any glass. And the pies tasted great." He moved to the sink and washed his hands. "Anyway, these fajitas are pretty simple. And if it makes you feel better, I'll make sure you know when the stove is on." He winked. "Just in case."

"If you say so."

I washed my hands while he went to a drawer and pulled out two aprons.

As I put on a fluffy pink apron, I couldn't help but wonder if this was a regular thing for him, cooking with a girl. Had Kelsie been his sous chef at Cornell? I shook away the thoughts, knowing I shouldn't care. It was just hard not to care when it was Jess.

"So we're cooking fajitas?" I asked, trying to push my thoughts away. "Chicken or beef?"

"Chicken. That's your favorite, right?" Jess moved to the fridge and hesitated before opening it, waiting for my answer.

"Yeah." When did Jess start remembering things like that? Did normal best friends remember details like what kind of meat I preferred in my favorite food? Probably.

He opened the fridge and pulled out some chicken breasts, two red bell peppers, two green bell peppers, and two onions. "We'll start with the chicken first so it'll have time to sit in the marinade. How do you feel about handling raw chicken?"

I scrunched up my nose. Raw chicken was slimy and squishy and cold. There was nothing good about that.

"I'm guessing that means *I* should cut it."

"If you don't mind." I tried to smile sweetly. "I think it'll be safer that way."

"Safer? What do you mean by that?"

"Maybe not necessarily safer, but definitely less gross. I wouldn't want to barf all over everyone's food."

"In that case, you can prepare the marinade for me." He set a bottle of Italian dressing on the counter and grabbed the chili powder from the spice rack. "Put one-half cup of the dressing, and one teaspoon of the chili powder in this bag." He handed me a gallon-sized Ziploc bag. "And I'll chop up the chicken to add in."

"Aye-aye, Chef." I saluted him like he was a captain of sorts. Yeah, I'm that cool. He grinned at my stupidity and got to work on the counter space next to the sink.

If I was acting like this already, I definitely shouldn't attempt to flirt with him. I could barely handle acting normal.

Okay, new goal. Act normal. Be normal. Be yourself. Isn't that what you're supposed to do anyway when you like someone?

I searched the kitchen drawers to find the measuring spoons and liquid measuring cup, and then measured the ingredients out and mixed them in the baggie. When I was finished, I plopped the bag on the counter next to Jess's cutting board and watched him cut the chicken into strips.

"Doesn't touching that super slimy meat gross you out?" *That sounded normal enough, right?*

Jess shook his head as he continued slicing. "You get used to it. Plus, what kind of man would I be if it did?"

"You have a point there."

Once the chicken was added to the marinade, and the bag

stored away in the fridge, I jumped up and sat on the counter as Jess got the veggies ready. I figured I was done with my part.

But he turned to me. "Your turn now." He smiled, his eyes almost level with mine.

I gawked at the chef's knife he'd pulled out. The shiny silver blade was almost a foot long. "What do you expect me to do with a weapon like that?" I asked with wide eyes. Jess laughed, so I went on. "How do you even cut with a knife that size?"

"It's easier than you think. In fact, this is my favorite kind of knife."

"Why?" I squinted, skeptical. "Does it make you sleep better, knowing you have something to defend yourself with in case bad guys ambush the house?"

"Har, har." Jess clasped his hands on either side of my waist and lifted me off the counter. My heart banged against my ribcage at his unexpected touch. "I'll teach you how to use it safely," he said close to my ear.

"Okay." It was all I could say, and it came out more like a gasp than an actual word.

Jess chuckled as he moved his hands from my hips to my shoulders and spun me around so my back was to his chest. "So if I were to demonstrate before letting you loose, do you think you'd be all right? Or would you rather have the more hands-on lesson?"

Hands-on lesson? Well, if he was offering...

"I think I'll need all the help I can get." I peeked over my shoulder.

"Hands-on lesson it is." He winked and smiled in what might be considered a flirtatious way...but it could have been my imagination.

"I'm guessing I start with the peppers?" I asked, trying to push away the attraction bubbling under the surface. But my pulse was throbbing so hard in my temples that it was hard to ignore the way being so close to Jess made me feel—all jittery, nervous, and excited.

He nodded. "Stand them up on the cutting board and cut them down the middle so you can remove the seeds and stem."

I gingerly picked up the knife's sleek black handle and did as he said. Once I'd cleaned all four peppers out, I set the two halves down flat on the cutting board to chop them up.

Jess leaned against the counter as he watched me, but I must have been doing something wrong because his hands reached over to still my own.

"The beauty of the chef's knife is that you can move it quickly through foods and chop them up much faster than with a smaller knife. You see, instead of cutting with a back-and-forth motion, you use an up-and-down rocking motion." Jess moved behind me again, his chest grazing my shoulder. "I'll help you with the basic motion then you'll be on your own." He cleared his throat. Maybe he was as affected by our nearness as I was. "Let's start with the green pepper first—that way if you slice your finger, we'll be able to tell where the blood is." I heard the smile in his voice and felt his chest move as he chuckled.

I drew in a shaky breath. "Maybe you should do this if you think I'm that dangerous." I was definitely not in a safe frame of mind at the moment.

"No, no. Your turn."

He instructed me on how to hold the knife in my right hand, and the pepper in my left, with my fingertips curled under my knuckles. He covered my right hand with his and helped me slice it through the pepper, in a continuous motion. My body flooded with heat. Having Jess's arms around me was far from the safest way to chop anything. My mind scrambling, I barely remembered to move the fingers back on my other hand as the knife inched closer.

We were in the middle of chopping the red pepper when Jess

said, "You smell good today. Is that your shampoo or perfume?" He took in a deep breath.

I stopped chopping. "It's probably my body wash." I hadn't put any perfume on. Didn't think I'd have a reason to. "You smell nice too." Too nice. His cologne seemed to be making me delirious, because my mind was running away with the thought that Jess was openly flirting with me. This had never happened before.

"It's the cologne you and Ashlyn picked out for me last Christmas."

"Well, we have good taste," I managed to say. Then I busied myself with the knife again. Once the peppers and onions were all chopped, without a drop of blood shed, we threw them into the frying pan, sautéing them with Italian dressing. The rest of the meal came together rather easily after that. Jess finished working on the fajitas while I set the table, and I was happy to make it through without making a complete fool of myself.

BECAUSE EVERYONE else had skipped out on the meal preparation, they offered to clean up and do the dishes. I wasn't about to argue with that, so I was more than happy to take a walk to the lake when Jess invited me. It hadn't started raining yet, so the ground was still dry, which was really nice. We sat on the bench Jess's dad had put in years ago, right at the edge of their property overlooking the water.

The lake was beautiful, a shimmering dark blue under the afternoon sky. The trees around the perimeter had already lost most of their leaves, with only a few orange and brown ones dangling from their branches. We sat in silence for a while, enjoying the scenery. When I peeked at Jess, he looked deep in thought. His lips were downturned.

Was he regretting breaking up with Kelsie?

I really should make sure to figure that out before I got my hopes up.

"Are you really okay after last night? It has to be hard to break up with someone after dating them for so long."

That seemed to push Jess out of his trance. "No. I'm good. Really good. It should have happened a long time ago." He smiled, and he really did seem fine. I'd known him for a long time and would have been able to tell if he was faking it. But he wasn't. His eyes were bright, and he seemed relaxed with his legs stretched out before him. "I feel like this big heavy collar has been snapped off my neck. I'm free."

"I'm glad that you're happy. That's all I ever wanted. And I can't say that I'm not happy that you guys are done."

"Well, that makes two of us."

"Yeah, but who do you think is more relieved?" I clamped my mouth shut. Why had I said that? That was as good as saying, 'Now that you're free, you should totally be into me.' I internally punched myself. *Stupid, stupid, stupid.*

"I kind of figured you'd be fine with it. You and Ashlyn weren't exactly Kelsie's biggest fans."

I shrugged, thankful he hadn't read more into my relief. "Sorry, not sorry."

Jess laughed. He let out a loud howl and completely lost it, bent over until he was grabbing his sides because he was laughing so hard.

"I'm sorry," he said, through his hysteria. "It wasn't that funny, I know. I think I'm just so tired that the crazy side is coming out."

I just watched him and smiled. His laugh was so funny. I'd always loved it. It was so contagious, the kind of laugh that made you smile more because of how it sounded rather than the reason behind it.

After a full minute, he wiped at his eyes and blew out a long breath. "Whoa, sorry about that."

"When did you finally get to bed last night?"

His face sobered. "Probably after three, breaking up took way too long." He shot his hand out at a falling leaf, missing it, of course, because he was too slow. "You'd think that after breaking up with someone, they wouldn't want to talk for so long. But Kelsie wouldn't let me get off the phone. I finally just had to say goodbye. It wouldn't surprise me if she tried to talk to me about it again. She's persistent."

I shook my head and watched the lake—the water was becoming choppier than it had been when we first came out. The promised storm was almost here.

"Oh, and before I forget again, I did actually get you a birthday present." Jess reached into his back pocket and pulled out a white envelope. "Sorry it's late."

I hooked my thumb under the flap and opened the envelope. It was an airplane voucher to Dominica.

"What's this?" I frowned at Jess.

He beamed at me. "That is a ticket to your senior trip."

"Huh?"

"Well, I still haven't decided if I'm going to take a semester off to work at my grandparents' resort, but I'm for sure planning to work there this summer. So, I thought it would be fun for you to come visit me after graduation. I mean, every senior deserves an amazing senior trip, and my grandma already said you'll have a suite of your own."

My jaw went slack. "But this...this is way too much for a birthday gift. I can't accept it." I tried to give it back, but he stopped me.

"Eliana, it really was no big deal. My parents have tons of frequent flier miles that needed to be used. Please let me do this for you." Of course. His family still had piles of money. This was, like, nothing for them.

I stared at the voucher in my hand, just thinking about the freedom it held. I could get out of Uncle Peter's house for a whole week after graduating. It sounded too good to be true.

"I'm starting to get offended," Jess joked.

"Are you really sure your grandparents are fine with me staying at their resort?"

"Of course. But if you feel guilty about it, I could hook you up with a job. They're always looking for maids."

I laughed. "Thank you so much." I threw my arms around his neck and hugged him. "This is seriously the best birthday present you could have gotten me."

Jess squeezed me back. "Don't think I'm not being selfish by giving this to you. This just means I get to hang out with you all summer."

"All summer?" I leaned back.

His eyes were so bright and happy. "Well, for as long as you decide to make your senior trip. I was serious about you getting a job there if you wanted."

"Wow. I—" I shook my head, bewildered at the thought of getting away from my problems three months earlier than I thought. If I worked at the resort all summer, I could save a lot of money for tuition or housing...and escape from home.

"Just say you'll come." His eyes looked different than usual, more vulnerable. Did these tickets mean more to him than just a time to hang out? Was he planning something more?

I really hoped so.

I gave him my biggest, most sincere smile, hoping I was reading him right. "I'm tempted to go home and pack my bags now."

Jess grinned before pulling me in for another hug. "I have a feeling this is going to be the best summer ever."

CHAPTER SIXTEEN

LATER THAT EVENING, we were all just sitting around the lake house when Ashlyn suggested we play the old pickup line game we always played when I used to live next door. It was kind of a ridiculous game, one best played when you were so tired that everything suddenly became funny. We weren't nearly to that point yet, but Ashlyn seemed determined to finally teach it to Luke, Ryan, and Bridgett who had missed out on our late-night nonsense.

"For those of you who haven't played this game before," Ashlyn said once everyone had settled into their seats, "we basically go around the circle and take turns saying a pickup line that hasn't already been said." She held up a finger to indicate rule number one. "If you repeat a pickup line, you're out." She lifted a second finger. "And if you take longer than ten seconds when it's your turn, you're out. Last one standing is the winner." She looked at Jess and me because she knew we were probably her toughest competition. We'd played this game so often, we had dozens of lines memorized and could go on forever. Although, Ryan did seem the type to have a few up his sleeve.

Jess lifted his hand. "And let's try to keep it clean—remember, my little sis is in the room."

Ashlyn stuck her tongue out at him. He smirked at her.

"Dang it." Luke snapped his fingers. "Those are the only kind I know."

Ashlyn elbowed him in the side.

Luke held up his hands and grinned. "I'm kidding."

"You better be." Ashlyn raised her eyebrows at him then turned to the rest of us. "Who wants to go first?"

"I will." Ryan raised his hand high in the air. "I figure I better start before someone can steal the few I know." He sat up straighter on the couch.

"Okay, Ryan. You're up," Jess said.

Ryan got a huge smile on his lips and turned to his girlfriend. "So, Bridgett," he paused for effect as he let his eyes look her up and down. "You must be exhausted."

"Why?" she asked, playing along.

"Because you've been running through my mind all day long." He ended with a wink.

She shook her head and laughed, a blush rising to her cheeks. It was cute that he could still have that effect on her even though they'd been dating for a while.

Bridgett cleared her throat, attempting to keep a straight face. She said to her boyfriend, "I heard you like water, Ryan, which is good because you already like 70 percent of me."

"Nice," Ryan said, draping his arm around her. "You're up, Eliana."

I tucked some hair behind my ear and tried not to blush as I turned toward Jess. "I don't have a library card, but do you mind if I check you out?"

"Not at all." Jess smiled and pulled out his cell phone. "But first, I forgot my phone number...can I have yours?"

And of course my face burned, betraying me. This was such an awkward game to play now that I had feelings for Jess.

Luke and Ashlyn finished up the round with, "If you were a booger, I'd pick you first." and "You're single? I'm single. Coincidence? I think not."

Ryan started off the next round with, "Kiss me if I'm wrong, but dinosaurs still exist, right?"

That round went perfectly until it was Luke's turn and he couldn't think of anything.

Bridgett was booted out during the third round and Ryan lost out on the fourth.

It was down to Ashlyn, Jess, and me. I began the round off with, "You look so familiar...didn't we take a class together? I could've sworn we had chemistry."

Jess's lips quirked up into a smile, probably remembering the time he'd used that line at a middle school dance, and Ashlyn and I had made fun of him for weeks after.

It was his turn. "Are you a parking ticket? 'Cause you've got fine written all over you."

Ashlyn bust up at that one. Back in the day she usually lost because she couldn't stop laughing long enough to get her next line out before the ten seconds had passed. I hoped it would be the case this time, because I was running low on pickup lines and Jess knew most of mine already.

Jess started the countdown after a few seconds. "And five, four, three—"

"If kisses were snowflakes, I'd send you a blizzard!" Ashlyn blurted out to Luke.

Dang it!

I wracked my brain for the next line. Finally, I said to no one in particular, "Do you live in a cornfield, 'cause I'm stalking you." Okay, that one was lame. But it worked.

We went on like that for a couple more rounds before Ashlyn finally lost.

Before we could start the next round, Ashlyn had Ryan and Bridgett get off the couch to sit on the floor. Apparently, she wanted everyone to have the best view of the showdown between Jess and me. I scooted to the other end of the couch to face Jess, who also turned in his seat so we faced each other head on.

"Okay, Eliana," Ashlyn said. "Your turn begins now."

Now that it was just Jess and me, this game felt even more awkward. It was weird saying all these things to Jess, knowing they held some truth, for me at least.

I drew in a deep breath and started with a line that I found oddly romantic. "If I were a cat I'd spend all nine lives with you."

Jess smiled at that, a hint of a competitive spirit glinting in his eyes. "I'm not trying to impress you or anything...but I'm actually Batman."

Oh yeah? "I thought you were a camera? Because every time I look at you, I smile."

Jess leaned his arm along the back of the couch and his next line rolled off his tongue. "I'm not a photographer, but I can picture me and you together."

"Well, excuse me," I said, leaning toward Jess as my competitive spirit fired up. I would not let him win this game. "I think you have something in your eye." I squinted as I gave his eyes a good inspection. Then I leaned back and relaxed my gaze. "Oh wait, it's just a sparkle."

Jess grinned before moving on. "If I were a stop light, I'd turn red every time you pass by, just so I could stare at you longer."

Okay, that one was good. It probably would have worked on me in real life.

"Do you have a map? I'm getting lost in your eyes." *Enough with the eyes.* I shook my head. Jess's eyes were hypnotizing me or something, because I no longer noticed anyone else in the room. It was just me and him, and this joke of a game we were playing.

Jess glanced at me with a hint of mischief. "Can I take a picture to show Santa what I want for Christmas?"

"Your hand looks heavy. Let me hold it for you."

"I value my breath, so it'd be nice if you'd stop taking it away every time you walk by."

"Okay, I'm here. What were your other two wishes?"

Jess scooted closer and lowered his voice just above a whisper. "I tried my best not to feel anything for you. Guess what? I failed."

My mind went blank—completely wiped clean. My head buzzed as I tried to formulate some sort of comeback, but all my brain seemed interested in was taking his words at face value.

But we were just playing a game, right?

Jess wasn't serious, was he?

He couldn't be.

But his strategy was excellent, because I knew I'd lost. In the background of my fuzzy head I could hear our friends counting down. "Four, three, two, one."

Their cheering broke me from the spell I'd fallen under. I forced a smile when everyone cheered and congratulated us on a game well played. When I looked back at Jess, he was still staring at me with those captivating eyes of his. Heat flashed all over my body, followed by a pins-and-needles feeling all over.

A moment later, I was pulled to my feet and Ryan was giving me a high five. "That was awesome!" he said. "I had no idea of all the pickup-line possibilities."

Jess stood from the couch. Ryan gave him a high five as well. "I am officially impressed!"

"Thanks, man," Jess said, his eyes briefly locking with mine as he flashed me a triumphant grin. "It's taken many years of practice. Too bad they never seem to work in real life."

Ryan laughed and slapped Jess on the back. "You should try that last one you used. I'm sure any girl would fall for it. I mean, you saw the effect it had on Eliana. She knew it was a game, and she was still speechless."

My face burned hotter. I hoped no one else had read too much into my reaction.

"Yeah, well," Jess said, his eyes darting to me again. "I'll have to try that one again sometime."

ASHLYN AND LUKE ended up taking Bridgett and Ryan back with them a little later, since Bridgett's parents were expecting her to be home soon. Jess and I followed shortly, after locking and securing the house.

I climbed into the regular passenger seat of the Silverado, no more super squishing, since we stashed the cooler in the backseat this time.

"Thanks for putting this all together," I said once we were on the road. "It was way more fun than my actual birthday."

Jess turned his head to glance at me, the lights of an oncoming vehicle lighting up his face. "I'm glad we could do this, and I'm really glad I decided to come home this weekend."

"Me too." We were quiet for a while, listening to the radio and watching the winding road in the darkness. I should have felt tranquil, since we were driving in the rain and there was always something so peaceful about that, but I couldn't relax. Jess would be going back to Ithaca tomorrow. Today was my last chance to make something happen, if it was going to ever happen. Who knew how many girls at Cornell had been waiting for him to break up with Kelsie too.

"What does this song remind you of?" Jess interrupted my

thoughts when a popular pop song from three years ago came on the radio.

I listened to the song for a minute.

"It reminds me of going to football games my sophomore year," I finally said.

"Same for me. Every time I hear this song, I'm instantly taken back to the homecoming game that year, when you and I loaded up at the snack shack and tried to see who could drink the most soda before having to go pee."

"Yet another bet I never had a chance at winning." I smiled, being taken back to that time. "I don't know why I kept trying to beat you. I always ended up getting so sick."

"Good times, good times."

I played with my fingers in my lap. "It's funny how songs can be so powerful like that. Only a few notes and you are taken back in time."

"We should pick a song to remember this trip by," Jess said. "If you could choose any song to remind you of your eighteenth birthday weekend, what would it be?"

I thought for a moment. What song would completely encompass everything this trip had made me feel—everything from happiness to longing and desire? Nothing popped into my head. "I have no idea." Did they even make songs about wanting your best friend to fall in love with you?

"What's your favorite song right now?" he suggested.

"You're not gonna like it. It's country."

Jess groaned like I'd committed the biggest crime in the world. "Country?"

"See, I knew you wouldn't like it." I smiled sweetly back at him. "But you know what, it's about time you got over this country phobia of yours. So I'm glad you asked me. I have a ton of country songs that are my favorites right now."

"But why country?" he whined.

"Because country is awesome."

"Awesome?" He raised his eyebrows, skeptical. "So you want to remember this trip forever by listening to a bunch of songs about how your dog died when you were twelve. Or how your boyfriend cheated on you so now you want to go and bash his car in before lighting it on fire."

"Not all country songs are like that. Plus my current favorite, by Terrence Thorne, is more like a country...pop? Ballad?" I thought for a second, trying to figure out how to explain the way Terrence Thorne's songs made me feel. I knew where Jess was coming from with the twangy, angry-ex type songs; I didn't like those ones myself. But some songs were so beautifully written, so heartfelt, that they had the ability to transport me to another time and place where I could imagine how beautiful love could be. "The songs I like are the ones that tell a story. For example, *More Than I Wanted* from Terrence Thorne's first album is probably the most romantic song I've ever listened to."

Jess appeared to mull this over as he tapped his fingers on the top of the steering wheel. "Was that the one playing on the radio all last spring?"

I nodded, happy he'd at least heard of it.

"What makes it so romantic in your opinion?"

"I don't know, it's just..." I trailed off, wishing I'd had the foresight to pick a different song. Why in the world had I named a love song when talking to him of all people? But I needed to get past my awkwardness if I was ever gonna make something happen, plus that song would be perfect for remembering this weekend. I just hoped I could make it out of this truck without completely humiliating myself.

I finally said, "How about we listen to it. You can decide for yourself if it's a good song for this trip." I hoped he'd think it was a good song anyway.

"Okay." Jess connected his phone to the truck's speakers, and soon, after a little search, *More Than I Wanted* started playing. I listened at the familiar piano-and-guitar intro. A moment later, Terrence sang:

You know this year's been rough without you
Don't know how I made it through
Each day I thought about you
Wishing that you wanted me too

You make my world so much brighter
You're the sun that warms up my heart
When storm clouds burst all around me
That's when I find shelter with you

I wanna hold you close
Need to kiss your lips
Let you know that you're wanted
And as the years pass by
I want you by my side, forever
And never let you forget it
Because you're so much more than I wanted

As we listened, I thought about how much it sounded like a fairytale. To have someone feel that way about me, *really* feel that way about me, was impossible to imagine. No one had ever cared about me like that. How could I even hope Jess might?

"What are you thinking about?" Jess asked as Terrence sang the next verse.

"I'm thinking about how wonderful it must feel to have someone want you like that." My face burned with embarrassment when our eyes met. "You must think that's stupid."

"No. I was thinking the same thing," he said. The look on his face was one I didn't see often. It was a quiet look, like he was pondering the words Terrence sang. "I guess I can imagine feeling that way about someone. But I don't know what it would be like to have those feelings reciprocated."

"Did you feel that way about Kelsie?"

Jess chuckled and shook his head. "No, I definitely didn't feel that way about Kelsie. And I know for a fact that I'm not everything *she* wants in a guy, it was obvious by the way she treated me."

"So you really are glad you broke up with her?"

He nodded. "I kind of wish I could go back and tell myself not to go on that first date with her. Things might have been so different if I hadn't."

What did he mean by that? I had to ask him the question that had taunted me since last spring.

I ran my fingers along my seatbelt, trying to gain courage. "Why did you start dating her in the first place?"

Jess pursed his lips and thought for a moment, sucking in a deep breath. "I think I dated her because I didn't have the self-confidence to go after someone better."

Who? Could it be me? I had to know!

"Are you talking about a specific someone, or someone in the general sense?"

I held my breath.

"Specific." He looked pointedly into my eyes, as if communicating much more than that one word said.

My insides turned to mush, twisting and contracting so much that I felt like I was falling off a ten-story building.

"I-I wish you'd chosen the other girl, too."

Silence.

Silence on the outside anyway. It felt like the walls of the truck were closing in on me as the rain pounded on the windshield. My mind screamed. *What did you do? Why did you put yourself out there like that? What if he was talking about someone completely different?*

But then Jess looked at me in a way that told me he felt EXACTLY the same way.

I waited. Finally, he cleared his throat and asked, "Do you want to go back to my house for some hot chocolate before I take you home?"

CHAPTER SEVENTEEN

THE BROOKS' house was mostly dark when we arrived, except for the porch light that was left on, a welcoming sight.

"They're probably still at Macey's ballet recital," Jess said as he unlocked the front door and flicked on the entryway light.

"Do you think Ashlyn's back yet?" I shut the door behind me, still feeling anxious about our conversation in the car.

"Probably not, she said she and Luke were planning to watch a movie tonight at his house." Jess led the way into the kitchen. "Go ahead and make yourself comfortable on the porch and I'll come out when the hot chocolate is ready."

I sighed, relieved I'd have a moment to gather my wits before moving on to the next portion of the night. Which was...? I still didn't know. But I was hoping it would be good. So I made my way to the bench in the enclosed porch. The rain had stopped, and the clouds had somehow already cleared to reveal the stars. They were bright tonight, and I had a clear view of them from where I sat. Growing up, Jess, Ashlyn, and I frequently sat here, looking at the stars. I drew in a deep breath, letting the quiet night calm my nerves.

When Jess came out with our mugs, he smelled like he'd freshened up his cologne. My insides got all twisted up at the thought of him doing that for me.

"One cinnamon hot chocolate for you," he said, handing me a big teal-blue mug.

"Thank you." I tested it to make sure it wasn't too hot before taking a bigger sip. It was so good, with just the right amount of cinnamon.

Jess sat down next to me, close enough that his leg pressed against mine. I didn't move my leg away.

We were quiet for a while as I tried to figure out something to say. I was pretty sure he'd hinted at liking me in the truck, but what was I supposed to do now?

I gazed up at the sky and finally had an idea.

"Do you still remember all those constellations you used to talk about?"

He nodded, seeming relieved that I'd broken the awkward silence. "Do you want me to show you a few?"

"Yeah." I set my mug on the ground. "I think it's about time I learn how to find more than the Big Dipper."

"I'll say." Jess gestured at the window. "Let's go out on the deck. We can see more from there."

We walked outside to the deck, zipping our coats for more warmth.

"First, let's find Orion's Belt." He pulled me up to where he was, and pointed ahead of him. "Do you see those three bright stars in a row?"

I gazed in the direction he was pointing, but the stars all looked the same to me. "Not really."

"Let's try this." He moved to stand directly behind me. He placed his head over my shoulder so his cheek rested against mine, his scruff tickling my cheek.

I told myself he was doing this so we would be looking from

the same vantage point, but that didn't keep my heart from going from a gallop to a sprint in a matter of seconds.

He took my hand and positioned one of my fingers until it was where he wanted it to be. "You should be pointing at the middle star of Orion's Belt. Now do you see it?"

"Yeah," I breathed. "I can see it."

"Great." Jess moved my arm, his fingers trembling slightly. Was he as nervous as I was? Why were we so nervous? "That star there is called Alnitak. That one is Alnilam. And that one is Mintaka." He guided my finger to find each star in Orion's Belt.

I managed to nod, feeling tongue-tied. Jess let my arm drop to my side.

He stepped back, settling beside me, which left me feeling chilled without the warmth of his body next to mine.

I wrapped my arms around myself as I shivered.

"It is kinda cold out here, huh?" Jess looked at me as if debating what to do next.

I nodded, and he hesitantly came back and wrapped his arms around my waist. I tensed when his hot breath crept over my neck as he rested his face next to mine again. "Is this any better?"

"Much better," I whispered. But he was certainly making it hard for me to breathe.

"Good." He tilted his face toward the sky again.

Jess showed me Betelgeuse and Bellatrix next, which I learned were the stars at Orion's shoulders.

"Do you know what the brightest star in the sky is?" Jess asked after going over the rest of Orion.

"The North Star?" I had no clue.

"You mean, Polaris?" he asked.

"Sure."

"Actually no, that's not the brightest. Sirius is." He pointed southwest of Orion. "It's also called the Dog Star."

I stood there in quiet awe as Jess continued. I could almost feel my mind expanding. It was amazing how much was out there in the universe that I didn't know about. There were millions of stars, so incredibly far away, and yet we could still see them and learn about them. "How do you know all this stuff?"

"Have you forgotten already?" Jess said quietly next to my ear. "Don't you remember what a nerd I was growing up? I always had my nose stuck in a book or was looking things up on Wikipedia."

"You were not a nerd." I glanced over my shoulder. "You were smart."

"I sure looked like a nerd."

I shook my head. He'd been insecure about his looks for way too long. "You look great, Jess. I've always thought so." And to an even greater degree these past months.

"Really?" His voice was swamped with disbelief. "I seem to remember you daydreaming about the buff guys from that reality dating show you and Ashlyn always watched. You know, the ones who put us regular guys to shame."

"You don't give yourself enough credit...or me, for that matter. And anyway, you look more like a rugged mountain man today."

"That's what I was going for." I heard the smile in his voice. "So is the lumberjack look one I should repeat?"

I bit my lip, remembering how I'd had such a hard time keeping my eyes off him today.

"I'll take that as a yes." He squeezed me briefly.

His phone vibrated in his pocket. He pulled it out, looked at the screen, and sent the call to voicemail. The screen had showed an image of Kelsie smiling at him.

"Do you mind if we play that song again?" he asked, pressing the buttons on his phone to open his playlist.

"I'm pretty sure I could listen to that song all night."

Once the song was playing, he set it down on the deck's railing. As the intro played, Jess slipped his arms around my waist again, and we rocked side to side to the beat.

"I know I wasn't so sure about listening to a country song earlier," Jess whispered in my ear, sending chills down my spine. "But I think this song is perfect."

My stomach tangled up in knots.

We swayed for a time as we listened to the music.

As Terrence sang the chorus, Jess lightly pressed his lips to my neck.

I wanna hold you close,
Need to kiss your lips,
Let you know that you're wanted.

I tilted my head to the side, and Jess swept my hair back before kissing my neck again. His beard tickled my skin as he moved to the spot below my ear.

He spoke, and there was a roughness in his voice that I'd never heard before. "I should probably take you home now."

I swallowed. "Why?"

"Because if we don't leave now, things are going to change." He loosened his arms from around my waist, allowing me to turn and face him.

"What if I want things to change?" I asked, lifting my eyes to his, which were practically smoldering.

His Adam's apple shifted and his eyes seemed to ask if I meant it.

Jess took a deep breath and finally said, "Then I'd have to tell you how beautiful you are." He lifted a hand to my face and ran his thumb along my cheek. "How I have a hard time keeping my eyes off you whenever we're together."

I let my head rest against his hand, trying to tell him with my eyes how much I wanted him to continue.

"And I'd have to tell you that I've wanted you for a long time."

My body went tingly all over, my heart thudding in my chest. "Really?"

He leaned closer, his eyes burning into me as he spoke just above a whisper. "Really."

His mouth came down on mine and he kissed me softly, slowly. Electricity surged through my veins as he coaxed my lips to move with his.

I wrapped my arms around his neck. He was warm and strong, and when his hands flattened against my back, pressing me against him, I knew my dreams were finally coming true. I pushed up on my toes, needing to be even closer to him.

"You still taste like strawberries," Jess said after a minute. It took a moment for my brain to realize he must be talking about my strawberry lip gloss.

Had he remembered my lip gloss from our kiss last spring?

"H-have you thought about that kiss since then?" I asked, hesitantly.

He pulled me closer. "Lots of times."

"Lots of times?" *What?* My head was spinning. I thought I was the only one who ever thought about that.

"Yeah," he breathed.

The rest of the world fell away as he kissed me again. It didn't matter that we'd been friends since we were kids. It didn't matter that he had just broken up with someone. I only cared that Jess was kissing me. ME. And he seemed to want this as much as I did.

"Are you cold?" I mumbled against his lips, knowing we should stop soon so we could talk about this.

"No." He kissed me again, shaking his head as he leaned against the rail, pulling me snugly against him. "What about you?"

I sighed. "Nope."

Minutes flew by. Our kisses were slow, igniting with passion.

I needed to put a stop to this before I lost my self-control. "We have to talk about what's going on, Jess."

He didn't seem to hear me.

"Jess..."

"We can talk later. I've waited way too long to kiss you like this." He nuzzled his face into my hair, breathing me in. "You seriously smell so good." His fingers found my hair, and he wrapped a lock around his finger.

Was he trying to distract me? If he was, it worked. He found my lips again and moved a hand to cradle my head. He murmured, "Do you really want to talk now? We can, if you do."

I tried to think about it, but my mind couldn't focus on anything other than how good it felt to be in his arms, kissing him. So I shook my head and said, "We can talk later."

I felt his lips quirk up into a smile. "I like that plan."

Not thinking, I grabbed his shirt through his open coat and slid my hands up his chest and along his shoulders. "Do you wanna watch a movie?" I asked between kisses.

"I'm pretty sure we've already watched all the movies." Was he out of breath? Because of me?

"Hmm...wait, what?" It was a lie, but I didn't care to argue.

"I don't wanna watch a movie." He slowly led me back through the porch door and to the bench again where we managed to sit down without kicking over our mugs. "But I'm sure we'll come up with something in a minute."

"Yeah." My voice quivered. This was insane! I seemed to be hypnotized, like my mind had detached itself from my body somehow and melted my inhibitions away. I knew I should push him away soon, but I didn't want to. I wanted to kiss Jess, and I wanted to kiss him for a long, long time.

I didn't know how long we sat on the bench, but I came back

to my senses when I heard the door creak open behind us. Jess and I broke apart. Ashen-faced, I looked toward the door, knowing we'd been caught by someone in his family. I hoped it wasn't his mom. When I saw who was there, my hand flew to my lips. I gasped.

Standing a few feet away in her high-heeled boots and tailored white wool coat was Kelsie. Her eyes were wide as she stared at us with a look of complete horror.

CHAPTER EIGHTEEN

"KELSIE! WHAT ARE YOU DOING HERE?" Jess jumped to his feet and stood in front of me, as if trying to hide me from her view. But I knew she'd already seen me.

She folded her arms and arched her eyebrows way up. "This is why you tried to break up with me over the phone? So you could make out with your little slut without feeling guilty?" Her glare turned to me. "How long has this been going on? I knew I couldn't trust you to keep your hands off him."

"Whoa, Kelsie!" Jess raised his hands in front of him. "Calm down!"

"Don't tell me to calm down!" Kelsie stomped. "I'm not the bad guy here."

Jess turned back to me. He didn't look like he felt guilty, or regretted kissing me. He said in a low voice, "I better talk to her, I'll be back in a bit." He ushered Kelsie inside the house, leaving me to wonder what he would say to her.

I watched them through the windows. Jess took Kelsie into the family room and turned on a lamp before sitting on the couch with her. Why was Kelsie here anyway? Was she hoping to get him back?

The cold air that had been nipping at my toes all night was finally too much for me, now that I didn't have Jess keeping me warm.

I looked around for a blanket in the basket by the bench, but it was empty. I couldn't go in the house and interrupt them—that would be awkward and would probably make things worse.

Instead, I opened the porch door and snuck out the back gate. Jess and I would figure things out later. If I hurried I could probably make it on the last bus of the night. I didn't know what Jess was going to do. But he had kissed me. He liked me! I should feel bad for what Kelsie was going through, but I couldn't care about Kelsie when things were finally so great for me.

WHEN I SLIPPED through the back door, I found my mom sitting in the dark. I flicked on the light. She was sitting at the kitchen table with a cigarette in her left hand. When had she started smoking? My stomach knotted. What else did I not know about her anymore?

Her other hand held a glass of red wine. An empty bottle sat on the table. I hoped she hadn't drained the whole thing in one sitting.

She squinted in the bright lights and seemed to take in my appearance. "What are you so happy about?"

I didn't know if I wanted to open up to her, after how little she'd seemed to want me these past few months, so I pretended not to hear as I cleared the empty bottle from the table, tossing it in the trash. When I turned around, she asked again, "What put that smile on your face when you walked in here a minute ago? Was Brandt still out there?"

"Ew, Mom! I was with Jess."

In what universe would seeing Brandt make me smile?

My mom took a drag from her cigarette and blew the smoke in my direction.

"Well, isn't that nice." Her voice was void of emotion.

"Yeah," I said carefully. "He likes me."

Mom pursed her lips into a smirk as she tapped the ashes off her cigarette into a bowl. "Sure he does."

Sure he does?

"What do you mean by that?"

"I'm sure he says he likes you now, but that's what all men say. You should know that by now. They'll say anything to get what they want—that's what all men do. And then they leave. Your father did it. Brandt did it tonight. It's better to stay away from them. They're all the same."

I scrunched up my nose and shook my head. "You're wrong, Mom. Maybe Dad and Brandt did those things, but Jess would never do that. He's different. He's a good guy."

"Didn't he date like ten different girls last year? You are so naive."

It was only eight. And that didn't mean anything, he didn't like them anymore. "He's been dating Kelsie for over six months."

"Now *that's* even better." She guffawed, which turned into a cough. A horrible, hacking cough. She took a drink from her glass. Once her coughing fit stopped, she continued, "He cheated on his girlfriend to be with you. And you expect him to be faithful?"

He didn't cheat. They were broken up—maybe for less than twenty-four hours...but they were still broken up. Knowing it was useless to try and explain everything, I said, "It's different with me." She didn't even know. She had no idea what was going on between us—what had been there for months.

"Sure, it is. I bet he tells you you're special. That you're the only one for him—the one he's wanted to be with all along."

A sliver of doubt crept past the shield I'd been holding up between my mom's accusations and me. He *had* said those things. Was that a line he used on all the girls he'd dated in the past?

Mom smiled, seeing her words were finally getting through to me.

She took a long sip from her glass, her eyes staying on me the whole time. They seemed to soften as she set her drink back on the table. "I'm sorry to be the one to break it to you, but isn't it better that you know this now, before he's taken everything away from you?"

I fought the tears forming behind my eyes. How could she say these things? Why did she have to try to take away the last bit of happiness in my life? Couldn't she let me live in my dreamland for a while?

She was bitter. That's what it was. She was a bitter woman who wanted to bring me down. Misery loves company. I looked at her—this woman in front of me was a shell of the woman she'd been a year ago. Her eyes were sunken in; her skin, once vibrant and healthy, was now sallow. She didn't look well. Where my dad's disappearance had rocked my world, it had destroyed hers. It was so sad to see, especially since despite everything that had happened and everything she'd said, I still loved her.

But I wasn't about to let her wreck my life even more.

"I'm sorry Dad left us," I said, my hands clenched in fists to keep me from losing my resolve. "I'm sorry you lost everything. And I'm sorry you made some stupid decisions because of that. But I'm not going to let you ruin my chance at being happy. You lost the chance to give me advice the day you started drinking again."

"How dare you speak to me like that!" Mom squished her cigarette into the bowl. "Get out of here. I won't have you disrespecting me like that anymore."

She was so messed up that she couldn't see things right. "If you want me to respect you, Mom, act respectable," I said before running up the stairs.

My mom was wrong. Jess was not like Dad, and he was definitely not like Brandt. He was finishing things off with Kelsie right now, and things would work out between us.

Mom came clumping up the stairs after me. "I said don't talk to me that way, young lady. And don't walk away when I'm talking to you," she slurred. Did she even know how terrible she sounded?

She was so unsteady that even though I wanted to run to my room, I was worried she was going to fall down the stairs. So I balled my hands at my sides, trudged down the stairs, and grabbed her arm to help her up to her room.

"Let me go!" she yelled sloppily, trying to jerk herself away from me. But my grip was firm.

"I'm helping you to bed," I spoke quietly, hoping to get a better reaction from her this time.

"I said, LET ME GO!" Her hand smacked my cheek. Hard. So hard it tingled and burned at the same time.

"No, Mom." I worked to keep my voice steady, but it shook despite my best efforts. Tears threatened to topple out. "You need help."

But I did let go of her arm, opting to follow one step behind her, just in case. We were almost to the top when she missed a step and stumbled back. I grabbed her arm to steady her, but she didn't like that and suddenly shook me off her. The force behind her tantrum made me lose my balance. I tried to right myself, to grab the banister for support but I couldn't reach it. A second later, I tumbled down the stairs, crashing to the ground with a bruising thud. I wailed, my back screaming with pain where it had banged against the wooden stairs.

I sat up, rubbing my back, and caught my mom gaping at me from the top of the stairs.

"Eliana? Oh, baby, I'm so sorry. Mommy didn't mean it."

Tears sprang to my eyes. It was happening again. Life with drunk Mom 2.0.

She stumbled down the stairs to help me, but I shook my head, scrambled to my feet, and grabbed the car keys before bolting out the back door.

I DROVE straight to Jess's house, barely able to see the road through my tears. I didn't care if he was still talking to Kelsie. I *needed* him right now. I didn't know what I was going to say, but I needed him to make everything okay.

Kelsie's Jag was parked out front when I got there, so I made my way through the back gate again, trying to wipe away my tears as I snuck into the deck and the enclosed porch area.

When I peeked through the window, Jess and Kelsie were still sitting on the couch. Jess's back was to me, Kelsie was facing the window I was looking through. I didn't think she noticed me. She didn't look quite as angry now. Maybe she accepted their breaking up was for the best.

I rubbed my back as I tried to decide what to do. My whole backside would probably be black and blue tomorrow. And my head was splitting with a headache. I hurt so bad, and thoughts of my childhood kept rushing through my mind. My mom was as bad as she was before, if not worse. And this time my dad wasn't around to help.

"Jess," I whispered, barely peeking my head inside. I didn't care if Kelsie saw me like this. I needed Jess now.

"Eliana?" he turned, confusion all over his face. He walked to the door. "What's going on? I went to check on you and you were gone."

"I was. But..." I eyed Kelsie who sat on the couch with an irritated expression. "I needed you." I didn't even try to hide the pleading in my voice.

Jess's face screwed up with alarm. "You need me?" His gaze darted between me and Kelsie.

"Back for more?" Kelsie crossed her arms.

Jess's shoulders straightened. "I'm going to have to say goodnight to you, Kelsie. I think we've already said pretty much everything that needed to be said."

Kelsie pouted but pulled her coat on anyway.

While Jess walked her out, I sat on the couch, hugging myself while trying to take a deep breath.

It wasn't working.

"What's going on?" Jess sat next to me and pulled me into a hug.

I flinched in pain at first before leaning into him, letting his arms give me the comfort I so desperately needed. Finally, I drew in a calming breath.

"My mom and I had a fight. It was really bad."

"I'm so sorry. Was she mad I kept you out so late?" Jess squeezed me.

Ow! I stiffened, my bruised body complaining against his touch.

"Did that hurt?" Jess pulled back and inspected my face.

I bit my lip. "After our fight, I r-ran up the stairs too fast and ended up tripping and falling down."

Why couldn't I tell him about my mom? Why couldn't I tell him everything?

"You fell down the stairs?" His eyebrows scrunched like he didn't think he heard me right.

I felt a hitch in my chest.

Keep yourself to yourself, my dad's words sounded in my mind again.

"I-I'll be okay. But I can't go back there tonight. Is it okay if I stay here?'

"Of course." He pulled me against his chest more gently this time and kissed my forehead. "You can stay here as long as you need."

I sighed against him, letting his comfort envelop me.

I wished I could stay here forever.

CHAPTER NINETEEN

I WOKE to the midmorning sun streaming through the Brooks' guest bedroom windows. I stretched, hoping it might help with the soreness from the night before. My back cracked and shoulders popped. I was still so sore, maybe even more so. I walked to the vanity mirror attached to the dark wooden dresser to see what I looked like.

I looked terrible. Much worse than my usual morning, thanks to the leftover mascara all smudged under my eyes. I lifted the hem of my shirt to wipe the black smudges, and that's when I saw the bruise. A big, blotchy red-and-purple bruise on my side where I'd hit the stairs last night. I lifted my shirt higher to find another bruise. Upon further inspection, I found more bruises on my shoulder, my butt, and on the back of my legs.

I guess it was lucky they were in places the kids at school wouldn't see tomorrow.

After a trip to the bathroom to wash my face and freshen up, I found Ashlyn in her bedroom. Her hair was wet like she'd just gotten out of the shower.

"Jess told me you were here." Ashlyn gestured for me to join her in her room. "He said you and your mom had a fight, are you okay?"

"I'll be fine." I sat on the pink-and-gold comforter of her queen-sized bed and watched her put makeup on at her vanity. "What time did *you* get home? I didn't go to bed until about two."

She grinned and set the purple mascara tube down, looking at me through the mirror. "A little after that. Haven't I told you what a good kisser Luke is?"

I shook my head and resisted the urge to tell her that Luke wasn't the only guy around with good lips.

As if sensing my thoughts, Jess peeked his head in. "I thought you might be in here." He smiled at me, his eyes warm and happy. With everything that had happened the night before, we still hadn't talked about what had happened between us. That kiss.

My heart blipped when I thought of it. I could almost feel his hot breath on my neck again.

Jess interrupted my thoughts. "Your mom called a few minutes ago to see if you and her car were here."

My hand went to my back pocket to where I usually kept my phone. It was dead, of course.

"Did she sound mad?"

"Mad and worried."

Good! She should be worried. She had just knocked her only daughter down the stairs the night before. I hoped she felt bad...if she even remembered it.

"I better take her car back."

"Do you want me to follow you? I have to go back to Ithaca tonight, but I think we have some things we didn't get to talk about last night." There was an anticipation in his eyes that I hadn't seen before. And wait, was he blushing? His cheeks were more pink than usual.

"Yeah, I'll, uh..." I stood, patting around my pockets for no reason. "I'll go home and shower. Pick me up in forty minutes?"

"Yeah."

I glanced at Ashlyn who had watched the whole exchange. Her eyes were so big and her mouth had gone slack.

I walked to where she sat, gave her a hug and whispered, "We'll have to talk more when I get back."

I PUT the keys on the counter before rushing upstairs. My mom's door was closed, but Uncle Peter was just leaving the bathroom in his robe. It was always so awkward when we met like this.

"Hey," he nodded as I slipped past him.

"Hi," I said over my shoulder.

"Hey, wait, Eliana." He put a palm on the door as I was shutting it. "I heard what happened last night."

"You did?"

He nodded. "I'm sorry. I swear I never knew she had a drinking problem before. I never would've encouraged her and Brandt to go get that wine for her anniversary if I'd known. I thought I was helping her loosen up on a bad night."

I looked down as I processed what he said.

"I really am sorry. I'm gonna stop throwing parties all the time."

Yeah right.

"Don't you think all your friends will miss all the free booze?"

"Nah." He waved the thought away. "Davey got a new job anyway. He only started coming over because he and his wife were fighting, stressed about money." He shrugged. "And Brandt, well, I don't think he'll want to keep coming over here after what happened between him and your mom."

"Okay," was all I could think to say. I wanted to believe him, but I'd learned long ago not to get my hopes up. "Tell Davey congrats on the new job. I hope things get better for them." I really did. When we'd first moved here, all I could see were the negative things about this neighborhood. I focused on the parties, the ramshackle appearance of the houses, and the fighting neighbors. I hadn't realized that most of the neighbors were normal people who worked hard every day to make a living. And that some were dealing with things I didn't even know about, like Davey and his wife. Maybe if I hadn't judged them so quickly, I would have understood why they were acting the way they were. Out of fear. And stress.

Could things get better for my mom and me if I made more of an effort to be there for her? And help her instead of always trying to get away from the situation?

Probably not. But maybe I should try harder.

WHEN I CLIMBED in Jess's car, I noticed that he was all cleaned up and wearing a sea-green t-shirt that brought out the color of his eyes.

"You shaved your beard!"

He rubbed his fingers along his jaw and shrugged. "No-shave November ended. It was time."

"Did you take a picture first?"

"Of course!"

"Good." I'd have to ask him for a copy of it sometime.

"How are things with your mom today? Are you still fighting?"

I shrugged. "She was in her room, so I left her alone. I'll talk to her later."

Jess pulled onto the road and we drove in companionable silence. I couldn't help but compare it to the last car ride we'd had after kissing. There was a peaceful energy in the car this time. An excited energy, of course, but peaceful. Last time was pure anxiety. And instead of switching the radio from every love song it played, Jess had Terrence Thorne's first album playing. That had to be a good sign.

When we pulled into his family's driveway, Jess hesitated before unbuckling his seatbelt.

"I need to tell you something before we go inside."

"Okay." His guilty expression was not reassuring at all.

"I told Ashlyn about last night. She practically attacked me as soon as you left."

"Which part did you tell her about?" I managed to ask.

"The part on the deck."

My pulse skyrocketed at the look in his eyes. I swallowed. "And how'd she take it?"

His lips quirked up into a half smile. "You'll see."

"What about the rest of your family? Did your parents hear?" My palms felt sweaty. Jess's mom had always been a fan of Kelsie. A big fan. Would she be mad they'd broken up?

Jess opened his door. "I have a feeling they'll find out soon, if Ashlyn hasn't already said anything."

He jumped out before I could freak out on him. But when he opened my door for me, I said, "Should I be worried?"

"No. Just be happy. I know I am." He hesitantly slid his hand in mine, intertwining our fingers, and I melted.

We barely made it through the front door before I heard Ashlyn yell, "Elianaaaaaa!" followed by her rapid footsteps on the entry hall's tile floor. A second later she barreled into us and flung her arms around me, almost knocking me over. I clung to her to keep from falling backward. "I'm. So. Happy. For you guys!" she said. "Finally!"

I smoothed my clothes back down once she stepped back. I asked Jess, "So she's okay with it?"

He grinned. "I'd say so."

"Of course I am! I've only been waiting like two years for Jess to man up."

I narrowed my gaze and gave Jess a questioning smile. "Two years?"

He shrugged. "Give or take a few days."

"What's going on back there?" Mrs. Brooks' voice called down the hall. "It sounds like the circus broke through the wall."

"It's just us, Mom," Jess called.

My stomach dropped, my hand trembling as I thought about how his mom might react.

Jess reached over to squeeze my hand. "It'll be fine," he whispered. "She's known you practically your whole life."

I know. But that was as the little neighbor girl next door. Not the girl who made out with her son and came back to spend the night.

I was gonna be sick.

Mrs. Brooks came around the corner holding a string of Christmas lights, her blonde hair and designer clothes immaculate as always. When she saw Jess and I holding hands together, she did a double take, her eyes darkening.

"Hi, Mrs. Brooks," I squeaked.

She nodded at me, her eyes dipping to our hands once more. "Good to see you, Eliana." She looked down at the string of Christmas lights she was working to unknot. Then at Jess, her gaze firm. "Jess, can I have a word with you? In my room, please?"

This couldn't be good. She was not happy to see her darling Kelsie had been replaced.

Jess turned to me. "I'll be right back." He squeezed my hand again before leaving. My hand felt so lonely on its own. And the shaking had returned.

Ashlyn looped her arm through mine and pulled me into the family room. The large room was full of boxes and boxes of

Christmas decorations that they'd been bringing out of storage when I left this morning. The twelve-foot tree already stood in its usual spot, in front of the big wall of windows. It was half lit, with a ladder standing next to it.

"You can help me and Macey untangle the lights while you dish on last night." Ashlyn led me through the maze of boxes to where her thirteen-year-old sister was sitting with a pile of lights in her lap.

"Hey, Macey," I said as I sat on the carpet beside her and grabbed a string of lights from the box in the middle. Macey was like a miniature version of Ashlyn, with long blonde hair, high cheekbones, and light blue eyes.

"Is it true that Jess dumped Kelsie to date you?" Macey blurted out.

I glared at Ashlyn.

"Sorry," Ashlyn said with a grin. "I had to tell someone the glorious news."

"I don't know if I'd call it dumping." I turned to Macey. "More like he decided to date me instead, and she, um, found out...while it was happening." My words fizzled out as I realized how bad I'd made that sound.

"How did she find out?" Macey asked with her bright, innocent eyes.

"Yeah, Eliana, tell her what Kelsie saw." Ashlyn nudged me with her elbow.

My face flushed. "We were just...discussing the matter on the back porch when Kelsie showed up."

Ashlyn put a hand to her mouth and mock-whispered, "When she says discussing, she actually means making out."

I smacked Ashlyn's arm as Macey's jaw dropped. "Kelsie caught you guys kissing?"

I bit my lip and Ashlyn laughed at my embarrassment. She was enjoying this way too much.

"Oh, I wish I could have seen the look on Kelsie's face," Macey said.

"That makes one of us."

"That bad?" Ashlyn asked.

"Bad would be an understatement. She looked like she was about to explode."

Ashlyn grinned. "I wouldn't mind seeing that look on her. It's probably a big improvement from the fake smile she usually sports."

"Possibly." I shrugged. "So, uh...what did Jess say to you about last night?"

"He said Kelsie was no fun to deal with." Ashlyn looked at me with an amused smile. "Oh, were you wondering what he said about the part with *you*?"

I nodded, trying not to roll my eyes.

"We better go upstairs for that." She eyed Macey, apparently not wanting to discuss this in front of her younger sister after all. "We'll be right back, Mace." Ashlyn stood and pulled me up with her before heading out of the room. We ended up in her bedroom again. She made a show of shutting the door before plopping down on her bed. "So how are you feeling about all of this?" She patted a spot next to her.

I sank down beside her. "I don't know. I've wished something like this would happen since last spring, so, yeah, I'm happy."

"Good, good."

"What did Jess say about it?" I asked.

"In my entire life, I've never seen him so excited about something. He said he wished he made his move a long time ago."

The nervous feeling in my chest was replaced with euphoria.

"Knock, knock." Jess's voice came from the other side of the door along with the sound of him knocking.

"Come in," Ashlyn called and stood. Jess walked in the room

looking slightly irritated after his conversation with his mom. What did she say to him?

"I'll leave you two alone." Ashlyn moved toward the door. "You probably have a lot to talk about." She disappeared around the corner only to peek her head through the door a second later. "Just leave the door open, will ya? I don't want you making out in my room."

My cheeks heated up and I noticed Jess eyed me anxiously as well.

When Ashlyn was gone, Jess said, "So we should probably have that talk we were supposed to have on my deck last night, huh?"

I cleared my throat. "Yeah. We should probably do that."

"But let's get out of Ashlyn's room."

He led me across the hall to his bedroom. I hadn't been in his room since he'd left for college. It hadn't changed much. He still had the same red-and-blue striped quilt on his bed, and his old basketball was stuffed in one of the built-in cubbies that framed his headboard. I smiled when I saw he still had the picture of him, Ashlyn, and me on his dresser.

I went to the window to check if I could see into my old bedroom across the way. I couldn't help but wonder how my room looked now. But there was nothing to see because the curtains were closed.

"Remember when we used to write notes on whiteboards and show them to each other through the windows?" Jess asked, coming to stand behind me.

I sighed. "Those were the days." Living next door to Jess and Ashlyn had been such a great way to grow up. "Remember when you tried to convince me that you saw someone in my closet?"

Jess laughed. "That was awesome. I've never seen you move so fast."

I elbowed his stomach. "I still can't go to sleep without

checking my closet before bed." The hair on the back of my neck still raised every time I thought about how I'd bolted out of the room, thinking some guy was going to come after me with a knife.

"Sorry. I couldn't resist."

"I still need to get you back for that....and about a billion other things you did to torture me growing up."

He moved his lips near my ear. "I'm pretty sure seeing you across the way every day, not thinking we'd ever be more than friends was torture enough."

My temperature spiked. I turned and looked up into his penetrating green eyes. "You know, coming from anyone else that would sound creepy."

"I know." He cleared his throat. "But coming from me, how did it sound?"

A smile lifted the corner of my lip. "Really nice." My smile broadened as relief showed on his face. "I'm pretty sure you just made my day."

He stepped closer, leaning his forehead against mine.

"You know what would make my day?"

"What?"

"This." He bent his head down and kissed me, his lips slowly grazing my bottom lip, coaxing my mouth to part. My head swam, muddled with heat as I traced my fingers along his smooth jaw.

He threaded one hand into the hair at the nape of my neck, seeming to need this kiss in a way—like it was helping him fight whatever had been bothering him after his conversation with his mom. I felt his frustration melt away as it was replaced with desire.

"Is this for real?" I broke away for a second, still not believing this was happening.

"Yes," Jess said. "In fact, I don't have any plans for today, so..."

He moved to kiss the skin along my jaw, working his way down my neck.

Chills ran down my spine all the way to my toes.

"Jess," I finally said.

"Hmmm?" he said as he found my lips again.

"We still need to talk about everything." I placed my hands on his chest, working hard to keep my mind from giving into the foggy daze it was drowning in.

"We're communicating just fine," he mumbled against my lips.

I gave in for a few minutes longer, because there was no way I could resist him. But eventually we did break apart and sat on the window seat.

Jess draped his arm around me and pulled me against his side. "What do you want to *talk* about?"

"I don't know. Everything."

"Well, let's see." He pursed his lips. "I like you. And I'm hoping you like me."

I nodded shyly.

"Looks like we've got it covered." He shrugged. "That was easy."

"Well, I guess since your questions are satisfied, I'll ask mine. Starting with: What did Kelsie want last night anyway?"

His demeanor immediately went from carefree to brooding. "I think she was coming to get me to change my mind."

"Awesome. I bet that went over real well after what she saw."

"You could say that." He sighed. "She was super mad, but I told her it's over and that I'm with you now." He squeezed my shoulder.

I still felt guilty for how everything had gone down. It didn't look good at all to have Kelsie walk in on her newly-ex-boyfriend making out with me.

Jess was keeping something from me, though. I could tell.

"Is there something else?"

"Well, when we were dating I promised to be her escort for this debutante ball thing in New York." Jess swallowed. "I still have to go."

"What?"

Jess's eyes met mine, looking pained. "She doesn't have anyone else to go with. It's a super fancy thing, and since we were still dating then, she didn't go to the bachelor's brunch to find another escort." Jess shook his head. "And she was crying because growing up she'd planned to have her brother, Kason, take her, but of course that can't happen."

No, that definitely couldn't happen since he'd OD'd last year.

I did feel kind of bad for her. Maybe Jess did owe her this at least.

"Is everything okay between you and your mom?" I asked, remembering back to his earlier mood.

"Sure. It will be anyway."

"Yeah?"

He shrugged. "She'll come around."

"Come around?"

He shook his head, his frustration coming back. "She's not happy with the way I handled things. She wanted to know what was going on with you and me." A guarded look crossed his face. "And she wanted to make sure I wasn't leaving Kelsie hanging, ranting on and on about how her family spent over twenty-five thousand dollars on this ball, and stuff."

I clenched my teeth. Of course his mom would make sure he was still going. She loved Kelsie. She and Kelsie had bonded over their love of fashion. She probably shuddered at the idea of her son dating a girl who didn't even know how to pronounce the words "haute couture" properly, let alone afford it.

I inhaled deeply. This would be okay. It was only one night.

One night in New York City. Surrounded by all sorts of one-percenters, flaunting their daughters in diamonds and designer dresses.

Jess reached over to hold my hand. "It'll be fine. It's not a big deal. And if it makes you feel any better, I'll be miserable the whole time, wishing I was dancing with you."

So he was planning to dance with Kelsie?

Of course I knew that's how it worked. That's what people did at balls. I just didn't like the idea. At all.

I leaned my head back on his shoulder and sighed, trying to push my jealousy away. I just got Jess back from Kelsie. I didn't want her to get her claws on him again.

Jess kissed me on the forehead. "Remember, as soon as the ball is over we have my family's New Year's Eve party. And this year, I'm hoping we'll both have someone to kiss when midnight strikes."

Butterflies danced in my stomach. "I like the sound of that."

I just had to make it through the next few weeks.

CHAPTER TWENTY

JESS and I spent the rest of the day together. Even with everything that happened with my mom, it turned out to be the happiest weekend I'd had in months, if not the happiest ever. But that night he had to go back to Ithaca. And I had to go back to my life.

Mom was waiting for me in the living room when Jess dropped me off.

"We need to talk," she said when she saw me. Her eyes were sad and puffy, as if she'd been crying. I cleared some dirty socks off the couch cushion and sat opposite of my mother with my arms folded across my chest.

"I..." she started. She glanced around the room, looking like she was warring with her emotions. "I'm sorry about last night."

I nodded and bit my lip, focusing on the crumbling plaster in the corner of the wall behind her.

"I was just so upset about Brandt that I took it out on you."

I kept staring at the crumbling wall.

My mom sighed. "Are you going to say anything? I apologized, Eliana."

"Are you going to quit drinking?"

She looked at the clock on the wall. "I'm going to cut back. I only drank with Brandt because it was fun. But now that he's gone, I guess it shouldn't be a problem anymore."

"Yeah. Okay. Whatever, Mom." I rolled my eyes.

"I'm going to stop, Eliana. I just need a drink sometimes to take away the edge."

"Don't they say admitting you have a problem is the first step to recovery?"

"I'm working on it."

"Okay, well, like I've been saying, if you ever need a ride to AA I'd be happy to take you there." I stood to leave.

I was almost out of the room when I heard my mom whisper, "*I'm sorry I forgot your birthday.*"

I GOT my first text from Kelsie the next night. It was a photo of Jess talking to a girl somewhere on the Cornell campus. The caption read, ***He cheated on me, he'll cheat on you too.***

I studied the photo closely. Jess was leaning against a building, smiling as he looked down at the girl he was talking to. I couldn't see much of the girl's face from the angle of the picture, but her head was turned up and the way she was standing was definitely not a closed-off stance. But Jess wouldn't flirt with another girl, would he? They probably had a class together. Kelsie was trying to get into my head.

I called Jess that night to ask how his day was.

"I'm pretty sure my brain is going to turn into goo before these next two weeks are over," he complained.

"Sounds exciting."

"About as exciting as the Henderson-Hasselbach Equation."

"Did you run into Kelsie?" I asked, jumping to the subject.

He paused for a moment before answering, "I saw her when I was at the library, but it was from a distance."

That must have been where Kelsie had snapped the photo. "So you didn't talk to her?"

"Nope."

"That's good." I sighed. "She probably would have made a scene."

He sighed, too. "Probably."

Should I tell him that Kelsie had texted me? Should I ask him about the girl in the photo? Or would that make me look jealous?

Yeah, that would definitely make me look jealous, and I didn't want Jess to think I was going to turn into a possessive drama queen like his last girlfriend.

How did people do this long-distance relationship stuff? We'd only been apart for a day, and I was already insecure.

But I couldn't help it. That's what happens when you date someone as awesome as Jess. He probably had tons of girls wishing they could date him. And I still had a hard time believing that out of all the other girls he could date, he had picked me.

KELSIE TOOK the next few days off from texting me. She must have been busy with finals like Jess. But on Thursday night she made up for lost time and kept sending one after another.

Buzz

You're a slut.

Buzz

Your dad left because he didn't love you anymore.

Buzz

I saw your dad with another woman before he disappeared.

Buzz

Jess feels bad for you. You're a pity date.

Buzz

He's going to get bored. Guys like him will ALWAYS want girls like me.

I started to text Kelsie a response, to tell her to shut up, but her texts kept coming before I could get anything typed. I didn't want to read them, but I couldn't look away.

Buzz

You're not good enough for him and his mom agrees.

Buzz

He'll come to his senses soon.

Buzz

Whore.

Buzz

Ugly.

Tears poured down my cheeks as I tried to figure out how to block her from sending me any more texts. Even though I knew most of them were said out of spite, some of those words hit me harder than most. Dad had left us, and he wouldn't have done that if he still loved us...if he still loved me.

As for Jess, I knew he liked me. But a tiny part inside my brain couldn't help but wonder if maybe, just maybe, he truly did feel sorry for me. If his pity motivated him to be kinder, to make him feel obligated to come to my rescue.

That night, when Jess called, I told him I wasn't feeling well and needed to go to sleep.

CHAPTER TWENTY-ONE

TWO DAYS BEFORE CHRISTMAS, Jess invited me to go to the mall to help him figure out what gifts to get everyone in his family.

The mall teemed with people of all ages doing their last-minute holiday shopping. Christmas music played cheerfully through the speakers, lights were strung on all the shops, and red and green were everywhere.

We ended up in the jewelry shop first. It didn't take long for him to find a necklace with matching earrings for his mother. The next stop was for Ashlyn—he got her a gift card to Chic Girl Boutique, Ashlyn's favorite clothing store.

Macey was next on the list. She was into art right now, so we headed to the little art shop upstairs. It was nice and quiet in there, and oh so colorful. Rows of paints, pencils, and paper of all sizes were stacked on shelves and in bins—so much art and creativity waiting to be unleashed.

Jess browsed until he found a kit of pastels with forty-five different colors in it.

"This should keep her happy for a while," he said as he tucked it under his arm and pulled me toward another aisle.

As we left the pastels I spotted a white wool coat outside the store.

It couldn't be.

I pulled Jess behind a corner so Kelsie wouldn't spot us.

"What are we hiding from?" Jess leaned in close, his voice low and suggestive. "We can't make out right here. Give me an hour and I'm yours for the rest of the day." He winked and nuzzled into my neck, kissing me there.

"Jess." I braced my palms against his chest and gently pushed, but he didn't budge. I shot my gaze around to see if anyone in the store could see us. Jess may not care about PDA, but I didn't want to get caught. He was making his way toward my lips when the white coat came into view again.

I pushed Jess away, making him lose his balance for a second. His eyes, which had been dazed, instantly focused once he saw who stood next to us.

"Kelsie?" It was like déjà vu.

"Hey, Jess." Kelsie smiled sweetly, seemingly unbothered by what she'd seen. So much different from the last time. "Hi, Eliana." Her smile remained, but there was a hardness in her eyes.

"What are you doing here?" Jess asked. I couldn't help but notice that he took a step away from me.

"Shopping, of course." She raised the bags in her hands. She must have been to at least five stores already. "Just getting some last-minute things for the ball."

I inspected the bags more closely, trying to guess what they contained. My stomach clenched when I spotted a bag from a lingerie store.

"That's an awful lot of stuff for one evening." Jess's eyes widened when he took in the bags.

Kelsie tapped one hand on his shoulder. "It's not all for one night, silly." I wanted to gag at her attempt to be cute. It was nauseating. "You remember there are also a bunch of parties to go to before."

What? He would be with her for more than one night?

Jess pursed his lips. "I guess I forgot."

Kelsie's gaze slid to me. "Typical guy. I don't know how they survive without us." If she was attempting to commiserate with me, she wouldn't have the satisfaction of having me return the gesture. It was ridiculous how she was acting, like she'd never texted any of those horrible things to me. Was she always so fake?

Of course she was. This was Kelsie: the queen of duplicity.

How did Jess not see through that before?

Could he even see through it now?

"Anyway," Kelsie continued talking to Jess. "Your tux should be ready for pick up on the twenty-seventh."

"I already have a tux."

"Not one with tails. Escorts only wear tuxes with tails. Remember? We went over this weeks ago."

Kelsie reminded Jess of a few more details before leaving with one of those fake smiles flashed my way.

Jess raised his eyebrows after she was gone. "That went surprisingly well. Maybe the whole debutante ball won't be so bad after all."

I scoffed. "She's putting on a show for you. When you're not around, her other side comes out."

Confusion formed on his face. "What do you mean?"

I'd been trying to keep it to myself, not wanting to add to the drama. But now I had to tell him. I peeked around to make sure no one in the store was listening.

"She sent me a bunch of texts." I then told him what she'd written me.

"Why didn't you tell me sooner?" He looked angry.

I shrugged and pretended to be interested in the row of watercolors. "I blocked her. I figured it wasn't a problem anymore."

"Do you think she was telling the truth about your dad and another woman? Should I try to ask her about it at the ball?"

"You still want to go with her?" How could he go with her after hearing what she'd done?

"What? No!" He ran a hand through his hair. "I *have* to go." Jess grabbed my hand and led me toward an aisle with different kinds of paper. "I can't leave her hanging a week before the ball. It's my fault she doesn't have anyone else to go with."

I felt like I'd been punched in the gut.

Kelsie was still the only one whose feelings mattered. She'd been a beast to him the whole time they were dating, but because he hadn't broken up with her at the right time, she was the one we should all feel sorry for?

"As soon as this dumb ball is over with, we'll never talk about Kelsie again." Jess looked at me softly and covered my hand with his.

I nodded, wiping at the moisture trying to fill my eyes. "I hope not, because I really don't like her."

Jess squeezed my hand. "I'll use the time with her to my advantage. I'll find out what she knows about your dad, and then we'll be done with her."

CHRISTMAS EVE WAS much quieter than it had been in years past. Knowing my mom and Uncle Peter wouldn't put much effort into the holiday, I pulled together the best meal I could with my limited cooking skills: cranberry chicken, microwaved broccoli, and instant mashed potatoes. For dessert, I made a simple chocolate trifle from an online recipe. I was actually quite proud of how it turned out. Maybe Jess's skills were rubbing off on me.

Things with my mom were getting better, and it did seem like she was trying to quit drinking. Uncle Peter was true to his word and hadn't brought booze home since our conversation. So dinner went surprisingly well. Uncle Peter and Mom talked about things they did growing up. For the first time since moving in, it seemed like we were kind of like a family. After dinner, she even stuck around to watch our traditional movie, *Charlotte's Christmas Dream*. It wasn't the usual Christmas Eve I'd grown up with, but my mom had been sober and we didn't fight the whole evening, so it was a good night.

Jess left for New York City a few days later. Kelsie had tried to get him to go down a few days early with her and her family, but when he found out he would be sitting around until the debutante's cocktail party on the twenty-eighth, he opted to drive himself. I didn't like thinking about Jess spending so much time with his ex-girlfriend, especially one who seemed to want him back. I couldn't understand why she would want him back after he'd left her the way he did. Maybe she was trying to get back at me? Or was I reading into everything? I hated how much Kelsie was messing with my head.

JESS HURRIED HOME the day after the ball and picked me up before going to his house. I was excited to have so much time with him before he went back to Cornell in a couple of weeks. After seeing he had passed all his finals, he decided to give pre-med and Cornell another chance.

Jess looked exhausted when he knocked on my door after his three-and-a-half hour drive.

"How did the ball go last night? Was it weird being with

Kelsie again?" I asked when I climbed into his car. He'd texted me most of the time that he was gone, but he hadn't been able to text me during the actual ball.

"It was okay. Kelsie was nice enough, I guess."

I waited for more but he left it there.

He furrowed his brow. "Are you asking for, like, a play-by-play or something?"

"I wouldn't mind it."

He drummed his finger along the steering wheel as we waited at a stoplight on the corner by the high school I almost had to attend. "Well, first off, I asked her about what she'd said about your dad, and it turns out she was lying about the whole thing."

"She never saw him with another woman?"

"No." The light turned green, and Jess pulled through the intersection and headed up a hill.

I was quiet for a moment while I processed this, watching the trees drooping with heavy snow as we passed them. Should I be happy or sad that Kelsie lied? I didn't know. I was happy because he might not have cheated on my mom. But sad because it still left me clueless as to what happened with my dad and why he left.

I decided to change the subject back to the ball before I could wonder about my dad longer. I'd already exhausted myself so many times speculating about what he might be up to. "Was the dinner any good?"

Jess nodded. "Yeah."

At $17,000 a table, it had better be so delicious that even the most proper of debutantes couldn't resist licking her plate. "What did you eat?"

"Um, a beef filet with some sort of sauce and potatoes. You would have loved the dessert, chocolate raspberry something."

"Oh. Sounds yummy." I couldn't help but think that with his

newfound love of cooking he would have paid extra attention to the fine food. "What did Kelsie's dress look like?"

He seemed to think for a moment, his eyes intent on the road as he wound through the slush-filled streets. "White…fluffy?"

"Did you have to dance with her all night?"

A dark look passed across his face, but it was soon smoothed away by one of nonchalance. "We danced once or twice, but I was able to pass her off to her dad and other guys most of the night."

"Well, that's good." I sighed, feeling a light, airiness drop over me. We were finally done with Kelsie.

CHAPTER TWENTY-TWO

THE BROOKS' annual New Year's Eve party was something I'd looked forward to every year, and this year promised to be another great event. Mrs. Brooks had stopped me on my way out the other day and handed me a personalized invitation. "How's your mother?" she'd asked kindly, and we talked for a minute—nothing too heavy, just small talk, but she was really nice. Maybe she was finally okay with me dating her son. Or maybe I was wrong about her preferring Kelsie. Either way, I felt lighter and more hopeful.

When I showed Mom the card, she decided to come too. She stopped moping around the house right after Christmas. Maybe that dinner we had together as a "family" had shown her that someone still cared about her: me. I needed to try to do more things with her in the future. Even if my dad never came back, there was still hope for my mom's and my relationship.

Mrs. Brooks greeted us at the door when we arrived.

"Come in," she said, beckoning us in. "What a surprise. I didn't know if you'd be able to make it," she said to my mother. I couldn't tell if her smile was genuine or forced, but she invited us in all the same.

"Thank you for the invite," Mom said, her voice coming out slightly strained as she tucked a loose piece of hair behind her ear. "I wouldn't miss it."

We walked into the brightly lit entryway of the Brooks' home, music floating down the hall from the living room.

"Let me take your coats," Mrs. Brooks offered. We handed her our coats and she disappeared into the music room before leading us down the hall.

The great room was bustling with all of our old friends and neighbors. Mom gripped my arm as she took in the scene. I didn't think she'd seen any of her friends since we'd moved away from the neighborhood. Her shaking fingers told me she was nervous.

"It'll be fine," I whispered to her. "They'll be excited to see you."

She nodded and smoothed a hand down the front of her dress.

"You look great," I said. And she did. She wore one of her favorite dresses from back when she and my dad attended a lot of parties like this. It was a floor-length black dress, with a lace overlay. It didn't fit quite as perfectly as it had a year ago, because of the weight she'd lost, but it still looked good on her.

"Annette!" a voice called from across the room. A tall woman with ultra-toned muscular arms was taking huge strides in our direction—Mrs. Hillyard. When she reached us, she wrapped my mom in a tight hug. "It's so good to see you, Annie. Oh, so good to see you." She pulled away and held my mom at arm's length, looking her over.

Once she recovered from the lung-crushing embrace, Mom smiled. Mrs. Hillyard was like the neighborhood mother and would help her feel comfortable with her friends once again. My mom would now be okay at the party and I could hang out with my friends without worrying about her for the rest of the evening.

As soon as I saw my mom being taken into an old group of friends, I went to find Ashlyn and Jess.

"Hey." Jess gave me a hug when I made it to their theater room. "I was wondering when you'd get here."

"I wanted to make sure my mom was okay before I came back here." I pulled back and peeked around the room, finding that it was just us. "Where's Ashlyn?"

Jess sat down and patted the spot next to him on the reclining loveseat. "Luke got home from his trip early and asked her on a special surprise date. She told me to apologize for her skipping out on us...but I think she was excited about not being a third wheel."

I shrugged and plopped down next to him on the cushion. "Third wheel? It's not like we never used to hang out just the three of us before."

"Yeah, but now I think she feels like she's in the way."

"In the way of what?"

A smirk lifted his lips as he put his arm around me, pulling me against him to whisper in my ear. "Stuff that would be awkward for us to do when she's sitting right next to us."

Electricity ran down my spine, and I smiled when he pressed his lips below my ear. I made a play at pushing him away, but my heart wasn't in it at all.

After a few kisses, I pushed myself back. "Is Ashlyn weirded out by us?"

"Of course not." He waved the thought away. "She thinks we're *so cute* together." It was amazing how well he could mimic his sister's voice. He took my hand in his and started the movie we'd planned on watching.

A few minutes later, the screen on Jess's phone, which was sitting on the other side of me, lit up. I peeked at it, curious, and saw he'd been tagged by @cornellkelsie in a photo that she posted on Instagram.

It's probably just pictures from the debutante ball.

A minute later his screen lit up with the same thing.

By the fourth or fifth time, I was so annoyed that I picked up his phone and handed it to him. "Here. It keeps lighting up."

Jess took the phone, looked at it, and frowned. He swiped his finger across the screen, opening his Instagram app, to look at the picture. I only saw the picture for a second before he pushed the lock button and shoved the phone between him and the couch.

"What was it?" I asked.

"Oh, nothing important." His knee bounced.

I hoped a picture of him dancing with Kelsie wasn't important.

A few minutes later, the yelling began.

"*You think you're so much better than me, don't you*?" The irate voice of my mother sounded through the door, immediately stealing my attention away from Jess's phone. "*I still own that home, you know*!" Pause. "*I could move back in there any day if I wanted to*."

I sat up and scooted away from where I'd been cuddled up on the couch with Jess. "I better go check on my mom." My cheeks burned flaming hot. Had she been drinking? I thought she was doing better.

"D-do you want me to go with you?" Jess asked, readying to stand.

"No. It's okay, I'll probably be right back." I slipped down the hall and stuck my nose around the corner to see what was going on. She couldn't be that drunk already. We hadn't been here long enough for that...unless she was already buzzed before we got here and had hid it from me. She'd always been good at that.

Mom was standing in the middle of the room. One arm waved in big arcs, as she pointed and yelled at Mrs. Reyes. "I never liked you anyway. I don't know why I pretended to. I saw the way you looked at Paulo."

"How dare you speak to my wife like that!" Mr. Reyes said, his champagne sloshing over the top of his glass as he stepped forward.

"Don't pretend to be all innocent," she spat. "I know *all* about your open relationship."

Mr. and Mrs. Reyes' jaws dropped at my mom's accusations.

Mom took another swig from her glass and spoke to the crowd, "How many of you have been approached by these two to go on their special couples' weekends?"

Mrs. Brooks rushed through the crowd, set two hands on my mom's shoulders and whispered something in her ear. When she tried to maneuver Mom out of the room, my mom yanked herself away, tripping on her own dress. She would have landed on her face if Mr. Hillyard hadn't caught her.

I heard footsteps on the floor behind me. I glanced back to see Jess about halfway down the hall. Not thinking, I sped into the crowd, my eyes trained down on the floor to avoid looking any of the guests in the eye, and grabbed my mom's arm with two hands.

"We need to leave." I tugged on her.

"Don't treat me like a child, Eliana!" she yelled, trying to jerk herself away from me, just as she had to Mrs. Brooks. But my grip was firm.

"You've said enough. We need to go." I spoke in a low voice, hoping to get her out of here quietly.

"LET GO OF ME!" Mom slapped my cheek, so hard tears shot to my eyes. But I didn't let go. Why was this scene so familiar? Why were we doing this again?

"No." I worked hard to keep my voice steady, but it shook despite my best efforts and the tears were threatening to topple out. "You've had enough for one night."

I was thankful when Mrs. Hillyard took my mom's other arm and helped me drag her out of the room.

"Eliana. Wait." Jess gripped my arm before I could collide into him. "Let me help."

"No, it's okay. Mrs. Hillyard's helping us." I couldn't look at him. I didn't want to see the sadness, or pity that might be in his eyes now that he knew what my mom was like. Now that he knew she was a drunk.

I was so sick of people feeling sorry for me. So sick of feeling this way.

"We'll be fine. Stay inside where it's warm," I gasped, working hard to hold in the sob bubbling in my throat.

He didn't move.

"Please," I pleaded at him through the tears in my eyes. "I need to do this without you."

Jess slowly dropped his hand, and I hurried my mom out to the car.

"I need my coat," Mom said in a flat voice after Mrs. Hillyard and I had buckled her in.

I looked at Mrs. Hillyard, who was holding her arms to keep the cold away.

"I'll stay with her while you get it," Mrs. Hillyard said through chattering teeth.

"Okay, I'll be right back." I trudged back up the snow-covered walk.

I grabbed our coats from the music room and was about to leave when I overheard Mrs. Brooks' voice.

"I never should have extended the invitation. I was feeling charitable when I invited them, but I'm sorry you had to witness such a scene tonight. I don't know where that came from." I peeked around the corner only to immediately pull my head back in the room. Jess's mom was talking to his grandma in the entryway. Mrs. Brooks was standing by the window next to the front door, probably making sure my mom was in the car and away from her guests. "That family has gone downhill this past year, ever since Paulo ran off. You know he's the reason my sister had to sell her house in the Hamptons."

"Everyone has their bad nights." Jess's grandma patted Mrs. Brooks' forearm. "Heaven knows I've had my fair share of things I wish I could do over."

Mrs. Brooks shook her head. "Eliana's a nice girl and all. I feel bad for her, really I do. We all do. But I don't know why my son is dating her. If you ask me, I think he feels sorry for the girl." Humiliation slipped over me, thick and suffocating, as I listened. *Is this what his conversation with his mom had really been about that day?* "He's being a good friend, but she's going to hold him back if they keep dating. He almost went to culinary school because she encouraged it." The disdain in her voice was heavy. "He'll come to his senses soon though and get back with Kelsie." Her voice brightened as if nothing would bring her more happiness than having Jess dump me. "Now that's a girl going somewhere. His future would be bright, tied to that family."

I couldn't listen to her anymore. I stepped out from my hiding place, wielding the coats like a shield over my chest. When Mrs. Brooks saw me, she gasped, her hand to her chest. Jess's grandma's eyes flashed with sympathy. Or was it pity? I couldn't be sure, and I didn't wait to figure it out. So I held my head as high as I could and whisked past them and out the door.

"I'M SORRY, ELIANA," my mom said when I set her at the table at Uncle Peter's house. Mascara tears had run down her cheeks, her dress was torn at the bottom from when she'd tripped earlier, and her eyes were puffy red. She looked terrible. "I thought I could handle tonight on my own."

I didn't say anything as I pulled out a mug from the cupboard and set it in front of her while the coffee maker got to work.

She was hunched over, running a shaky hand through her hair. "It's just, it was the first time I'd been with all those people since your dad left us. They were all whispering about me."

"Do you think that maybe they were whispering because you were drunk?"

She slumped back in her chair and crossed her arms. "If they were my friends, they wouldn't have dropped me because I moved away."

I didn't even have energy for this. I thought things were getting better, not worse.

"I'm going to bed, Mom. Don't burn yourself with the coffee." I pushed myself away from the counter and headed for the stairs. "Happy New Year."

Once in my room, I plopped on my bed, wiping at the tears brimming in my eyes. I was done crying over this. It was stupid.

My phone vibrated with a text.

Jess: **Can I come over? I still want to ring in the New Year with you.**

I sighed and texted him back.

Me: **Sure.**

I lay back on my pillow, huffing out a big breath. Then I remembered how Jess's phone had lit up all evening. I unlocked my phone again and navigated my way to Kelsie's Instagram page: @cornellkelsie. I wasn't an official follower of hers, but I'd checked her page enough in the past year that her profile was familiar.

As I scrolled down her page, I saw photo after photo of Kelsie in a fancy white ballgown—a beautiful dress covered in Chantilly lace, and layer after layer of tulle. I clenched my teeth, wanting to think she looked ridiculous in such an ostentatious gown, but she was gorgeous. Had Jess thought she was beautiful too? I shook the thoughts away and scrolled further through the photos.

Some of the photos were of her and her parents. Others were of her and other girls in white dresses. And even more were of her with Jess. I touched the first picture with Jess in it, not caring about the other photos that had nothing to do with my boyfriend.

The picture enlarged—Jess and Kelsie, arm in arm as they walked down the aisle with a bunch of other debs and their escorts. I clicked out of that picture and moved onto the next. This one was of her doing her curtsy for the crowd, Jess holding her hand for balance. I gritted my teeth as I swiped to the next photo, one of them dancing in a crowd of ball attendees. The next ones were other shots of them dancing—each slightly different from the next. In one, they were cheek to cheek, dancing really close. In another she was resting her head on his shoulder. Another had her speaking into his ear, his head tipped toward her, a slight smirk showing on her face.

I thought he said they barely danced.

My heart raced as I scrolled further down her feed. Each picture looked more intimate than the next. I came to a video with the caption: *Thanks @jessbrooks93 for the magical night.* I tapped on the video and watched multiple clips that had been edited together on the single video. There was a short clip of her being presented to the crowd, and a clip of her dancing with her father, a clip of her standing with a group of girls, another of her and Jess dancing—they looked similar to the photos I'd already seen. The last clip showed her with her arms wrapped behind Jess's neck, her face tilted up, his face tipped down. They kissed, and the video ended.

The blood drained from my face. They kissed? Jess kissed Kelsie?

My heart pounded as I scrolled the video back a few seconds.

Kelsie smiled at him. He dipped his head down. She tilted her face up. Their lips touched. The video cut off.

I rewound it again, and again, trying to figure out exactly what had taken place.

He was smiling at her as she whispered something in his ear and rubbed the back of his neck.

Jess was still in love with Kelsie. His mom was right. This whole thing was a sham.

My heart tried to tell me that I was jumping to crazy conclusions, but my mind couldn't ignore the facts. Not when they were staring me in the face.

Knock. Knock.

Jess.

CHAPTER TWENTY-THREE

"HEY, your mom told me to come up. I hope you're decent." Jess walked in, shutting the door behind him. He strode toward where I sat on my bed and plopped down next to me, leaning in to give me a kiss.

I shot my hand up and stopped his lips with my fingers. "Don't."

"Why?" Confusion formed in his eyes, along with hurt.

"Did you kiss Kelsie?" The question came out sounding strangled. I cleared my throat. "At the ball?"

"What? Of course not! Why would you even ask that?"

His lies sliced through my stomach. He hadn't even hesitated. How many other things had he lied to me about?

"You promise you didn't kiss her?"

"Yes, I promise. I barely danced with her, there's no way I would kiss her." He must have seen the distrust in my eyes because he asked, "Why don't you believe me?"

I shoved my phone in front of his face, my hand shaking. "Because of this." I pushed the play button so he could see the same clip I'd watched over and over.

He took the phone and leaned back to watch the screen. Once he realized what he was watching, his eyes widened and a look of horror took shape on his face.

The words rushed out of him like a hurricane. "I-it's not what it looks like. I promise. She set me up."

"How could this be a set-up? You guys are kissing."

Jess shook his head. "*She* kissed *me*. I was just doing what I'd agreed to—dancing with her—when she kissed me." He pushed a hand through his hair. "You have to believe me. As soon as I knew what she was doing, I stopped it and went back to my hotel room."

My heart wanted to soften at his words. *But how could I believe him when he'd lied straight to my face a second ago?*

"If what you're saying is true, why didn't you tell me about it?"

He raised his hands. "I'd already dealt with it, and it was never going to happen again. I didn't want you to worry over nothing. You were already so paranoid about me even going. I didn't want to make things worse."

"Or did you just hope I'd never find out?"

Jess sat there with his mouth hanging open, his eyes concentrating as he tried to think of an excuse. Finally, he said, "I didn't kiss her. You have to believe me."

"You've done things like this before."

"But I wouldn't do that to you, Eliana. Not to us. I care more about you than I ever—"

I held up a hand to stop him. I couldn't have him saying how much he cared about me. "Even if that's true, I overheard your mom talking to your grandma tonight. She hates me. She hates what my dad did to her sister."

Jess stared at the floor, and I knew it was true.

"Is that what she wanted to talk to you about that day?"

"I don't care what my mom thinks. I'm nineteen. I can make my own decisions about who I date."

I shook my head as his mother's words played through my mind. *Jess is just being kind to the poor girl. He's being a good friend.*

"It seems like we have the whole world fighting to break us apart." My breath caught in my throat, and I barely choked out my next words. "Maybe we should start listening." I looked at the wall behind him, unable to meet his eyes. "I think we were better off when we were just friends."

Jess flinched like I'd slapped him across the face. "No." He stood with a force of emotion. "This isn't happening. You're not thinking straight. You had a bad night and are making rash decisions."

"I can't be in a relationship with someone I don't trust. It wouldn't be fair to you or to me."

His face changed, frustration dominating his features where desperation had been before. "Maybe things would be better if you stopped looking for something to go wrong," he spat.

Now it was my fault?

I crossed my arms and looked at the wall. "I can't deal with this right now."

"Why can't you do this, Eliana?" He let out a harsh breath, and when I looked at him, his eyes were deader than I'd ever seen them. "Do you know how hard it was for me to put everything out there again after our first kiss? I bared my soul to you, and now you're throwing it all away...because you care what my mom thinks? Because Kelsie is crazy and posting crap on the internet to break us up? I thought we were stronger than that!"

I wish I was that strong. But I'm not...I'm just not.

His face hardened into stone when I didn't say anything. "You're my *best* friend. No one gets me the way you do. Not my family. Not

Ashlyn. Not anyone." He closed his eyes and took in a deep breath before looking at me again with his tortured green eyes. "It would be so easy between us if you let it." He sighed. "Like breathing."

But it's not. Nothing about my life was easy. "We can still be best friends. That doesn't have to change."

"Friends?" Jess scoffed, looking down as he scuffed his shoe along my carpet. "I don't know if I can be your friend anymore. Not after this." He backed away and moved to the door.

"So you're leaving?" A sudden anxiety filled me. This night wasn't supposed to end like this. "You're throwing away fourteen years of friendship, just because I can't date you? Is the real reason why you went through so many girls last year because you don't have the guts to stick something out?"

"I'm not the one breaking up here!" A vein bulged on his forehead. "You dumped me!"

"But I still want to be friends!" I yelled back. "I'm mature enough to stay with someone even when things get rocky."

Jess shook his head. "You don't even realize what you're saying, Eliana. Things did get rocky, and you decided to take the *easy* way out and be content with just being friends. You're not willing to take the risk."

"Well, I'm sorry if I'm a little scared to do that right now. It's not like you have the best track record. Any girl would be crazy not to be worried about dating you in the long run. You do have a reputation of being a terrible boyfriend."

Jess's mouth hung open and you'd think I'd just slapped him from the shocked look on his face.

After a long moment, he finally spoke, "Thank you for helping me understand your point. I don't think there's much else for me to say now. I've already made a complete fool of myself." Jess looked like he wanted to say something more but pressed his lips together instead, biting down on the words before they could escape.

Regret instantly burned through me. I tried to think of something to make things better between us but came up empty.

He put his hand on the doorknob and looked over his shoulder. "Goodbye, Eliana."

And he walked out of the door.

The alarm on my phone went off as the door clicked shut. It was midnight.

Happy New Year.

What had I done?

CHAPTER TWENTY-FOUR

ASHLYN BURST into my room the next morning in an oversized t-shirt and sweatpants. "Where's Jess?" Her eyes scanned my room as she turned around. She ran to my closet and looked inside. "Where is he? Did he stay here last night?"

"Of course not. Why would you think—"

"He didn't come home last night." Her eyes were wild with worry.

"What? He left here at midnight. I thought he went home."

She shook her head violently. "He never made it. We've been calling him all night, calling you too, but neither of you picked up. So we thought..."

"We broke up," I said, my stomach shrinking.

The blood drained from Ashlyn's face. "You what?" Her eyes turned hard. "How could you? How could you do that to my brother?"

"He kissed Kelsie. He cheated on me and lied about it. I couldn't trust him and I was going crazy." I couldn't handle any more crazy in my life.

She shook her head. "He wouldn't do that. You're overreacting."

"I saw it on Instagram. He was smiling. She was gorgeous."

Ashlyn dug through her purse and pulled out her phone. She pushed the screen a few times, and after a moment, the video I'd seen last night was playing.

Ashlyn's face went from curious to confused then to angry as the video played. Then, like I had done, she slid the video back and watched the end again. "Jess wouldn't do this." She pointed at the screen. "He told me he wished he hadn't gone on the trip."

"Because he regretted cheating on me with his ex-girlfriend?"

Ashlyn looked like she wanted to shake me. "Jess would never cheat on you! He loves you! Kelsie probably set this whole thing up. She's a pro at twisting things around."

I shook my head. I couldn't believe it.

"What was he like when he left here last night?" she asked. "Was he mad?"

The image of his stone-cold face pushed itself into my mind. "Yes."

Had he been so upset that he'd driven recklessly after leaving here? Had he been in an accident? My breath caught in my throat. The roads were slippery last night. It was late when he left, and there were probably drunk drivers all over the road after ringing in the New Year. My heart pounded against my ribs as panic set in. And from the look in Ashlyn's eyes, her mind had gone to the same place.

"He still hasn't called me back." A hand went to her stomach and her voice trembled when she spoke. "If he's hurt I'll never forgive you." She lifted the phone to her ear and waited, but Jess didn't pick up.

I sunk to my bed and ran my hands through my hair as my vision blurred with tears. "What did I do?" Was that the last time I'd ever see him? A hole ripped through my chest and I tried to draw in a breath, but I couldn't. I was too hard on him last night. Why hadn't I listened? Had I blown up the whole thing with Kelsie when I shouldn't have?

"Did you get a hold of Jess yet?" I looked up through my watery eyes and saw Ashlyn was on her phone again. Talking to her parents? "He's not with Eliana. She broke up with him and he left here a complete wreck."

More guilt piled on.

"You need to call him." She pointed at me after hanging up.

I searched the nightstand for my phone. It wasn't there. I shuffled around my bed, looking under pillows and under my blankets. I finally found my phone on the floor between my bed and nightstand. "It's dead."

"No wonder we couldn't get a hold of you."

"Sorry, I was kind of a mess last night." I plugged in my phone with shaking hands.

As soon as my phone started coming back from the dead, I punched in my passcode and found Jess's name at the top of my favorites list. The phone rang and rang then went to voicemail.

"He's not answering me either."

"Call again." She gestured with frustrated hands.

I did, but again there was no answer. This time I left a message, my heart racing and heat flashing over me as I said, "Jess. I hope you're okay. I'm sorry about last night. Everyone's worried about you. I understand if you don't want to talk to me, but please let your family know you're okay. We're all so worried."

Ashlyn called her mom and told her that Jess wasn't answering me either. When she hung up, she grabbed her keys and said, "We're gonna go look for Jess, and you're coming with me. There's no way I'm going to find my brother's dead body alone."

THE ROADS WERE TERRIBLE. All the snow from last night had frozen into ice. Ashlyn guided her black Mercedes as best she could through the streets, somehow managing to make it through town without losing control. But we still hadn't found Jess. He wasn't at the park. He wasn't at the cabin. We drove by his grandparent's hotel to see if his car was there, but we didn't see it. As panic set in deeper, we had the idea to check Little York Lake, hoping to find Jess at his thinking spot. But when we got there, the parking area was empty.

"I don't know where else to look." Ashlyn hit her steering wheel. "Are there any other spots you used to go to?"

I shook my head. "We already checked them all."

Where was he?

It would almost be a relief to find him at Kelsie's, at least he'd still be alive.

DING! Ashlyn's phone sounded loud in the car, nearly giving me a heart attack.

Ashlyn scrambled for her phone. "It's from Jess!" A hand flew to her chest.

"What does he say?"

The phone almost slipped from her shaking hand. "He says: 'I'm in Ithaca. Had a bad night. Tell mom to stop freaking out.'"

Ashlyn wrapped me in her arms and we both sobbed. "He's okay," Ashlyn cried.

I clung to her, relief washing over me so fiercely I could barely stay upright. Jess was safe. *Thank you. Thank you. Thank you.*

Once we were stable enough to drive again, Ashlyn turned her car around and headed toward town. We stopped at Emrie's Frozen Treats for some frozen yogurt and talked about everything that had happened between me, Jess, Mrs. Brooks, and Kelsie.

"Sorry I got so mad about you and Jess earlier. I still think there's something we don't know about that night. Jess loves you."

I wanted to believe her, but I knew I wasn't ready to even think about that. I needed to get my life in order before I could consider being in a relationship with anyone.

CHAPTER TWENTY-FIVE

TALKING with Ashlyn helped me realize how badly I'd overreacted with Jess the night before. I should have let him talk and give me his side of the story, instead of automatically flipping out over what Kelsie posted online. It was entirely possible that Kelsie had planned the whole thing. She hated Jess and me together. Why had I fallen for her trick? Why had I believed her over the most important person in my life? I was so mad at myself for letting everything that had happened that night to influence the relationship that brought me the most happiness.

As soon as Ashlyn dropped me off I dialed Jess's number. We would figure this out. We would get past this. He had to forgive me.

But the call went to voicemail.

I called three more times before leaving a message, "Hey Jess, I know you don't want to talk to me right now. I'm sorry for the way everything went last night. I overreacted. Please call me back so we can figure things out."

I hung up. Hoping he would call me back soon.

But he never called.

Hours went by. Long, heart-wrenching hours and I still didn't hear anything from him.

Had I messed everything up so badly that he refused to talk to me again?

I called Ashlyn next, desperate to fix everything. Maybe she could drive me to Ithaca and I could talk to Jess face to face. Maybe he would see how much I regretted last night.

She picked up after the third ring. "Hello?"

"Jess isn't answering any of my calls," I blurted out. "I'm worried if I don't talk to him today he'll never forgive me."

There was a pause on the line. Then Ashlyn's voice spoke quietly, "Jess is gone. He called us to say that he's deferring from Cornell to work at my grandparents' resort for a while."

"What? No! He can't do that. He can't leave!"

"He's already on the plane, Eliana. It's too late."

I collapsed onto my bed, feeling like a weight had been dropped on my chest. *Jess was gone?*

I tried to draw in a deep breath but I couldn't, it was like trying to suck air through a straw.

"Are you okay, Eliana?"

I was going to pass out. *Breathe, Eliana. Just breathe.*

Finally, I was able to draw in a decent breath.

"Are you okay?" Ashlyn asked again, worry evident in her tone.

I gasped. "Yeah...I'll be okay." I sucked air through my nose. *Breathe in. Breathe out.* As I did my breathing exercise, Ashlyn sighed.

"I think you broke my brother's heart."

CHAPTER TWENTY-SIX

I TRIED CALLING and texting Jess all the next week. I even tried emailing him, just in case he had blocked my number. After seven days of silence from him, I finally received a message.

Jess: **Please stop trying to contact me.**

And my heart, which had been hanging on through everything that I'd been through with my parents and life, finally broke.

He didn't want me anymore either.

CHAPTER TWENTY-SEVEN

OVER THE NEXT MONTH, I was brimming with all kinds of emotions. First, it was disbelief. Then sadness. Loss. Hurt. Depression. And then I got mad. Really mad. How could he give up so fast? How could he throw fourteen years of friendship out the window because of one big fight? Did he ever care about me at all?

But then, of course, my anger faded away as the weeks passed on and all I was really left to feel was forgotten.

MY FIRST ACCEPTANCE letter came in February. I was offered a partial scholarship to SUNY Cortland. Originally it had sounded like a great place—I could go to school with Ashlyn and still be close to Cornell, but somehow it wasn't far enough away anymore. Ithaca College's acceptance along with a full-ride scholarship came next. But that would put me even closer to Jess when he came back, so I hid the letter in the bottom of my underwear drawer. It was possible to be in the same town as someone, and never run into them...especially if you went to two different schools. But not seeing him again when it was so easy would have made me feel even worse than I already felt.

But with the scholarship, I could afford to move away from home. Getting out of Uncle Peter's house would be worth it, right?

So I let Ithaca College know of my intention to start there next fall and hoped by the time it came around, Jess and I may have figured out how to be friends again. And if not, I hoped I'd be reconciled enough to find his replacement.

AT THE END OF FEBRUARY, I finally decided to go through the pile of junk mail that had stacked up to ridiculous amounts on the kitchen counter. If I was going to move on and make my life better, I might as well quit waiting around for college and start by making this house more livable.

As I went through the pile, I was surprised to see my name on a few of the envelopes. Did companies magically know I had turned eighteen this year? I'd never received so much junk mail of my own.

I opened the first envelope with the company name, Credit City, on it. Playing with the idea of getting my first credit card, I slipped my finger under the folded top and opened it. My dad had taught me when I was younger how, when handled responsibly, credit cards could be a good way to build your credit score. Maybe it was time for me to do that.

Inside had all kinds of information on why getting a card with Credit City would be a great idea. I set it aside, deciding that with the stack I had, I might as well find the one with the best rates and rewards.

After opening a few more letters from credit card companies,

I found an envelope from the Army. I tossed it in the trash. Sure it would be great to serve my country and all, but yeah, the Army was not the place for me.

The next envelope was from a company called Hayward Auto Loans. The inside of this letter was different from the rest. There was a single sheet. No return envelope. No privacy policy and other random papers companies sent to cover their butts.

I opened the letter. My hands shook when I read the first line.

Tesorina mia Eliana,

My dad was the only one I knew who would start a letter like that.

I don't know if you have read any of my letters, since I've disguised them as junk mail, but I have to try again.

I'll be brief.

I'm sorry. I'm so sorry for leaving you and your mother. What I did is unforgivable. You two are the sun and the moon in my life, my everything, and I don't deserve your forgiveness after leaving you the way I did. But I love you. I love you with all my heart and I wish for the day when I can come back. I know I messed things up even worse by leaving, but I'm working to fix things.

It is selfish for me to think that you would want to hear from me again. I had to try one last time.

I will always love you,

Papà

Tears were streaming out my eyes so fast I could barely read the last line.

I tore through the pile of letters after that, desperate to see if he had truly sent other letters to me.

There was only one more. Had one of us accidentally thrown away the others, not knowing what was inside? I tried not to feel the loss as I ripped open the letter.

Tesorina mia Eliana,

Happy Birthday! Happy Birthday to my beautiful Baby Girl. You are 18 today! I couldn't be more proud of the amazing person you are becoming.

I wish I could be there to celebrate with you, we would eat our delicious French toast and I would drive you to school on my way to work, talking about all the fun things we had planned for the evening.

It is my prayer that you and your mother are still able to do those things. I am a terrible father for not being there. I feel horrible about that. I should be there, and if I was a better man I would be. But I don't want to talk about that anymore, I'm sure you already heard enough from my other letters...if you are getting any of these at all.

So for today, please let me write of happy things, for you are 18 and the world is yours! You have always been such a joy in my life, excelling at everything you set your mind to. You are kind and loving and even though I messed up on a lot of things, knowing that I helped guide you into the wonderful person that you are brings me some comfort in this mess I have created.

You are always on my mind and in my heart. Do not think I could ever forget you.

I love you with all my soul.

Papà

A loud sob burst from me with those last words. My dad hadn't forgotten me. He still loved me. He still wanted me.

CHAPTER TWENTY-EIGHT

THAT EVENING, Mom found me in a pile of papers and envelopes when she walked in after work.

"What's going on here?" she asked, her mouth hanging open at the mess.

I held up the three letters from Hayward Auto Loans that were addressed to her.

"I think you'll want to open these."

She took them from my hands and inspected them. "Why would I care about getting an auto loan? You know we can't afford to get you a car."

"They're not what they look like." I bit my lip and looked at her hesitantly. "They're letters from Dad."

"DO YOU THINK THERE WERE MORE?" Mom asked after she'd finished reading her letters, her eyes wet.

I shrugged in my chair next to her at the table. "It sounded like it, but we probably threw them away."

She nodded, staring at the three letters my dad had written her. She sniffled and wiped at her eyes with trembling fingers.

"He's trying to figure out how to fix things," I said, hopeful. "Maybe he'll be back soon."

My mom pinched her eyes closed and drew in a shaky breath before releasing it in a loud huff.

"Those are beautiful promises made by a desperate man," she finally said. "Let's not get our hopes up yet."

She stood and walked up the stairs, but she took her letters with her.

MY NEXT INSTINCT was to text Jess the good news, celebrate this happy moment after all the hard times he'd helped me through. But I remembered that we didn't talk anymore. Didn't even text anymore. So I did the next best thing. I texted Ashlyn.

Me: **My dad wrote me!**

Ashlyn: **What?!?**

She, of course, called me for details, asking me to read the letters word for word.

"Are you going to contact him?" she asked.

"I tried looking up the address but I'm pretty sure it's a fake. I'm guessing he might have someone forwarding the letters to us since the postage stamp says New York."

"Dang!" She sighed. "Do you think you could contact him through the Internet somehow? Do you think he ever checks social media?"

"My dad never liked social media. He thought it was a waste of time."

She was quiet for a minute. "But do you think he might check yours? He had to know you moved to your uncle's house somehow."

She was right. Maybe he had checked up on me that way.

As soon as we hung up I posted a picture of myself holding the envelope with the caption, "Think I should get a car for college?"

Of course, I couldn't afford a car, but if my dad was paying attention, he would know I had read his letters. He would know how I wished he was with us. And maybe he'd try harder to come back.

CHAPTER TWENTY-NINE

THE NEXT FEW months passed with no further word from my dad. I tried not to be too sad about it because at least I had the letters he had sent. At least I knew he still loved me. And maybe, just maybe someday we'd be together again somehow. He said he was working on it. Something like this might take a lot more time than I thought.

And even if it took a really long time, those letters had created a miracle. Something had changed in my mom. Something had given her a reason, one she hadn't been able to find before, to go to her AA meetings and actually try to get sober again.

So even if my dad never found a way to come back to us, and even if Jess never wanted to talk to me again, at least my mom was trying. And I would take her effort and cling to it with everything I had. I would work with what I had and be grateful for it this time.

"ARE you going to work at the movie theater again this summer?" Ashlyn asked me as we walked around the mall one afternoon in June. School was almost out, and she suggested we pick out something special for graduation.

"I think so," I answered. "You're going to be there again, right?"

A huge smile spread across her lips as we walked into Chic Girl Boutique. "Actually, no." She led me to the back wall of the store which was covered with necklaces and bracelets. "My grandparents called last night and asked if I wanted to come work at the resort this summer."

"Oh." I focused my attention on a rack of bracelets, hoping she couldn't see the disappointment in my face. I had been looking forward to one last summer with her before we went to our separate colleges. Her to SUNY Cortland with Luke. Me to IC.

"It's going to be awesome. I've been dying to visit again especially since Jess told me how wonderful it was to work there."

"He's enjoying himself then?" I bit my lip, holding my breath for news of my old friend. Over the past few months, Ashlyn and I had tried to stay in the safe zone of not talking about him. There were just too many feelings where Jess was involved.

She pulled a necklace from the rack and held it against her neck while she studied her reflection in the mirror. "He says it's gorgeous there and it's been nice for him to get away from everything here in New York." She put the necklace back and combed through the others.

"So he's doing better now? He's happy?" I picked up a gold bracelet and tried it on, watching her through the corner of my eye for signs of what was really going on with her brother these days.

"I think he's happy. He says he's still not ready to come home yet." She shrugged. "I don't blame him, though. My parents were furious with him for dropping out of Cornell."

"I thought you said he deferred."

"It's pretty much the same thing as 'dropping out' in my family." She sighed. "I wish you guys would talk to each other. I'm so tired of this dumb fight."

"It's not like I've been ignoring his calls or anything."

She shook her head and moved to another display in the shop. We browsed the jewelry in silence for a few minutes before she turned to me with bright eyes.

"I have the best idea!"

I looked at her hesitantly. "You do?"

"Do you still have the vouchers to Dominica?"

"They're sitting in my underwear drawer. In fact, they'll probably live there until they finally disintegrate." If Jess didn't want to talk to me, he sure as heck didn't want me showing up at his resort in paradise for my senior trip.

Ashlyn didn't seem to notice my apprehension. She grabbed my arms excitedly. "You should come with me to the resort! I'm sure I can talk to my grandma and get you a job. Then you and Jess can figure out how to put this whole misunderstanding behind you."

Excitement warred with uncertainty in my brain. "I don't know. That's kind of a lot to ask them."

Apparently, my words fell on deaf ears because Ashlyn went on. "This is exactly what you guys need!" She smiled hugely at her genius and took my hands in hers. "I'll call my grandma tonight and let you know when to pack your bags."

"But..." I tried to say.

She held up a finger. "No buts. I *know* this will work." She grabbed a handful of bracelets and took them to the checkout counter. "You just wait, Eliana. You're about to have the best summer of your life!"

CHAPTER THIRTY

A FEW HOURS after dropping me off at home, Ashlyn called to tell me that her grandparents had a job for me if I wanted it. I could start the Monday after graduation.

I knocked on my mom's bedroom door as soon as I got off the phone with Ashlyn.

"Come in," she called from the other side of the door. She was sitting up in bed, watching TV. My heart ached when I noticed she was wearing one of Dad's old t-shirts. "What do you need, honey?" She hit the power button on the remote and the room was suddenly quiet.

I stepped inside, hovering near the door. I took in her bedroom. I hadn't been in here much since the move; she had the curtains pulled back so the late evening sunlight was streaming through the windows. Her giant dresser took up almost the whole wall in front of her bed, but amazingly enough, it was clean. Ever since she went back to her AA meetings, she'd been taking more care in helping to keep Uncle Peter's house tidy—doing more dishes, washing laundry—all the things she did before Dad left. It had been nice to have some things go back to normal.

"Are you just going to stand there?" she asked with a laugh in her voice.

I cleared my throat and forced some courage into my bones. "Ashlyn asked me to work at her grandparents' resort with her this summer."

Mom was quiet as shock registered on her face. "She did?" she finally asked.

I nodded, moving away from the doorway to sit next to her feet on the bed. "I already have a voucher for the flights, so that won't be an issue."

"Is that where Jess is?" Her eyes were cautious.

I looked away. "Yeah. He might not want me there, but...I don't know. I think it would be a good experience, and I have to at least try to fix things between us. I need to give it one more try."

And if he still didn't want me I would have to accept that this was the way things were going to be.

"You should go." She was smiling. "You deserve to have a vacation, especially after everything your father and I put you through."

"Are you sure? I know you're just getting everything back to normal, will you be okay with me gone?" Things were going so much better now, I didn't want her to slip up again because I left her.

"Your uncle has promised to keep helping me. And you'll be leaving in a few months anyway for college. I'll be okay."

"Thank you!" I leaned forward to give her a hug, feeling comforted to smell her favorite perfume instead of alcohol when she pulled me close. And from the way she seemed to melt into the hug, it made me wish I'd done this long ago. We had needed each other all along.

When we pulled away, my mom made me look her in the eyes. "I'm so sorry for all the pain I caused you, Eliana. You deserve to be happy."

My eyes stung with the promise of tears as I nodded. "We both deserve to be happy."

THE LAST WEEK of school came quickly. Life was chaotic as I tried to get everything ready for my summer trip.

Graduation day finally came. Mom dropped me at the entrance to the Elizabeth Eastmond Arena at Ridgewater Community College before one o'clock. I rushed inside while she parked the car so I could find Ashlyn and get a few pictures together in our caps and gowns before everything got started.

I was hurrying down a busy hall that was crowded with fellow graduates and their families when I turned the corner and nearly barreled into someone. I looked up and dropped my gold academic stole sash when I saw who it was.

Standing there with a very bronzed face was Jess.

"What are you doing here?" I jumped back, my breath catching in my throat.

Jess blinked a few times, as surprised as I was that we were standing face to face.

Once he recovered, he said, "I flew back for Ashlyn's graduation."

I nodded. "Of course. Sorry. I-I wasn't expecting to see you here." I breathed deeply to collect myself. I should have realized he wasn't here to see me too. Just Ashlyn.

Jess nodded once, his lips set in a firm line.

Why did he have to look so indifferent to seeing me again when I was having a hard time controlling my breathing and quieting my galloping heart? He looked like the people in old photographs, unsmiling and somewhat ornery.

"Well, don't let me keep you from where you were going." He stepped to the side, making ready to leave.

“Yeah, I’ll, uh, go now.” My face burned as I bent over to pick up the sash still resting at my feet.

I slipped the sash over my head, feeling very small when I stood next to my ex-best friend in the busy hall with people chattering all around us. I was about to walk away when my curiosity got the better of me.

I turned back to him. “Are you home for good?”

“No, it’s just a quick trip. I’ll be flying back this weekend.”

“Oh. I was just wondering—”

He crossed his arms and sighed. “Wondering what?”

“I thought that maybe you heard I was going to be working for your grandparents and that’s why you left.”

His arms dropped as bewilderment registered on his face. “I-I actually hadn’t heard about that.”

So Ashlyn wanted it to be a surprise.

I pursed my lips. “Is that gonna be weird?”

His face went stoic again. “Why would it be? You can do whatever you want, Eliana.”

Is that how he really felt? How had we come so far from where we’d been before? I used to be able to tell exactly what he was thinking from his intonation, or the way he shifted his body. But this, this was something I’d never experienced before. It was like I was standing in the big hall with a stranger. He was tanner, buffer, maybe even a little taller, and his hair was sun-bleached a few shades lighter. The only thing that hadn’t changed at all was the color of his eyes, but even they were stormier than I remembered.

“O-okay,” I said, feeling awkward. He wasn’t even looking at me anymore. He’d pulled his phone out and was studying the screen. “Sorry to waste your time. I’ll go now.”

“Sure.” He lifted his eyes from his phone for the briefest second before putting it to his ear. Then he turned and headed in the opposite direction.

I walked toward the spot Ashlyn said we should meet, all the way wondering if I'd be able to survive a summer around a Jess who didn't seem to care whether I was dead or alive.

"What's wrong?" Ashlyn asked as soon as I found her standing with Macey, Luke, and her parents. "You look like you've seen a ghost."

"Not a ghost." I shook my head and gasped. "Jess."

"Jess?" She grabbed my arms, her face lighting up. "Jess is here?"

"You didn't know?"

"No." The look on her face was one of pure excitement. "Where is he? I can't believe he's here!" She turned around to scan the arena. Twenty seconds later, she did a little jump and pointed. "There he is." She called his name and waved her arms high above her head.

He noticed her and switched his direction to join his family.

"I'm gonna get in line," I told Ashlyn, "I'll see you down there."

"Are you sure you don't want to wait? I'll just be a minute."

The memory of our interaction a few minutes ago was too fresh in my brain. "No, that's okay. I'm gonna go."

I left the Brooks as Jess swept his sister up into his arms, remembering a time when he would have greeted me the same way.

I could barely concentrate on the ceremony. My mind kept wandering to thoughts of this summer and what it'd be like to be around a Jess that hated me. As the student body president, Aiden, talked about this past school year, and how awesome it had been, I couldn't help but think how different my year had gone. I would not miss high school or this town. I was more ready than ever to leave everything behind and start fresh in the fall.

When Aiden reminisced about homecoming week and how amazing it had been, my gaze flicked to Jess. He seemed to be looking at me too. Was he thinking about the dance? And if he was, was that memory still a good one, or was it now tainted with regret? He looked away before I could get a read on anything he might be thinking or feeling. And maybe that was it. Maybe he wasn't thinking about it at all.

It was then that I noticed someone else sitting with the Brooks' family. My mom. She was sitting between Jess and Macey.

What?

How did she end up sitting with them? I didn't think Mrs. Brooks had said a word to her after the scene she caused at their New Year's Eve party. Mom tentatively smiled at me when she saw me gawking at her. Did Jess see her sitting alone so he invited her to sit with them?

But that was something the old Jess would do.

Maybe he figured having her there would keep his parents' attention off his sudden reappearance? Ashlyn had told me how frustrated they were with him still.

The rest of the ceremony went as expected. I stood in line until it was time to walk across the stage and receive my diploma. When it was my turn, I was just happy I made it across the stage without dropping my diploma or tripping on my gown before quietly finding my seat.

After the ceremony, I hurried over to my mom, but Jess suddenly found an excuse to go say hi to Ryan, thus effectively avoiding me.

I tried to smile it off, but it ripped me apart inside to see how he was so obviously avoiding me.

CHAPTER THIRTY-ONE

THE FLIGHT WAS LONG, but Ashlyn and I eventually made it to the resort. It was dark and I was tired, so I didn't get to see much of the island. A middle-aged woman showed Ashlyn and me to our rooms, which were right next to each other. I walked in, locked the door, and collapsed on the large four-poster bed, surrounded by pillows. Within a few minutes, I was dead to the world.

In the morning, I woke to the sound of someone knocking. I got up and smoothed my tangled hair on my way to the door. I expected to find Ashlyn coming to check in on me, but found a beautiful maid instead, with long dark hair and the darkest eyes I'd ever seen. She was holding a breakfast tray.

"Good morning, Miss Costa," she said in her accented voice. "Mrs. Brooks asked me to bring breakfast and welcome you to the resort."

"Wow." I put a hand to my chest. "That is so thoughtful. Thank you." I took the tray from her and set it on the small table in my room.

I looked around my suite as I ate, savoring each bite of my

strawberry French toast, yogurt, and apple juice. The room was spacious—at least twice the size of my room at Uncle Peter's. Ashlyn told me that I'd be staying in one of the special suites at the resort, reserved for close friends and family, but I had no idea I'd get something this nice. There was a white wardrobe and a dressing table along one wall. Across the bed was a large flat screen TV with a love seat and chair in front of it. It was such a light and airy room. I absolutely loved it.

I was transferring clothes from my suitcase to the wardrobe when there was another knock at the door.

"How did you sleep?" Ashlyn danced into my room wearing a light pink blouse and white shorts. She eyed my bed. The white comforter was still pulled neatly over the pillows. "You did sleep, right?"

"Of course I slept." This was probably the first time Ashlyn had seen a bed I'd slept in not in disarray. "I was so exhausted last night that I simply collapsed on top of the bed." I placed the last of my clothes in the wardrobe.

"I see." She smiled and plopped down on the love seat. "Are you ready for your grand tour of the resort?"

"That depends on who will be giving us this tour?" *Please don't say Jess.* I zipped up my suitcase and stood it against the wardrobe.

"Only the most knowledgeable tour guide we have here at Brooks Island Resort. His name is Amani," she said. "He's a native of the island and has the dreamiest brown eyes I've ever seen on a guy—aside from Luke's, of course."

"Sounds like he's qualified then, I mean if he's really that cute." I winked, pretending to be interested. I mean, maybe a summer fling with a cute guy was just what I needed.

"Oh, he is." She grinned.

Amani *was* really cute. He had rich, dark skin, shaggy brown hair, and a super laid back personality.

Amani showed us around the resort, which was much bigger than I'd imagined. The white Tuscan-inspired building had four stories and sat just off the bay. I'd always pictured a small, quaint building with maybe fifty rooms, so when Amani told us there were one-hundred eighty rooms, not including the spa, restaurants, banquet room, pools and any other fancy amenity you could imagine, I was stunned.

When Amani led us outside to see one of the pools, my heart stuttered. A few feet away was Jess, handing a drink to a lady at a table along the pool. He wore a white polo with the resort's logo on it, paired with navy blue shorts.

"When did Jess get here?" I whispered to Ashlyn as we got closer. I'd expected him to visit his family for at least a few days.

"I think he got in some time yesterday," Ashlyn said. "He took the red-eye right after graduation."

"Why the hurry to get back?"

Ashlyn shrugged. "He and my parents are still fighting about the whole dropping-out-of-school thing. He didn't feel like sticking around any longer than necessary."

Jess finished delivering the drinks on his tray and walked in our direction. He stopped when he saw us.

"Mom and Dad actually let you come?" Jess took a few steps toward us. "I thought they were worried about their prodigal son turning you over to the dark side."

Ashlyn laughed. "They know I'm already a hopeless case. They practically threw me out the door yesterday."

She turned to me with a hand to the side of her mouth. "Since Macey is at a dance camp all month, this is the first time in twenty-five years they'll have the house to themselves." She winked. "I don't think they'll be begging me to come back any time soon."

"Eww." I scrunched up my face. "Not the picture I wanted in my head right now."

"Yeah, Ashlyn," Jess said. "That's gross." He smiled at our shared feelings. A split second later, he seemed to realize that he'd acted friendly toward me for the first time in months and decided to remedy it. He cleared his throat and went back to ignoring me. "Well, I have work to get back to. I'll see you around." He gave Amani and Ashlyn each a warm smile, and glided his eyes over me, only to give me a curt nod.

After he left us, I let out a breath I hadn't realized I'd been holding and urged my heart to slow its pace as I watched his back retreat.

Ashlyn turned to me with a frustrated look on her face. "I can't believe Jess ignored you like that. Never before in my life has he been more excited to see me than you."

"He was probably in a hurry to get back to work." My mom had told me about how Jess had seen her sitting alone at graduation and had been kind enough to invite her to sit by him. Apparently, his kindness to her wasn't going to be misplaced on me anytime soon.

She let out a sigh. "My grandparents own the place. It's not like he's going to get fired for talking to his sister and lifelong friend."

I shrugged. If today was a sign of what was to come, this probably wasn't going to be the *best summer of my life* like Ashlyn had promised.

THAT NIGHT, there was a big bonfire on the beach for all the resort goers. Ashlyn, of course, insisted we get all glammed up for the evening. I felt funny walking down the beach in my flowy dress instead of shorts and a t-shirt, but when I saw everyone gathered on the beach I was happy I'd listened to her fashion advice. These rich resort guests vacationed in style.

I looked over the crowd of people and had to take a second look when I recognized someone.

"Is that Ryan over there?" I pointed in front of us.

"Yeah," Ashlyn replied. "I guess when Jess found out I got to bring a friend, he invited Ryan last minute so they could hang out."

"Wow. That's some short notice."

"Apparently, he and Bridgett broke up before graduation, so he was more than ready to get out of town. It's probably best if we don't say anything about her to him," she said under her breath.

"Thanks for the warning."

"Hey, Ryan!" Ashlyn called when we got closer.

"Ashlyn! It's so good to see you." Ryan wrapped her up in a big bear hug. "I've been waiting all day to see you guys." Ryan turned his brown eyes on me, his smile wide, showing off his perfect teeth.

When he bent down to give me a hug, I awkwardly hugged him back wondering why the sudden hugging. We never did this in New York. Not that I was complaining. Ryan smelled good.

When he stepped back, he lifted his hand to his sides. "I'm going to warn you up front...I decided to become a hugger last week. So, you're going to have to get used to that, I'm afraid."

"That's okay. Hugging is good." I laughed uncomfortably.

Ryan rubbed his palms together. "So have you guys found out what your job is while you're here?"

"My grandma wouldn't tell me. She said she wanted it to be a surprise." Ashlyn put her hands on her hips and pouted.

Ryan got a mischievous look on his face. "Then I won't ruin the surprise for you. From what Jess tells me, you're in for a real treat."

From the way he said it, I had the inkling that we might be doing something less than glamorous.

"Anyway, you guys should come join the party." He squeezed

himself between us and placed an arm across our shoulders, leading us to the fire.

"So, Ryan," Ashlyn said when we'd found a place to sit in the sand, just a few feet away from the fire. "Are you going to be here for the whole summer, or just a couple of weeks?"

"I'm here 'til August." Ryan leaned back on his palms. "I still can't believe we get paid to work here. I mean, sure I'll put in eight hours a day, but the rest of the time will seem like I'm on an exotic vacation."

"I know, right?" Ashlyn leaned back as well and angled her face to the moonlit sky. I could hear the smile in her voice as she spoke. "I'm sad Luke can't come until next month, but after that, this summer is going to be awesome."

"Totally," Ryan said.

"Have you found out what you'll be doing while you're here?" I asked Ryan.

"Lifeguarding."

"Lifeguarding?" My eyebrows arched. "You're a certified lifeguard?" He was full of surprises today.

He smiled that big, white smile of his. "I worked at a pool in New York all last summer."

"Wow, that's awesome!" I said.

"I bet tons of girls will fake-drown this summer to get a little mouth to mouth from you." Ashlyn laughed and nudged his shoulder with hers.

"Yeah, right." Ryan rolled his eyes and tossed a handful of sand.

We continued to catch up, finding out where everyone was headed for college in the fall. Ryan would be joining Luke and Ashlyn at SUNY Cortland, which made me wish I knew someone else going to IC.

"Hey," Ryan said, his face lighting up like he'd had the greatest thought on earth come into his head. "Cortland and

Ithaca are pretty close, so if our friend Jess ever decides to end this vacation of his, we could all totally hang out on the weekends."

"Totally!" Ashlyn said excitedly.

My chest, on the other hand, deflated at the thought. "I'm not so sure Jess would appreciate that idea. Well, at least not the part with me being there."

Ryan's brow squished together. "Why not?"

Ashlyn spoke up. "They aren't talking anymore." An annoyed expression crossed her face. "And Jess is being a butt about it."

"Why?" Ryan asked.

Ashlyn eyed me as if gauging whether to tell Ryan everything or not. Not many people knew Jess and I had even dated, since he'd been out of town most of the time, and we were on winter break for the rest of it.

"It's complicated," was all I said. If Jess wanted Ryan to know, he'd tell him.

Ashlyn was sweet, and she quickly changed the subject to all the things she planned to do when we weren't working this summer. Snorkeling. Hiking. Sightseeing. Lying on the beach. As we talked, my gaze continued to wander across the fire to where I noticed Jess talking to a petite girl with short blonde curls. A twinge of jealousy bit at me when I saw the way she touched his arm as they spoke. Was he dating her? He had been in a hurry to get back to the resort after his short visit to New York. Maybe this pretty blonde was the real reason why.

I realized I'd been caught staring when Jess looked in my direction. He made eye contact with me for a second then frowned as he looked at Ryan. His gaze flickered to me again before focusing on the girl at his side, laughing at something she must have said.

I clenched my jaw. I could shake him! Shake him good and

hard and tell him to stop being like this. He was acting like he didn't even know me. How could he pretend we hadn't been friends for fourteen years?

I excused myself and walked around the fire to confront Jess. We needed to figure out how to be in the same vicinity as each other without him scowling the whole time. When I was a few feet away, Jess looked past the girl to me. A look of annoyance crossed his face, but he said something to the girl and stepped around her anyway.

He folded his arms across his chest. "What do you want?"

"I wanted to talk to you." I sighed.

He uncrossed his arms and gestured for me to walk with him down the beach.

WE STOPPED in a place where there were large boulders scattered on the sand. I could only faintly hear the party over the sound of the ocean now. The only light we had to see by was from the moon.

Jess sat down on one of the boulders and crossed his arms.

I didn't know exactly what I was going to say. I hadn't had time to plan this out. Sure I'd thought of what I could say to him all last spring, but none of those things seemed to fit the situation I was in right now. In all the other scenarios I'd imagined, Jess had never been as angry with me as he seemed to be now.

"Well?" Jess asked, obviously impatient to get this over with. "What's this conversation you need to have with me?"

I shrugged. "I don't know exactly."

Jess scoffed.

"I just—" I paced in front of him. "I think that if we're going to work here together, we need to call a truce or something."

"A truce?"

"Yes, Jess." I stopped pacing and faced him. I was so short that even with him sitting, my head wasn't much higher than his. "Hasn't this gone on long enough? Why—" My voice threatened to falter with the emotions bottled up inside of me. I breathed deeply, the salty air calming me down slightly. "Why can't we be friends again?"

Jess's voice was quiet when he spoke. "I don't want to be your friend. I—" he stopped. "I know you're going to be here for the summer, and I can tolerate that, but don't think that means we're friends. We may be stuck hanging around each other for a while, but that doesn't mean we have to talk."

I felt like I'd been punched in the stomach. How could he say that?

A world couldn't exist where I saw Jess every day but didn't talk to him. It wasn't possible. "You don't mean that."

"I do." He stood and ran a hand through his windblown hair. "I don't know what I was thinking last winter. I must have been out of my mind."

I never knew words could hurt so much. My heart bled with each toothpick he stabbed in it. "So you regret breaking up with Kelsie then?" Maybe he blamed me for that and wanted to get back with her.

The look Jess gave me was incredulous, like it was the most ridiculous question to ask him. "Of course not. That, at least, was something I did right."

"But you regret what happened after?"

His eyes locked with mine as if he was remembering the same thing I was: his arms wound around me on his deck, our lips meshed together in a passionate kiss.

"Don't you?" His voice was husky as he glanced at me, at the sand, and then back at me again.

I looked away, unable to meet his gaze. Why did I bring that up?

"I regret what it did to our friendship," I finally said. He didn't say anything for a while, simply nodded and turned to watch the waves crash rhythmically against the shore. The moon was full tonight and outlined Jess's silhouette against the night sky.

I went and sat on the rock Jess had occupied earlier, feeling drained from all the emotions I felt: anger, frustration, hurt, confusion, and jealousy. But mostly I felt sadness.

I spoke to his back. "Who was that girl you were talking to? Is she your girlfriend?"

Jess turned back to me and sighed. "Her name is Layla. She's been at the resort with her family for about two weeks." His hands were stuffed in his pockets and he kicked a rock with his flip-flop. "She's not my girlfriend, but you never know what might happen."

"She's pretty." What else was there to say after that?

"She's cool, and she doesn't play games with guys' hearts. The world could use more girls like that."

Was that a personal jab? I was trying to be nice to Jess, and there he goes back to being a jerk again.

"It looked like you and Ryan were hitting it off." He dug his toe in the sand.

If he was going to play that game, then I might as well join in. "Yeah. Ryan's great."

"You do realize he just broke up with his girlfriend, right?"

"Of course." I tried to sound more sure of myself than I was.

"Then you know that he's on the rebound."

Tears pricked at the back of my eyes, and a lump filled my throat. I already knew I wasn't as pretty, or fun, and definitely not from an ideal family like other girls. But to know that Jess thought that too, it ripped a hole in my chest. "So in other words, he'd only be interested in me because of that. Otherwise, a guy like him would never look twice at a girl like me. Kind of like what happened with you."

Maybe I had just been a rebound to him.

I didn't think it was possible, but Jess had managed to insult me at a whole new level. Not only was I not friend material for *him*, but it was unfathomable for a guy like Ryan to even consider dating me under better circumstances. Jess was on a roll tonight.

"You know what?" I hugged my arms to my chest and stood, choking my tears back. "This conversation was a mistake. I don't know why I thought I wanted to be friends again." I left him in the dark and ran toward the resort to hide in my room.

CHAPTER THIRTY-TWO

THE NEXT MORNING, I started my job at the resort. Ashlyn and I cleaned rooms together for eight hours a day. It was disgusting cleaning someone else's hair out of the shower, but Ashlyn told me if we did a good job we might move up to more desirable positions later.

"Do you think we'll ever get used to this?" I asked Ashlyn. My back cracked as I stood from scrubbing a stain on the bathroom floor of the room we were working in. "When I imagined getting a job at an island resort, I imagined a lot more vacation-type activities than this. But apparently, work on an exotic island is as hard as anywhere else." The first week had gone by slowly, and by the end of each work day, I was too exhausted from cleaning to do much exploring of the island.

Ashlyn puffed a piece of hair away from her face as she scrubbed the tub. "I know. I'm so looking forward to sleeping in tomorrow." Tomorrow would be our first day off since starting.

"Sleeping in past six will be heavenly." I wrung the mop out in the bucket and pushed it around on the floor again.

"Maybe we should plan something fun for tomorrow. Amani did offer to take us snorkeling."

"I'm pretty sure Amani is hoping for a little more than snorkeling when it comes to you," I said. "You should probably tell him that your boyfriend will be coming to visit in a few weeks."

"Oh, I've told him. Amani is strangely determined though," Ashlyn said. "That's why I need you to come snorkeling with us."

"I'm up for hanging out with you guys, but is snorkeling the best idea?" I leaned against the vanity. "We should do something that doesn't involve going further than ten feet in the water." Who knew what kind of creatures were lurking in the ocean. My hands sweated thinking about it.

"Nooo." Ashlyn stared in disbelief. "Don't tell me you're still traumatized by what happened at our old cabin?"

"I was nine years old. Of course I'm still freaked out about that! Having hundreds of fish biting and wiggling along my body is not something I'll ever forget."

The summer after third grade, the Brooks invited my family to the cabin they used to own in Buffalo. They owned a few fish hatcheries back then as one of Mr. Brooks' many business adventures, so of course, the pond on their property was loaded with fish. There was a paddle boat at the pond, so my dad and I decided to take it for a spin that weekend. After a while, we jumped in the water for a swim.

A few minutes later, a ten-year-old Jess came running along the pond with an old ice cream pail in his hand. He reached inside the pail, which I soon learned was full of fish food pellets, and tossed a handful of them right where my dad and I were swimming.

Immediately, hundreds of fish swarmed to where we were and jumped around in the water, swimming through my legs and arms as I frantically tried to get back to the paddle boat. While I was screaming, Jess stood on the shore laughing, head thrown back and all.

Ever since that experience, I never dared go swimming in anything other than a swimming pool. If there was even the possibility of something alive swimming around me I stayed on dry land.

Ashlyn laughed. "Well, if you aren't willing to go, I'll see if Jess or Ryan want to join us." She studied me for a moment, biting her lip and squinting one eye. "Have you and Jess been able to talk this week?"

"Not since the bonfire." I'd been able to avoid seeing Jess since our train wreck of a conversation. It was sad that a life-long friendship could deteriorate so quickly, but since Jess didn't want to fix things there wasn't much else I could do.

In a way, I was grateful to be so tired from cleaning all day—at least that way I was too exhausted to spend much time thinking about Jess.

"Ugh," Ashlyn groaned. "What is wrong with him? Jess won't even talk to *me* about it."

I shrugged and pinched my lips. "We're better off not being friends anymore, I think." I probably should have given up long ago anyway.

THE NEXT WEEK passed quicker than the first. My body adjusted to my work schedule, so when I was done cleaning for the day, I still had enough energy to do some fun things. Ashlyn and I spent quite a bit of time at the beach. She worked on her tan and I read. It was like living in paradise, once my shift was over, and I didn't think I could ever tire of it.

Ashlyn and I hung out with Ryan a couple of evenings, which was fun. He seemed to be handling his breakup with Bridgett just fine, despite what Ashlyn said. I think he may have even flirted with me a couple of times. I couldn't be sure, though, because his whole personality was so flirty he probably hadn't even tried.

Ashlyn and I were getting her room ready for a movie night with Ryan when there was a knock on her door.

"Can you get that for me?" Ashlyn asked as she arranged the snacks we'd scrounged up on the table.

I went to answer the door, expecting to find Ryan. Instead, I stood face to face with Jess for the first time in two weeks.

Jess furrowed his brow. "Did I knock on the wrong door?" He leaned back to check the number plate on the wall. "Is this Ashlyn's room?"

I nodded dumbly, unable to find my voice.

"Come in, Jess," Ashlyn called as she opened a bag of pretzels.

I backed away from the door to let Jess in. As he walked past, I got a whiff of his cologne. He still smelled the same, and the memory of his scent took me back to a time when things were better between us.

Jess went to Ashlyn and asked her something that I couldn't hear. She turned to him with an impatient look on her face and said something back. I couldn't help but assume their hushed conversation had everything to do with me and the fact that Jess probably hadn't known I was going to be here tonight.

A moment later there was another knock on the door. Ryan stepped in and pulled me into his customary bear hug. "How was your day?" he asked.

"It was good," I answered and stepped away, feeling self-conscious at the thought of Jess seeing Ryan hug me. Even though I knew it meant nothing, that didn't mean Jess did.

Ryan settled into the corner of the couch and patted the spot next to him. I hesitated for a second before deciding that if I sat there, that would probably make things less awkward. Ashlyn could sit on the other side of me and Jess could take the chair.

Ryan draped his arm around me when I sat next to him, and the memory of Jess telling me that Ryan was on the rebound forced itself into my mind. I tried to push the thought away but couldn't help thinking Jess was possibly right. Ryan was being way friendlier than he'd ever been in Ridgewater. A frown settled on Jess's face, and I knew he was thinking along the same lines. After all, why else would Ryan be interested in me now after I'd been almost invisible to him all those years before?

"What movie are we watching tonight?" Ryan asked.

"I'm not sure." I turned to Ashlyn who was still standing. "Did you decide on the movie yet?"

"I sure did." Ashlyn smiled hugely as she switched on the TV to show the movie she'd downloaded. "And if I hear any complaints, I'll be more than happy to send any whiners on their merry way." When the screen lit up, I was pleased to see that she'd chosen the latest romantic comedy I'd been dying to watch.

Ryan groaned and let his head fall back on the couch when he saw it was a chick-flick. "Come on guys. I thought we were going to be watching blood and guts all night."

"Sorry, no blood and guts here." Ashlyn smirked.

Jess, of course, didn't complain. He'd endured so many girly movies with Ashlyn and me through the years that he knew it was pointless. I was comforted that he hadn't changed *completely*.

Ashlyn turned the movie on and practically jumped into the chair before Jess could sit there. I realized my mistake—I should have stolen the chair for myself. This left Jess the only empty seat next to me.

It honestly wouldn't have been surprising if he'd chosen to sit on the floor instead of beside me, but I was stunned when he took the last couch cushion. I was even more surprised when he didn't hug the armrest; instead, he sat so close there were only a few inches separating us.

The movie was pretty good, and I found myself laughing a lot, but that changed about halfway through the movie when Ryan reached for my hand during a romantic scene between the main characters. His hand was strong and warm, and I couldn't breathe. It's not that I didn't want to hold his hand—Ryan was great— but the timing messed me up. The way he'd intertwined his fingers with mine, running his thumb along the back of my hand as the characters kissed, brought on an onslaught of memories ranging from all the times I'd imagined him doing this all through middle school, to my own romantic moments with Jess, and then to thoughts of me being Ryan's potential rebound girl. I tried to push those thoughts away, but when I caught Jess sneaking a glance at me and Ryan from the corner of his eye, I couldn't take it anymore. My pulse pounded in my head, and my body flashed with heat. I needed to break away for a minute to collect myself.

I sat there, holding Ryan's hand a few minutes longer so he wouldn't think I was rejecting him, and then excused myself to get a drink of water.

I walked to the mini fridge, grabbed a water bottle, and took my time drinking it down. I was trying to think of a legitimate excuse to leave when Ashlyn came over.

"Why didn't you tell me Jess was going to be here?" I whispered to her.

"Would you have come if I had?" She raised her eyebrows as she grabbed a soda.

"Probably not."

"That's exactly why I didn't tell you. You two need to spend time together if you're ever going to learn to be friends again."

"There's one problem with your plan." I set my water bottle on the counter. "We have to want to fix things. And Jess has already made it clear he doesn't want to be friends with me. Not now, not ever."

"That's where you're wrong, Eliana. You may think he meant that, but I know my brother. As soon as he swallows his pride over what happened between the two of you, I know he'll change his mind."

I shook my head. "I appreciate the gesture. I do." I sighed. "Just don't get your hopes up. Okay?"

And like I'd expected, nothing changed between Jess and me that evening. We may have sat on the couch mere inches from each other, but I never spoke a single word to him that night.

THE NEXT AFTERNOON, Ashlyn invited me to go to this awesome place her grandma told her about. So after I changed out of my cleaning clothes, back into my regular shorts and t-shirt, I waited for her in the front lobby.

She had a huge smile on her face as she sashayed into the lobby wearing a royal blue romper. She held up a blindfold as she came closer.

"What's that for?" I asked.

"You, of course, silly." She laughed. "I also have earplugs."

"Earplugs?"

"Yes, earplugs. For my huge surprise to work, you need to be blindfolded and unable to hear certain sounds from around us. It's just part of the fun. I'll also need your phone."

"O-okay," I said, handing my phone over. I understood the blindfold part, but I'd never heard of anyone using earplugs as part of a surprise.

She had me place the earplugs in my ears, and she tied the blindfold around my head. Once I was both blind and deaf, she led me outside to the car her grandma was letting us borrow. A moment later we were in motion, headed toward who knows where, with the wind blowing my hair.

When we rolled to a stop about fifteen minutes later, I wanted to ask Ashlyn if I could remove the blindfold but realized that with the earplugs in, I probably wouldn't hear her answer. So instead, I waited for her to come to my side of the car and help me out. She continued to hold my hand as she led me down a sandy path.

Then she let go of my hand and left me there.

She better come back.

It was another minute or two before she was back and untying the blindfold.

When I opened my eyes, I was shocked to see that we weren't alone as I'd assumed. Jess stood a few feet from me wearing a blindfold as well. I glared at Ashlyn as I pulled the earplugs out and stuffed them in my pocket.

Now she was taking Jess and me on special surprise adventures together? She just took meddling to a whole new level.

She helped Jess remove his blindfold, and we just stood there staring at each other.

"What's going on, Ashlyn?" Jess spoke through his teeth after he'd removed his earplugs. "You never told me we'd have company. What happened to our brother-and-sister bonding time?"

"Well, I've tried to be nice about this. I even asked Ryan to help move things along, but nothing is working."

So had she asked Ryan to flirt with me in front of Jess? To make him jealous?

How could she do that to me!

Ashlyn continued, "There was just one thing left for me to do." She gestured behind me. I turned to see that we were in front of a little cottage. "I was talking to Grandma last week about how ridiculous the two of you have been acting, and she told me about this place. So after last night's failed attempt to get you two to talk, I decided to take Grandma's advice and bring you here to patch things up."

"What are you talking about?" Jess asked, furrowing his brow. "How is coming here going to fix anything?"

"Oh believe me. It will." She took a step back. Her eyes darted between Jess and me. "You see, when I told you I was going to lunch with Grandma this afternoon, I actually went to your rooms, stole some of your clothes, and packed your bags. Your things are waiting inside the cottage, along with enough food to last you a while. You need to stop avoiding each other and get this over with once and for all." She then broke out into a mad dash back to the car, jumped, in and started it. "I'll be back in a few days to check on you guys," she called as she put the car in gear and rolled away. "And don't worry about taking the days off. Grandma already cleared your schedules, so you won't be fired when you make it back."

With that, she disappeared around a bend in the road and left Jess and me behind, still wondering what the heck had just happened.

CHAPTER THIRTY-THREE

AFTER ASHLYN LEFT US, Jess and I made our way into the cottage separately. It was a cute little place with white walls and teal blue furniture in the living area which connected to a small kitchen. There was a bathroom down a short hall between two bedrooms. I peeked inside the first bedroom but found Jess's duffle bag sitting on the bed. I continued down the hall to the second bedroom. My suitcase was waiting for me on the bed.

I sighed as I plopped down and stared at the ceiling, trying to figure out what I was going to do while trapped in a cottage with Jess for days on end. How could Ashlyn do this?

I thought about trying to find my way back to the resort, but it would be dark soon and I didn't want to end up lost somewhere on the island. I had no idea where we were, anyway.

My stomach growled, so when I heard sounds of Jess moving things around in his room, I padded my way into the kitchen and found Ashlyn had left a pizza and salad in the fridge.

I made a plate up and sat at the small square table in the corner. The cottage was cozy, decorated with a nautical theme. There was a large lighthouse painting set as the focal point of the room, with sailboat models adorning the mantle above the fireplace.

I couldn't help but feel that this place would be the perfect getaway for a couple to escape to.

Too bad it was wasted on Jess and me.

Jess walked into the room and made himself a plate of food before bringing it to the table. He sat in the chair across from me.

I looked at him tentatively, wondering who would break the silence first. I searched my brain for something to say, but couldn't think of anything. It was like sitting across from a stranger.

His feet bumped into mine under the table. I quickly tucked my feet safely away under my chair.

"Sorry," he mumbled, stabbing his salad with a fork.

"It's okay." I took a bite of pizza and studied the Victorian rose tablecloth pattern.

"How long do you think Ashlyn will leave us here?" Jess asked after a while. "Do you think she's serious about this whole thing?"

I shrugged. "She's been pretty annoyed with us lately. I think she means business this time."

Jess sighed and tossed his napkin on the table. "I can't believe my grandma is in on this too. She knows how much work I have to do. I promised her and my grandpa that the website would have its facelift completed before the end of the summer, and that can't happen if I'm not there to arrange for the photoshoot that's been scheduled for next month."

"Photoshoot? Like with models?" I could only imagine what kinds of models he'd be using to advertise for an island resort: gorgeous women dressed in swimwear, with perfectly toned and bronzed bodies.

"Some with models, others to simply showcase the resort and

the island." He shrugged. "Maybe I'll just use this time away to explore the island for more locations to shoot."

I guess that would work out. He could continue avoiding me by leaving the cottage during the days, and I would stay behind and find something to occupy my time here. I had seen a stack of movies in one corner of the living room, and when I got through those there was always the large bookcase full of books.

When Ashlyn returned, we could pretend we'd patched things up, and then go on with our separate lives.

I SLEPT in the next morning, hoping Jess would be gone on his exploring adventure before I was awake. But it seemed like he might have had the same idea as well because he came into the kitchen just as I was finishing my late breakfast. I went back to my room to wait it out, but after what seemed like an eternity, I could still hear him shuffling around in the main part of the cottage.

Not wanting to be held prisoner in the tiny room any longer, I slipped into the living room to pretend like I wanted nothing more than to read a book on the couch all day. I was just leafing through the bookshelf when Jess finally threw a backpack over his shoulders and grabbed a water bottle from the fridge. I sighed, just a few more minutes and I'd have the cottage to myself. No more feeling like I was being smothered by Jess's disapproving looks.

His footsteps stopped, and I looked to see why he was still here.

"Are you planning to just stay here and read a book all day?" he asked, but there was something in his face that made me think he wanted to ask me something more. What it was, I couldn't tell.

"I'd rather not go hiking and end up getting lost somewhere."

Ashlyn wouldn't realize if I went missing for days, and Jess...well, Jess probably wouldn't care.

"Okay." He seemed relieved that I wasn't asking to go with him. "I'll probably be gone most of the day. I'm just gonna hike—"

"I don't need a play-by-play," I interrupted, letting my annoyance with him cover my voice.

He drew his head back, shocked that I was so short with him.

"I wasn't..." He cleared his throat and looked at me pointedly. "If Ashlyn happens to come back, tell her I'll be back before the sun sets."

"Okay." I turned back to the bookshelf and waited for him to leave.

Once he was gone, I grabbed a book with a girl and a dog on the front cover. *Maybe I should get a dog,* I pondered as I sat on the couch. Dogs are supposed to be man's best friend; maybe a dog would replace mine.

The book was boring. Dogs may make for great companions, but that particular story was snooze inducing. After about twenty minutes I caught myself just staring out the window. It was a beautiful day out there. It would be stupid to stay inside.

I found a backpack in a closet, sitting next to a battery-operated lantern. I put a swimsuit on under my clothes, just in case I decided to be adventurous and take a step into the ocean. Then I grabbed the pack, a couple of sandwiches, some cherimoyas, and headed out for an adventure.

The sun was high in the sky when I made it outside. After a quick jaunt around the cottage, I found an overgrown trail in the lush green rainforest. Everything was bursting with life. Brightly colored birds chirped from their perches in the trees. The leafy bushes hummed with all kinds of creatures I couldn't see. And in the distance, I thought I heard the soft rumble of water. It only took a second for me to make up my mind to tramp down the barely-there-trail.

Growing up in New York, I was familiar with waterfalls, having gone to my favorites, Taughannock Falls and Niagara Falls, more times than I could count. But I had yet to see one here in Dominica, and my heart thrilled at the thought of one being close by.

I wandered along that trail for twenty minutes until the rough path suddenly stopped at a wood fence. On the other side of the fence was a stone path. I climbed over the fence and glanced both ways, wondering which way I should go.

Footsteps came from the left. I looked up and saw Jess. His hair was wet, his shorts dripping water along the path.

"Anything good that way?" I asked as he drew near.

He shrugged, looking off into the distance. "It's the Emerald Pool. My grandparents took me there when we came over Thanksgiving Break."

Emerald Pool?

That sounded like it could be pretty.

"Cool. I'll have to check it out."

Jess was only a few steps away. "You don't have to give me a play-by-play, Eliana," he said over his shoulder before continuing past me.

My cheeks burned at his words, though I knew I shouldn't let them bother me since I had just used them on him that morning.

Once he was out of sight and my cheeks had cooled, I turned down the way he'd come from. A few minutes later I stopped in my tracks and gasped as the Emerald Pool came into view. Old trees with exposed roots crawled along the moss-covered, rocky landscape. And there in the center was a fall of water pouring into a greenish-blue pool. It was breathtaking!

I hurried down the path the rest of the way, an unrecognizable urge pushing me to get closer. When I looked into the greenish-blue water, I stopped. Part of me really, *really* wanted to jump in, to feel the water on my skin and dip my head under. But the other part was screaming for me to stay away.

What if there was something swimming in there? It didn't look very deep, but who knew what kind of creatures lived down here. I was from New York, not Dominica. There could be all kinds of dangerous things living in this water. And what if they bit me? I didn't have a first-aid kit, and I definitely didn't know what was poisonous around here and what wasn't.

I bent over to inspect the water again. No sea monsters swimming around. Plus, hadn't Jess's hair looked wet when I saw him? He wouldn't have gotten in if it was dangerous, would he? I'd been afraid of nature's pools for far too long. I slipped off my shirt and shorts until I was just wearing my swimsuit. Before I could scare myself out of it again, I crossed the slippery terrain and climbed into the water.

As I dunked my head under, I concentrated on the feel of the water. Cool, but comfortable. Refreshing. Not as scary as I'd thought it would be. Maybe I could overcome my fear of open water after all.

I swished my hair back and forth before lifting my feet up. I lay back in the pool, just floating and closing my eyes as the water falling from above sprinkled over my face. After a few seconds, I moved away from the falls and squeezed my eyes to get rid of the excess water before opening them to stare at the sky. For the first time in a long time, I felt at peace. There was something about climbing into the water and overcoming that long-time fear that made me feel stronger. Made me feel like I could handle whatever came next in my life. It didn't make sense, but somehow being alone in such a beautiful place made a small change inside of me. I thought back on the last year and a half, and on how much had changed in my life. I'd gone through some pretty crappy things, and yet I was still here. I was okay. Life was moving on, maybe not in the way I'd always imagined it would, but it was still an okay life. I was still able to go to college like I'd always planned. I still had Ashlyn for a good friend. And my mom was getting better.

If I could go back in time and change things so that my dad stayed, if I could go back and fix things with Jess before they ever went bad, my life would be different. Possibly better. Probably. But I wouldn't be the same person I was today. I wouldn't be nearly as strong. Going through tough things had a way of making a person stronger.

As I lay there, looking at the sky, the trees, and the waterfall above me, I made the conscious decision to wash away all the pain, hurt, and anger that I'd had over the past year. I finally realized how much I had let everything weigh me down. I'd let my circumstances make me feel like a victim who had no choice in what was happening to her. I had just been going through the motions of trying to get by, but I hadn't been living. Not *really* living.

I dipped my head under the water once more and as my head broke through the surface, my feet touching the pool floor, I drew in the first real breath I'd taken in a long time. Long and deep. Oxygen filled my bloodstream and coursed through my muscles. It was a cleansing sort of experience. And I was determined to let this be a turning point for me. This was the moment I would look back on as the one where I decided to change my life. I was stronger now than I had been a year ago. I refused to let other people's choices affect my life so much. I would be the one to decide how my path went from now on. And I would be okay.

CHAPTER THIRTY-FOUR

I STAYED at the Emerald Pool for another hour or so, just drinking in its beauty and soul-healing qualities. I was surprised that no one else on the island seemed interested in visiting such a beautiful place, but then the sky suddenly changed and it started to rain. Looks like everyone back at the resort had known what I hadn't: today's weather forecast.

I pulled my clothes over my swimsuit and started down the path I'd met Jess on. A few minutes later, the clouds dumped rain like someone was tipping over buckets up there. I walked for thirty minutes, searching for the dirt path I'd used earlier, but I couldn't find it anywhere. It seemed that getting into the water, which had been a big deal to me at the time, was a lot simpler than finding my way back to the cottage.

I finally admitted I was lost when I ended up at the sign for the Emerald Pool trail...*again*.

Welcome to
EMERALD POOL

MORNE TROIS PITONS NATIONAL PARK
WORLD HERITAGE SITE

NOTICE

-The hike to the pool takes about 15 minutes
-The loop trail is ¼-mile long with three main lookout points

-For your safety do not stray from the trail

THAT'S THE PROBLEM. I laughed tiredly at the last sentence. I *needed* to stray from this trail in order to find my way back to the cottage. If only I could find the right place to stray. Had it been so overgrown that it was impossible to find in the rain? Of course, it was. All the shrubbery had drooped and hidden my way back to shelter. And now I was wet and cold *and* hungry! I should have just stayed in the cottage instead of attempting to have an adventure. This was so stupid!

After a few more times halfway down and back, I gave up on ever finding the path. Maybe if I followed the road I would find the driveway to the cottage. It couldn't be that far of a walk, could it?

But first, I needed to sit down somewhere. All that walking and searching in the pouring rain was exhausting. I found a rock under a tree with decent coverage and rested my tired legs. I opened my backpack to see what I had left to eat. Sadly, I only had one cherimoya left. It may have been the best fruit known to man—according to Mark Twain—but it was not nearly as filling as my grumbling stomach needed it to be.

After finishing my fruit and draining the last of my water bottles, I decided to get a move on. The rain didn't seem like it was going to stop anytime soon and it was getting late. I slung my backpack onto my shoulders and clomped down the muddy, wet road in what I hoped was the right direction. Had Jess made it back to the cottage yet? Probably. He knew better than me to stay out of a storm—not that I had done it on purpose. It was simply taking me forever to find my way back.

Curse Ashlyn and her plans...and her blindfolds. This was her fault!

The wind picked up, making it impossible to keep my head up in the torrential rain. Could this be the beginning of a hurricane? I didn't know. I wished I'd paid more attention to this kind of stuff in the news. It seemed like Amani had said something about hurricanes coming to the island in the past. But didn't those things happen more in the later part of summer? We always got more rain in New York at that time anyway.

I jumped over a huge puddle. Jess was probably worried about me. It would serve him right after the way he treated me this summer. Maybe he'd finally come to his senses. That was, if he was even worried. I hoped he was. I hoped he was pacing inside the cottage, wondering if I was ever going to make it back from this crazy storm.

The sun had all but disappeared, and I was about ready to find some sort of cave to hide in when I saw a long driveway. I squinted my eyes in the rain to see if the cottage was down there. It was! The cottage! That glorious cottage had light. Warmth. A shower. And most importantly, pizza!

I quickened my pace, not caring about splashing in the puddles anymore—it's not like it mattered since I was already sopping wet. I jumped onto the porch, only stopping for a moment to wring out my wet clothes and hair. Then I thought about the pristine interior of Jess's grandparent's cottage, so I stripped down to my swimsuit before going inside. Hopefully, I wouldn't scare Jess too much with my wet-dog appearance.

But the front room was empty.

I didn't know why I had expected to find an anxious Jess pacing the floor, wondering where I'd been. He wasn't in the front room or kitchen at all. The light in his room was off and the bathroom was dark as well. Had he gone to bed, already?

So much for him worrying about my safety.

I peeked inside his room. His duffle bag sat on top of a made bed.

He had to have come back earlier, though, since I hadn't left all the lights on when I went on my hike. Where could he be?

He better be okay.

He probably would be. He seemed like he knew what he was doing earlier on the trail. Hopefully, he'd be back soon.

I went into the kitchen and grabbed a piece of leftover pizza, not taking the time to heat it up before inhaling it. I stuffed down a second piece as well, and then I took a shower to wash off all the mud from my legs.

Once I was clean and dressed, I went back to the living room area to see if Jess had made it back.

It was still empty.

I peeked at the clock. Nine-thirty. Where was he?

I hurried to the front window to see what it was like out there. I could barely see out the window, everything was so blurry with rain. The wind was blowing like crazy now, trees were bending over sideways, and there was so much water and mud.

Where could he be? I rapped my fingers on the glass as I looked for any sign of him. Had he gone back out in search of me? Had he gotten lost? Or hurt?

Why had I been so rude to him this morning? I should have been nice to him. It was so stupid! Would that be the last memory I had with him? I didn't even want to think about it. I took a deep breath and told myself I was overreacting.

Jess would be okay. He was fine. He had found some cave—a really strong hurricane-proof cave—to shelter in during this storm. He'd be back as soon as the storm stopped and we'd laugh about this experience.

A tree fell down about twenty feet away.

I yanked the curtains shut. I couldn't watch. Seeing the destruction outside would only make me go crazy.

I needed a distraction. I went to turn on the TV. Watching movies had always been a good distraction in the past. I was turning on the Blu-ray player when the lights went out.

I screamed.

Then I scrambled around for something, anything to give me some light. I was rummaging through all the kitchen cupboards when I remembered the lantern I'd seen in the closet earlier. I dashed toward the closet, stubbing my toe on a chair in the process, and looked for the lamp. But it was gone.

Had Jess taken it?

I was sitting on the couch, trying not to have a panic attack when I thought I heard a voice.

Eliana.

I barely heard the sound of my name over the storm.

"Eliana."

It was a little louder this time.

A dim light peeked up through the glass in the door.

Jess.

"JESS!"

I bolted to the door and flung it open to find a haggard-looking Jess, soaked and muddy with the lantern in one hand, my wet shirt lifted in his other hand.

When our eyes met, he was looking at me like I was a ghost.

"You're okay," he gasped, his chest heaving with labored breaths.

"You're okay," I sighed, my legs threatening to buckle under me.

We stood there for a moment, my heart pounding as the

tension evaporated from my limbs, making me even weaker. Jess was here. He was okay.

The lantern and my shirt crashed to the ground as he covered the distance between us in two long strides. He caught me up in an embrace, walking me backward until we collided with the wall in the dark entryway.

"Jess," I gasped as he pinned me between him and the wall with his rain-soaked body, his hands sliding up my shoulders and into my damp hair. His hot breath was on my face for a second before his mouth crushed onto mine, hard, wet, and hungry. My knees gave out and I melted, clinging to him to stay upright. Drops of water from his hair dripped down my cheek as he coaxed my lips into a give-and-take—the perfect melding of our mouths that swirled over me like the hurricane outside. He tasted like rain, and I wanted to quench my thirst with his kisses. I wanted to kiss him and stay in his arms forever. This was what I'd been missing. This was what I'd been wanting ever since he left me. I wanted Jess. My Jess. The piece of my heart that he'd taken when he left was finally back in place, swelling my chest so big I didn't know if my ribs could hold it in.

"I looked everywhere for you," he breathed against my lips. "I was so worried."

I smoothed a hand along his chest, feeling his heart strumming faster than a hummingbird's wings. "I was worried about you, too," I said before curling my fingers in his damp hair and pulling his lips back to mine. His arm slipped behind my waist, his hand flattening against the small of my back as he pulled me closer, pressing me to him. Our kisses grew deeper and deeper, as if we didn't need air, only each other. My body ached for him. A deep, longing that made me lose all sense of everything. There was only that moment. Only Jess. Only us. I had never felt anything like it.

And then the kiss changed—it slowed and Jess's lips were

soft, so soft. His fingers traced their way up my arms, my shoulders, and along my collarbone. Heat spread through the pit of my stomach as his mouth brushed along my chin, leaving a trail of fire where it went.

"Jess," I whispered, knowing I was so close to jumping off the edge with him.

When he didn't seem to hear me, I said his name again.

He sighed, his voice husky when he spoke, "I know."

He kissed my lips one more time before resting his forehead against mine so we could catch our breath. In the dark room, I could barely see his eyes, but what I could see told me he was feeling the same desire I was.

"Sorry for being such a butt this summer," he finally said, tucking my loose hair behind my ear.

"I'm sorry I didn't believe you. I—I never should have said those things and made you leave."

Jess's face softened and he pressed his lips to mine in a gentle lingering kiss. "It's okay. We're together now. That's all that matters."

"I HAVE something I need to tell you," I told Jess as we cuddled on the couch after he'd showered off all the mud and we'd both changed into dry clothes. If we were going to move forward we had to tell each other everything.

His eyes clouded with worry, but he nodded. "Yeah?"

"It's about my mom."

"Your mom?" He sighed, seeming relieved. "I thought you were gonna tell me we couldn't be together after all."

I smiled. "Never."

"Good."

I drew in a deep breath, trying to gain the courage to tell him everything I'd kept from him last year.

I could do hard things. I'd survived the Emerald Pool and a really bad storm, after all. I peeked up into his eyes. "You remember how she got drunk and yelled at everyone on New Year's Eve?"

He nodded, pursing his lips.

"That's not the first time she'd done something like that. She —," I sighed. Why was it still so hard to talk about this? She was getting better. It shouldn't be scary to talk about something that was in the past.

"Yes?" Jess prodded.

"She's been an alcoholic for a long time." I pinched my lips, trying to decide how far to go back.

In the end, I decided to go back to the beginning and tell him all about how it had been growing up with an alcoholic mother. I told him about her temper and neglect, told him the truth about my mom's fake visit to her aunt that was actually rehab, and ended with how it got so bad that she'd accidentally knocked me down the stairs the night we kissed on his deck.

"I ran away, to tell you everything, but when I got to your house...I still couldn't say the words out loud."

"Oh...Eliana." He pulled me to him, holding me tight against his chest. The tears flowed from my eyes and I started crying full on. "I didn't know," he whispered. "I didn't know." Jess rubbed my back up and down.

I pulled away, and studied him, needing to see if he looked at me any differently now that he knew everything.

I didn't see any sign of disapproval. In fact, he had tears in his eyes. "Why didn't you tell me?" His voice came out tortured sounding. "I would have been there for you." His voice cracked. "I would have taken you away from that place, and made sure she couldn't touch you ever again." His chest heaved up and down and his bottom lip trembled. It was heartbreaking to see Jess get so emotional over what had happened to me. "I never would have left town if I'd known."

"I know." I gave him a sad smile. "I just felt so broken and ashamed after everything. I didn't want anyone to know one more bad thing about my messy life."

"Did you at least tell someone? Ashlyn?"

I shook my head. "I didn't want her to accidentally slip and tell you."

"I never would have judged you, Eliana." Jess tucked a lock of hair behind my ear. "Don't you know how much you mean to me?"

"It just doesn't make sense." I shrugged helplessly. "I'm nobody."

"How can you not see yourself clearly? You are the most amazing girl I've ever known." He looked at me with those green eyes of his. "I had to escape to an island to get over you." He moved his hand down my arm until he found my hand and laced his fingers between mine. "And it still didn't work. I almost begged you to take me back when you first came here."

"You coulda fooled me." I rested my head against his shoulder. "I thought you hated me."

"I hated what you did to me. I hated that even though you'd broken up with me, I couldn't convince my heart that it was over."

"Probably because it wasn't over. Not really," I said.

We sat in silence for a while, lost in our own thoughts.

After a while, he asked, "Am I going to have to tell Ryan that I stole you from him?"

I smiled, loving that he knew just the right way to lighten the mood. "I don't think he'll mind. Didn't Ashlyn say he was only flirting with me because she asked him to?"

“Yeah, my sister sure was desperate to get us back together. I guess she thinks everyone should be as happy as her and Luke.”

“We should probably thank her.”

He shrugged. “Maybe later. For now, we can still be mad at her for deserting us when there was a tropical storm.”

I laughed again, happy to have moved past the hard conversation. “What about you? Is that girl I saw you talking to at the bonfire going to be heartbroken?”

"Are you talking about Layla?" He chuckled. "That girl's crazy!"

"But I thought you said she was cool." Yes, I specifically remembered him saying she was cool because she didn't play games with guys' hearts.

"I only said that because you and I were fighting, and I didn't want you to know about my non-existent dating life."

"You were embarrassed about not dating anyone?"

"Well, after everything that happened, I didn't want you to think I was just sitting at the resort being miserable."

"Were you?"

"Miserable? Of course. I'd severed ties with my lifelong best friend." He grazed his fingertips along my back. His touch was so light, yet it burned a path into my skin everywhere it went. "Tell me you were miserable too?"

"I was miserable."

"Do you mean it, or are you just saying that because I told you to?" His lip quirked up into a one-sided smile as he continued to trace his fingers along my spine.

"I've never had a longer six months of my life."

"Even compared to last year with everything that happened with your dad?"

I nodded. Losing my dad had been like falling into an empty well, but at least I'd had Jess there at the top to call to me and tell me everything would be okay. Losing Jess right after being humiliated by my drunk mother had been like falling into the well, and then drowning in the water.

ASHLYN PICKED us up first thing the next morning. Apparently, the storm had her worried sick about us the whole night before. I considered using her guilt against her, to make her feel bad about leaving Jess and me stranded in the middle of who-knew-where. But I decided to let it go since her plan *had* worked. Jess and I had made up, and in a roundabout way, we had Ashlyn to thank for it.

The next two weeks were magical. Jess took me all over the island and took care of me in a way I hadn't been taken care of in a very long time. He was amazing, and I thanked the stars every day that I was somehow lucky enough to call him mine.

One evening, we were settling down to watch a movie with Ashlyn and Ryan in Ashlyn's room when a quiet knock sounded on the door.

"Did you invite your grandparents, too?" Ryan smirked at Ashlyn.

"No." Ashlyn unfolded her legs from the couch and walked to the door. "Though I have no idea who else would show up so late—unless Luke decided to come a week early."

She swung the door open then gasped.

"What is it?" Ryan shifted in his chair as if readying to protect her from danger.

Ashlyn slowly moved one foot back then the other to reveal who had knocked on the door.

"Is my Eliana here?" my dad's voice sounded.

CHAPTER THIRTY-FIVE

"DAD?" My breath caught in my throat. I tried to pull myself up from the couch but my body had gone completely weak with shock. Jess gave me a push, and I stumbled toward the door. Toward my dad.

"*Papà*!" I cried as I fell into him, throwing my arms around his neck.

"My beautiful Baby Girl." His arms shook around me as he kissed my hair, my temple, and my cheek.

"You came back," I said it over and over again, each time becoming less understandable until I was sobbing into his shirt. "I didn't know if I'd ever see you again."

"I never wanted to leave you. I never wanted to leave my girls," he spoke into my hair.

I pulled back to see if he was real. I looked up into his warm brown eyes, which were wet with tears. He looked just as I remembered, the same crinkles at the corners of his eyes, the same mole on his left cheek, the same dark hair with a touch of gray in it. He even smelled the same, of aftershave and spice.

It was then that I noticed he wasn't by himself. My mom was standing in the doorway, her eyes full of happy tears.

"Mom!" I opened my arms for her to join the family hug.

She stepped into the hug and we all cried together, squeezing each other and laughing.

It wasn't until a full minute later that I remembered we weren't alone.

I turned back to my friends, wiping tears from my eyes. "My dad's back."

Jess, Ashlyn, and Ryan all smiled back at me. Then Jess came to stand by us. He held a hand out for my dad to shake. "It's so good to see you again, Mr. Costa."

"It's so good to see you, too." My dad ignored Jess's hand and pulled him into a bear hug. "Thank you for taking care of my girl."

"I would do anything for your daughter," Jess said.

Dad held him at arm's length. "I know. You are a good man. Much better than me."

My friends all excused themselves from the room, giving me a chance to talk to my parents alone.

"You're probably wondering where I've been all this time." My dad was the first one to break the silence after we all had taken a seat—me and him on the couch, my mom on the chair. "And I hope you'll still want me to be here after I tell you. I'm already so thankful your mom decided to give me a second chance."

I glanced at my mom. She looked so different from how she'd been the past year. Her eyes were bright again with hope, her skin vibrant. She looked healthy, which I could only assume meant she'd kept herself sober after I left. And she was gazing at me and my father with such love that my heart almost burst with the hope that things would be good again in our family.

Where had my dad been all this time? I wasn't sure I wanted

to hear his answer. But I needed to ask the hard questions. So I dug deep and pulled from the strength I'd felt that day at the Emerald Pool. "Where did you go? How could you leave us?"

He exhaled deeply. "It's a long story. And one that I'm afraid won't make me look good in your eyes."

I waited. If I was going to be strong, he needed to step up as well.

He licked his lips then swallowed. "The FBI was right. I did embezzle a lot of money from my clients."

He let that sink in like a sack of rocks before continuing.

"I didn't plan to do it, not really. But when I was chatting with a buddy of mine about how tight things had gotten in our finances, he told me about this scheme of his that promised a quick return on my investment. It was only supposed to take a few months, and I was going to pay all my clients back the money I borrowed. I convinced myself it was okay since my clients had asked me to invest their money anyway. If I tied it up for a few months longer, it wouldn't be that big of a deal to them. No one was supposed to get hurt." He shook his head.

"But the deal went sideways. My *buddy* took the money and disappeared. I tried to cover it up for a while with new clients' money, but it wasn't working. When I found out the FBI were looking into things at work, I panicked."

Despite how happy I'd been to see him a moment ago, anger still bubbled in my stomach, reminding me of everything my mom and I had gone through because of what he did. "So you figured you'd leave us to deal with the mess?"

"I wasn't thinking." Dad pinched his eyes shut. "I was in Wyoming before I fully realized what I'd done. I almost turned around, but then I thought about how I was facing twenty-five years in jail. I couldn't come back. I'd be just as bad off. I'd be in jail until I was seventy. I'd miss out on everything."

"So *you* were the only person who mattered? Who cares

about Mom and me, and how we got stuck facing the news media, the neighbors, the FBI, and all the rumors at school? We had to move in with Uncle Peter because we couldn't afford to live anywhere."

"Eliana!" My mom tried to hush me.

Maybe that Emerald Pool had made me a little too strong.

"No, Annette. She's right." My dad shook his head, and I noticed he was fighting back tears. "I'm a horrible father. A horrible husband. I don't deserve your forgiveness. I-I just wanted to see you one last time before I turn myself in."

My heart stuttered to a stop as his words registered in my head. "T-turn yourself in?"

He pressed his lips together. "I found out you were here and decided it was probably the only chance I'd have to talk to you without the police or anyone else getting involved. So I sent another letter to your mother a couple of weeks ago, asking her to meet me here. Then I, uh, I had an alternate passport made up so I could get here without flagging anything."

"You got a fake passport. You might as well say it." I gave him a half smile so he knew I was teasing.

"Yes, we may as well add forgery to my list of felonies."

My mom snorted. And I had to laugh too. It was the only thing we could do in this situation if we were going to keep from crying.

"Anyway, I was so thankful when your mom showed up this afternoon. We talked about everything..." he trailed off. His eyes peered into mine, communicating that he knew about everything that had gone on while he was away. He squeezed my knee. "You are such a strong girl, Eliana. I'm so sorry for what we put you through. It's more than anyone should have to deal with, let alone you, my beautiful *tesorina*."

My lip trembled as my emotions tried to get the better of me.

I wiped my shaky fingers under my eyes as the tears trickled over the brim.

My dad pulled me into a hug and kissed my hair. "I'm so sorry." He rubbed my back. "You deserve so much better."

I nodded into his chest. Yes, I did. I deserved better. But life didn't always give us what we thought we deserved. Sometimes it gave us really hard things. Sometimes it gave us a miracle. Sometimes it gave us both. This was both. My dad had come back. But, it was only for a moment. Not nearly long enough.

After a time, my tears stopped and I straightened on the couch. "So you're turning yourself in?"

My dad nodded, his eyes sorrowful. "I have to. We'll never be free of this if I don't."

I looked down at my hands. "I guess that's true."

"But I was able to track down Angelo. That's one of the reasons it took me so long to come back. I knew I needed something if I was going to make this mess a little better. I'm hoping that with him and the money he ran off with I can get my sentence reduced. I don't want to get my hopes up too high, but it's possible that I'll only have to spend five years in prison instead of twenty-five."

Five?

Five was better than twenty-five, but it was still a long time. I'd have graduated from college by then. Or I could even be married.

I couldn't imagine another five years without him in my life. My mom and I had barely survived one.

My dad took my hands in his. "I have to do this. It's the right thing. I played with the idea of taking you two into hiding with me, so we could be together. But this life on the run is no life at all. I couldn't ask you to do that for me."

I turned to my mom to see her reaction to all this. Would she be okay with this in our future? Or would this be one more thing to break her spirit?

She gave me a sad smile. "Your dad is right. He needs to make things right. It's the only way to move on."

But I just got him back! Five minutes back in my life and he was already talking about leaving?

"Can't you hide at the resort for the rest of the summer? I'm sure my friends will keep it a secret. And...and Jess's grandparents might be okay with it."

My dad shook his head sadly. "I've been on the run too long already. We have tonight, but I'm turning myself in in the morning."

Panic surged in my chest. "Why tomorrow?"

"I don't want to get you or anyone else in trouble for abetting a fugitive. I can't do that to you guys, too."

"So this is it?"

He nodded and gestured for my mom to join us on the couch. He draped his arms around us, his girls, pulling us all in for one of the last group hugs we'd have in much longer than I wanted to think about.

THE NEXT AFTERNOON I sat in my suite with my parents and Jess. We tried to prolong the morning, soaking up every moment we had together as a family, crying so many tears I was surprised I had any left. Around two o'clock, my dad decided that the time had finally come. He picked up the phone and dialed the local law enforcement.

"Yes, hi. My name is Paulo Costa," he said. "I'm a fugitive of the United States and am calling to turn myself in."

My whole body went weak at his words and my pulse thundered in my head.

Jess must have noticed that I was about to collapse because he put his arm around me and helped me sit down. Kissing my head, he whispered, "It's going to be okay. Your dad is doing the right thing."

But how could this be the right thing? It didn't feel right. It felt a lot like losing my father all over again.

Dad finished his phone call and held out his arms for my mom and me.

There was a knock on the door about ten minutes later. I clung to my dad, trying to commit everything about him to my memory. Who knew how long it would be until I could hug him again? I memorized his spicy scent, the way he was soft around the middle, the way I fit perfectly under his arm.

Jess opened the door. My dad kissed my forehead one more time, and kissed my mom and gave her a lingering hug. Then he straightened himself and faced the local policemen who were entering the room.

"Are you Paulo Costa?" an officer with dark, dark eyes and even darker skin asked.

My dad nodded. "I am."

"We're going to have to put you under arrest." The officer and his partner stepped closer. My dad didn't put up a fight, he simply held his hands behind his back and let them put the cool metal around his wrists. When he looked up again, there were tears in his eyes.

My mom was the first to break down, but it only took a moment for me to follow. We each took turns hugging him as the tears flowed, and then we held onto each other as my dad was escorted out of the room.

"*Vi amo per sempre. Siete la mia vita,*" Dad said as he walked out the door.

I love you forever. You are my life.

And then he was gone.

EPILOGUE

ONE YEAR LATER

"IT'S funny to think that this time last year we were being forced into a cottage by my meddling sister so we could get over ourselves and admit that we were in love with each other." Jess reached for my hand as we walked down the Emerald Pool trail together. So many things had changed since the first time I came here. One year ago, I was sure Jess and I would never be able to fix things between us, I never thought I'd see my dad again, and I was worried about my mom and her well-being.

Things still weren't perfect. After the local authorities took my dad, they made arrangements for him to be taken back to New York. Mom and I followed soon after to try and find the best lawyer and compile all the information my dad had given us. They held a trial a few months later. It was brutal. But thankfully, I had Jess and school to keep me from spending all my time worrying about my dad's future. When all was said and done, Dad was given a five-year jail sentence. Him taking the time to track down his buddy and the money had helped a lot, and my anger toward him over leaving us for so long slowly dissipated.

My mom was doing so much better these days. She moved back into our house, and with Uncle Peter's help, had found a much better job to support herself. It was great to see the light in her eyes again, and wonderful to talk to her about her hope for the future. Hope was something we'd both been missing for such a long time, and it was amazing to have that back in our lives.

Dating Jess was magical and he was perfect for me. Sure, I knew he wasn't *perfect*, but neither was I. Something we had in our favor, though, was the fact that we'd been friends for so long. We already knew everything about each other, so there weren't any unwelcome surprises to catch us off guard. The one thing I hadn't expected was how amazing of a boyfriend Jess was. He was so loving and supportive and always went out of his way to make me feel special. Plus, I couldn't get over the fact that I got to kiss him whenever I wanted to. Which was pretty much all the time.

The Emerald Pool came into view, filling me with as much awe as it had the first time I saw it. I couldn't help but compare how much had changed since my first time here.

We came down the last few steps and leaned against the wood railing to enjoy the serene beauty of our surroundings. A bird landed on one of the tree branches a few feet away. A brown lizard with a yellow throat scampered along the rocks to hide in a fern when it noticed us standing close by.

I had missed this island. New York was beautiful, but living in a rainforest for a few months was an experience I would never forget. And I was so happy Jess had arranged for us to come back again this year.

"I wish I could have shown my dad this place before he turned himself in. He would have loved it."

Jess squeezed my hand. "We'll have to bring him here to celebrate when he's released from jail."

I nodded. Four and a half years seemed like forever away, but it would be nice to show him my favorite place in the world once he was free. "Maybe my parents could have something like a second honeymoon here when that happens. I think they would love that."

Jess scratched his thumb against the wood railing. "About that." He slowly turned his gaze from the scenery back to me. There was something in his eyes, some kind of nervousness below the surface.

I waited, having no idea what he was going to say.

He swiveled and took both my hands in his. "Well, you see..." He paused. Then in a much quieter voice, he said, "I was hoping you might be interested in coming back here for *our* honeymoon."

Our honeymoon?

Our *honeymoon?*

I gasped as understanding pelted through me.

Jess stepped back and mouthed the words *I love you* as he lowered himself down on one knee. He pulled out a small white box, opening it to reveal the most beautiful diamond ring I'd ever seen.

I couldn't breathe! My knees threatened to give out on me as they wobbled on the dirt path.

"I know you always dreamed of having your dad walk you down the aisle. But I still have to ask. I want you to know that you're it for me. You're the one I want to be with forever." He smiled, hopeful. "I was your first kiss, and I want to be your last. When we're together, everything makes sense. I'm my best self when I'm with you and I want you to know that I'm yours. Forever."

I was finally able to draw in a deep breath and was about to say something when he continued.

"I understand if you want to wait, to set the date for a time when everyone you love can be there. But I *love* you, Eliana Costa. And I don't want to wait to plan our future together." He looked up at me with his big green eyes shining in the setting sunlight. "Will you marry me?"

"Yes! Of course I'll marry you, Jess." Tears escaped out of the corners of my eyes, and for the first time, I wasn't embarrassed by them.

Jess stood and pulled me into his arms. Then he kissed me. When we separated, he slid the sparkling ring onto my shaking finger.

"I love you, Eliana," he whispered against my neck as we embraced again.

"I love you, Jess. You have no idea how much," I said. "And I don't want to wait four and a half years. I want to marry you as soon as possible. I want us to live our life the way *we* want to. My dad will understand."

"I think you're right on that one." He almost said it like he knew my dad would understand. When he saw the question in my eyes he said, "You didn't think I'd ask you to marry me without consulting your dad first, did you?"

"But he's been in jail for six months. How...?"

Jess reached for my hands as the corner of his lip slipped up into the half smile I loved so much. "I asked him while he was still here. You remember how I took him aside for a few minutes before he called the authorities?"

I blinked. "Yeah?"

"I asked for his blessing then." Jess's smile broadened.

I gasped. "You knew then? But we'd barely started dating. How could you know?"

He wrapped his arms behind my waist and looked at me with such love that I couldn't help but feel adored. "I've known for years, Eliana. It just took me a while to convince you."

Join my VIP Reader's Club!
Find great deals on my books and other YA and Sweet Romances!
Get a FREE book just for signing up!
Grab your copy of When We Began HERE!

What's the first rule when staying at your best friend's house for the week? Don't fall for her older brother.

READ THE NEXT BOOK IN THE SERIES:
IT WAS ALWAYS YOU
NOAH AND LEXI'S STORY

What's the first rule in pretending to date your brother's best friend? Don't let feelings get involved.

Sixteen-year-old Lexi Stevens has never been kissed—never even been asked on a date. So when she humiliates herself in front of her crush and her brother's best friend offers to be her fake boyfriend for the week to make him jealous, she doesn't know if it's the stupidest idea ever, or a dream come true.

When Noah Taylor's abusive stepdad kicks him out of the house, the last thing he needs is for anyone at school to find out—not even his best friend. But when his new "girlfriend" discovers he's homeless and lets him sleep in her closet, he starts to wonder if he's found someone he can confide in after all.

Soon Noah and Lexi are putting on a big show in front of the whole school while sneaking around behind her overprotective father's back. It isn't long before feelings develop and it becomes harder and harder to discern between what's fake and what's real.

Grab your copy today!

ALSO BY JUDY CORRY

Ridgewater High Series:

When We Began (Cassie and Liam)

Meet Me There (Ashlyn and Luke)

Don't Forget Me (Eliana and Jess)

It Was Always You (Lexi and Noah)

My Second Chance (Juliette and Easton)

My Mistletoe Mix-Up (Raven and Logan)

Forever Yours (Alyssa and Jace)

Protect My Heart (Emma and Arie)

Kissing The Boy Next Door (Wes and Lauren)

A Second Chance for the Rich and Famous Series

The Billionaire Bachelor (Kate and Drew)

Hollywood and Ivy (Ivy and Justin)

Her Football Star Ex (Emerson and Vincent)

Coming Soon
Emerson and Vincent's Story

Join Judy's VIP Reader's Club to be notified when it's released!
www.subscribepage.com/judycorry

ACKNOWLEDGMENTS

Thank you so much to Jared for supporting me in this writing dream of mine, for encouraging me when I wanted to give up on this book, and then finally for reading it even though YA Contemporary Romance is not a genre you'd pick up for yourself.

Thanks to James, Janelle, Jonah, and Jade for letting me talk about my books and characters with you. I love how excited you are about my stories and how you make me feel like the coolest author mom in the world.

To my critique group—Mike Kelly, Kristina Starmer, David Baker and Wendy Jessen—thank you for helping me figure out the story I actually wanted to tell and pushing me to make it so much better than I imagined it would be.

To my beta-readers who gave me the much-needed encouragement to actually publish this thing: Jami Lyn Niles, Ruth Morris, Jeff Corry, Lindsey Corry, Kristin Clove, Katie Smith, Dedra Tregaskis, Michelle Carter, Arielle Hadfield, and Idena Ward.

To my editor, Precy Larkins, for once again making me look better than I really am. You are the best!

To my cover designer, Victorine E. Lieske, for making a beautiful cover.

To my parents for teaching me how to work hard and go after my dreams.

Thank you to all my family and friends for your love and support through this crazy adventure of mine. I couldn't do it without you.

Thank you to the members of my online writing community who have been so willing to share your wisdom and help make this publishing adventure so much less daunting than it would have been on my own.

I'm especially thankful to my Father in Heaven, for blessing me with a little talent and creativity, a healthy dose of inspiration and perseverance, and the insane amount of personal drive it takes to be a writer.

Last of all, to my Wattpad readers: thank you for believing in this book and telling me how much you loved it! Eliana and Jess's story would still be hiding on my computer if it wasn't for you!

ABOUT THE AUTHOR

Judy Corry has been addicted to love stories for as long as she can remember. She reads and writes YA and Clean Romance because she can't get enough of the feeling of falling in love. She graduated from Southern Utah University with a degree in Family Life and Human Development and loves to weave what she learned about the human experience into her stories. She believes in swoon-worthy kisses and happily ever afters.

Judy met her soul mate while in high school, and married him a few years later. She and her husband are raising four beautiful and crazy children in Southern Utah.